Tricia Linden

Somewhere to Belong

Llumina
Press

ISBN: 978-1-60594-853-9 (PB)
       978-1-60594-854-6 (EB)

Printed in the United States of America by Llumina Press

Library of Congress Control Number: 2012903082

Dedication

For C.C., the best beau a woman could ask for;
because I've always wanted one of these.

Chapter 1

*T*his was it, time to leave. Daniel had heard all he wanted to hear. Besides, he'd heard it all before, but now it was official. He just wished the damn meeting would end so he could get the hell out of there.

It was final. They were dropping the mounted patrol, another casualty of the city's budget cuts. The last team of horses would be pulled from the streets at the end of the month, and he'd be in a patrol car full-time. The way management spun it, he should be grateful he still had a job, even if it wasn't the job he wanted.

As soon as he and his colleagues were dismissed from the briefing room, he headed for the door to the parking garage. He didn't feel like hanging around to commiserate with his fellow patrol officers. Right now, he just wanted to put some distance between himself and the police headquarters. It was time to leave San Francisco behind for a while and rethink his life.

Sunlight from the exceptionally clear spring day was quickly giving way to streetlights and city glow as Daniel maneuvered his fire-engine red Ford Mustang onto the Bay Bridge and headed out toward the Oakland hills. On the other side was Over-Yonder, the place he called home, a large four-bedroom semi-rural ranch house sitting on twelve acres, tucked into the rolling hills of Diablo Valley. It was the house he'd grown up in, along with his two elder brothers and younger sister. The years had slipped by, his siblings had moved away, his parents had passed on, and Daniel had become a single thirty-one-year-old man living alone in a family home that no longer fit.

Rather than going straight home to the empty ranch, he decided to call his sister, Teressa, to see if she was up for a little company. He needed a dose of family right about now. He was just coming off the Bay Bridge and was hoping he could reach her before he passed through the Caldecott Tunnel. He hit his sister's number on the speed dial of his cell phone, which, thankfully, was still holding a charge.

"Hey, Sis, what's up?" he spoke loudly. He wasn't sure how well he could be heard when using the hands-free speaker function, and he felt rather awkward talking to thin air.

"Hi, Daniel. Rory and I were just going to pick up Chinese and rent a movie. What are you up to?" Teressa was the only one who called her husband Rory instead of Robert, and the reason was known only to the two of them.

"I'm just leaving work and was hoping I could stop by, if you don't mind. I'm just coming off the Bay Bridge."

"You're close. Come on over and join us. No use spending Friday night alone."

"You sure? I don't want to rain on your parade," he hedged, hoping she would call his bluff. This was one night he didn't want to spend home alone, but he didn't exactly like the idea of being a third wheel either.

"Don't worry. Rory and I get plenty of alone time. Even newlyweds like to relax with family sometimes. Come on over."

He paused for only a moment. After all, it was what he wanted, to be with family. "Okay, you talked me into it. Is there anything I can bring?"

"You can pick up something to drink, unless you're happy with tea or water. Is Chinese okay with you?"

"Yeah, I'm good as long as you include some hot and sour soup. I'll pick up a six-pack of beer, okay?"

"Rory will be glad to hear that. See you soon." Teressa clicked off her phone.

Daniel smiled as he turned north toward Berkeley.

◆　◆　◆

The remains of dinner covered the kitchen table, and the movie lay forgotten. Once Daniel started talking about his problems at work, he couldn't stop until his frustration was well vented. Teressa, being a relationship coach, was eager to listen and lend her advice.

"When I signed up for the police academy, the only thing I wanted was be part of the mounted patrol. Maybe I had some romantic notion of being an urban cowboy, dispensing justice from the back of a horse, but the idea of being stuck in a patrol car just doesn't exactly appeal to me."

"I know you, Daniel. I can't see you sitting in a car all day," Teressa agreed.

"And then there's the paperwork. With all these budget cuts, we have more paperwork than ever. The internal auditors are constantly breathing down our necks, making sure we dot our i's and cross our t's. It's ridiculous and I'm getting tired of it all."

"Why don't you take a break? Give yourself time to figure out what you want to do next," Teressa advised.

"I'm thinking that's a good idea. I've got a ton of vacation stored up. I didn't want to take any time off until I knew what was going to happen to my unit. I figured as long as I could go to work and sit on a horse, I would."

"You know, Rory and I are going back to Scotland in June. Why don't you come with us? We're leaving a couple of weeks after they shut down your unit. It'll be a perfect time for you to get away."

"Scotland? That's a bit of a trip. I was thinking someplace close, like Yosemite."

"Oh, come on. You've been to Yosemite a dozen times. You need something bigger than that. This could be a life-changing decision for you. Besides, you've never even been out of the country. It's time for you to see the world."

"You and Robert are going to be gone for at least two weeks. I can't be gone from the ranch that long."

"Sure you can. Rory told me his cousins Jenny and Jack are looking for a place to stay. They're moving here from Oregon. There's plenty of room at the ranch, and they can watch the place while you're gone. It wouldn't have to be forever, just until they find a place of their own."

Daniel looked over at his brother-in-law. He'd been sitting at the end of the table, quietly watching the siblings' debate.

"Works for me," Robert said with a shrug. "You would be doing us both a favor. I'd like to help them out but our place is too small."

"You know I'd like to help, but I need to think about it." He hadn't considered taking on housemates, but it sounded like a good idea, especially if they were anything like Robert. In the short time he'd known Teressa's husband, they had become like brothers.

"Come on, what's not to like? Jenny and Jack need a place to stay, and you can use the extra help. It's a win-win situation," Teressa continued her campaign.

"I'm surprised you're already planning to go back to Skye," Daniel said. Nearly a year ago, his sister had taken a trip to Scotland and had returned home with Robert, her new fiancé. At one o'clock in the morning on New Year's Day, Robert MacNicol and Teressa Ellers had become husband and wife. His sister claimed there wasn't a better way to start the New Year.

"Rory still has a home and a business over there. He needs to check on his fishing boats. What if I told you there's a great horse ranch on the island not far from Rory's cottage?"

Daniel looked to his brother-in-law for confirmation. "Would she lie to me just to get me to go?"

"Aye, she would, but no, she's not," Robert confirmed with a grin as he relaxed in his chair, his Scottish brogue as strong as ever. Apparently, he enjoyed watching his wife banter with her sibling.

Daniel appreciated his sister's efforts to sell him on the idea of a Scottish vacation, but he wouldn't put deception beyond her means to get her way. He figured she was using his love of horses as leverage to get him to say yes, and he had to admit it was working. Or maybe he was just looking for an excuse to say yes.

Not missing a beat, Teressa continued on, "It won't cost you much, only the price of the plane ticket. You'll be able to stay at Rory's house."

"Our house," Robert interrupted.

She smiled brightly at her husband. "Our house," she corrected. "We'll show you around, or you can go off on your own as much as you want. What do you think?"

"I think you're not going to let up until I say yes."

"See, I knew you were a smart man. I'll go on the Internet and book you a ticket on our flight right now before you can change your mind. I know if I leave it up to you, it'll never get done." She jumped up and grabbed her laptop.

She was right. The Internet wasn't his thing, along with most other technologies of the twenty-first century. He had to admit, the ease and convenience of a cell phone was worth the venture into modern technology, but he couldn't see the appeal of video games, computers, or the Internet. To him, they were just a time suck. And forget about e-mail, texting, IM, or all the other ways technology was trying to speed up people's lives. He was perfectly happy living life in the slow lane. Well, maybe not perfectly happy, but certainly better off. Heck, his car had windows that rolled down with a crank handle, not the push of an electric button.

Unfortunately, his lack of techno savvy was also a significant deterrent to any real success in the world of women and dating. More often than not, the women he met wanted the immediate gratification of being able to contact him electronically, and that just wasn't his style. Most of the time, he didn't even have his cell phone on unless he wanted to make a call, and it could be days before he listened to his voice messages. His cell phone battery had a tendency to die faster than he could remember to plug it in to be recharged. His family and closest friends had learned to accept his anti-technology quirk, but the rest of the world seemed much less forgiving.

"Okay, all set." Teressa looked up from her laptop, another modern convenience that didn't exist in Daniel's world, satisfied with her effort.

"We leave on the eighteenth of June. We'll be in Skye in time for the summer solstice."

"What's so special about the summer solstice?" Daniel asked.

"It's the first anniversary of the day we met," she said, exchanging a sly glance with Robert. They were grinning like two kids sharing a secret, and Daniel knew well enough when to leave secrets alone.

Chapter 2

A few weeks later, Daniel found himself on a plane sitting next to his sister and brother-in-law, questioning his choices. They were headed toward the Atlantic coast on their way to Glasgow. It wasn't that he didn't like to see new places. He'd traveled up and down the West Coast with his dad, visiting horse shows, and had been to Canada and Mexico; but this was the first time he was leaving the North American continent, and honestly, he found the prospect of a long transatlantic flight to be a bit unnerving. He didn't like knowing they would be spending the next few hours flying over miles of ocean before they reached land again and wondered how he had let his conniving little sister talk him into this adventure.

Dinner had been served, and the cabin lights were dimmed to encourage the passengers to sleep or rest quietly. Daniel figured it made the long hours of the flight a lot easier on the passengers and flight attendants, but it hardly helped quell his anxiety. He was uncomfortably aware of his seatmates as he tried not to fidget, but hell, a body wasn't meant to sit still in one place for so long.

Robert and Teressa were already sleeping, curled up under their airline-issued blankets. Apparently, they were okay with the long overnight flight, but Daniel was finding it much harder to settle in. The journey was long, and the large plane was nearly full for the nonstop flight. He was grateful that Teressa and Robert had used their frequent-flyer miles to upgrade to roomier seats, but the space was still cramped for his six-foot-three-inch frame. And the hum of the engines, instead of being a soothing white noise, created an annoying vibrating buzz in his ears.

He wanted to get up and stretch his legs, but he didn't want to disturb Teressa and Robert, so he sat staring out the small oval window into the reflective blackness of the nighttime sky, regretting his misfortune of getting stuck with the inside seat. When they were boarding, he had agreed to let Robert take the aisle seat, always being the nice guy; and as he knew, nice guys always finished last. He glanced again at Teressa, his younger sister, happily married to the man of her dreams (as she

6

called him), and he knew he was definitely finishing last. He was the last unmarried sibling and the last one still living at the ranch.

Daniel sat in the dim light cast by the overhead reading lamp, wondering what he could do to get some sleep, or at least relax enough to forget he was thirty thousand feet above endless ocean. Well, maybe not exactly endless ocean, but close enough.

He searched the seat back pocket in front of him and flipped through the airline's in-flight magazine. It was beyond boring and of no use for his insomnia. He looked over at the seat back pocket in front of Teressa and noticed her travel journal poking halfway out. She'd been writing in it earlier. When he had asked her about the journal, she had explained how she had started the travel journal during her first trip to the Isle of Skye. With each succeeding trip, she was adding to the journal, creating a memoir of her travels to Scotland.

Daniel didn't usually go snooping into his sister's personal stuff, but since she hadn't seemed particularly secretive when she had told him about her journal, he figured she wouldn't mind. Hopefully, it would tell him about the places they were planning to visit. It would be interesting and perhaps a little insightful to peek into his sister's opinions on their intended destination. With hardly a second thought, he reached for his sister's journal and started reading.

A few hours later, and after several disbelieving glances at the two people sleeping next to him, he wasn't sure if he had read a credible account of an incredible journey, or if his sister was a fantastic storyteller. She'd written about fairies, wizards, and time travel; and the kicker of it all was her belief that Robert (a.k.a. Rory) was the reincarnation of a thirteenth-century warrior and her soul mate. What the hell was she thinking? Although it had kept him enthralled for the past few hours, allowing him to completely forget his insomnia and discomfort with the overseas flight, it was darn near impossible to believe her fantastic tale. He wondered if Robert was aware of his wife's vivid imagination.

Daniel didn't know what to think of his sister's story except that it was simply unbelievable. Interesting, but unbelievable. He'd give her credit on one count: She and Robert seemed made for each other. Whether it was because they were soul mates across time or just lucky in love, he couldn't say, but they certainly seemed to belong together.

With a final shake of his head, Daniel tucked Teressa's journal back into the seat pocket in front of her and switched off his overhead light. It was time to close his eyes and rest even if he couldn't sleep. He paused a moment as he reached to close the shade of the little oval window next to him, and gazed out into the early morning sky.

The glow of the rising sun rushing to meet the eastward-flying plane was just beginning to leak above the horizon. A lone star still shone bright in his limited view of the vast endless sky. It occurred to him that this single star, shining alone in the vastness of space, had spent eons shining its light out into the cosmos, always existing exactly where it was meant to be. In a moment of honest confession, he softly whispered, "I wish I could find a place where I belong."

He dropped the shade, closed his eyes, and laid his head back to relax. A soft breeze danced across his forehead. Just before he fell into a deep and peaceful sleep, he heard a woman's soft voice faintly whisper, "A wish expressed, a favor bestowed."

Chapter 3

*K*ayla MacNicol sat at the outer edge of the family circle in a daze, cold as an icicle hanging from the eaves in the dead of winter. Shivering, she noted how her mother and brother seemed perfectly content to carry on with their conversation without her, discussing her life as if she wasn't even in the room. She was tempted to wave her arms and shout, "Hey, I'm here. Look at me. Listen to me." But she would never do that. It wasn't in her to cause a scene.

Her mother, Lady Lydia, was speaking to Duncan, chief of the MacNicol clan and Kayla's eldest brother. "Don't you think it's time to seek out a husband for Kayla?"

"I haven't really given it much thought," Duncan replied. Kayla believed her brother didn't care one way or another if she was married. He'd rather train men for battle than arrange betrothal and marriages.

"She's nearly two and twenty. She should be married by now, raising her own family, not tending to her brothers," her mother repeated her often-said words.

"Has she a suitor in mind?" Duncan asked. He glanced over to his wife, Janet, as if seeking her assistance. As usual, Janet remained quiet. She rarely spoke in matters that concerned the MacNicol clan except to support her husband. And she never questioned her mother-in-law, Lady Lydia.

Kayla opened her mouth to say nay, but her mother spoke first.

"I have a suitor in mind," Lady Lydia said, as if that was all that mattered. "I believe Arlin MacDonald would suit very well."

Kayla's jaw dropped, and her eyes shot open. Arlin MacDonald was an insensitive brute. He had never been nice to her, nor had he shown her the least indication of affection. She had no desire to marry Arlin.

"My brother Arlin?" Janet asked. She sounded as surprised as Kayla felt.

"Yes, your brother. It's only prudent for the MacNicols to pursue another marriage with the MacDonald clan. It will strengthen family ties and seal our alliance."

"I wasn't aware our alliance needed strengthening," Duncan said.

"Alliances can never be too strong. We've not had a strong leader since we lost our good King Alexander. King John is nothing more than a puppet for Edward. I do not trust the English. The Scottish clans must unite if they wish to remain strong."

"I've always favored our alliance with the MacLeods. Their fellowship has always served us well."

"But the MacLeods donna have any single sons available for marriage. We lost our only chance for a MacLeod marriage when Murdock last wed."

Kayla was appalled that her mother would bring up Murdock MacLeod, knowing how she had once favored him as a suitor. He, however, did not return her sentiments and found Merrie Lewis more to his liking.

Kayla wished she had the strength to argue with her mother, but she knew it would do no good. Lady Lydia rarely listened to her youngest child and only daughter. Instead, Kayla sat stunned, quietly watching her family plan her life, her eyes moving from face to face, seeing their mouths move but no longer registering their words. They were plotting her life—her life—and yet the conversation seemed beyond her.

Even though she was sitting near the warmth of the hearth, she felt a chilling cloak surround her. She wanted to flee, to be alone with her thoughts and feelings.

Dimly hearing the voices of her family as they carried on without her, she slipped out the door of the great hall and made her way to the stone steps climbing up along the castle wall. Treading her way along the battlement walkway, she sought a secluded refuge beside a large circular stone tower standing guard near the main castle gate. She rested her head against the cold hard grey stones and gazed out at the familiar landscape. This was her home, the only land she had ever known. The thought of leaving her home and her family tore at her heart.

Her thoughts were a mass of confusion swirling in her head. It didn't seem reasonable that they wanted her to marry Arlin MacDonald. They didn't need another marriage to secure an alliance. Duncan was already married to Janet MacDonald. And Duncan was the MacNicol chief. It wasn't like Arlin was in line to be the MacDonald chief. He had three elder brothers and at least a couple of nephews standing between him and Hugh MacDonald, the chief of their clan. Of course, she understood that another marriage between the families would strengthen the clan ties. And, aye, she was aware there were limited—make that no other—matches available, but she didn't want to marry Arlin. In the end, that was the thought that surfaced above all others: she simply did not want to marry Arlin MacDonald.

She hated the whining voice speaking in her head, and yet there was no use denying that the always-dutiful daughter of Lady Lydia and Chief Kennon MacNicol did not want to do her family's bidding. For all of her two and twenty years, she had always done everything that was expected of her, especially where her family was concerned. Everything except get married.

She had always believed she would marry; it just hadn't happened yet. She knew being married brought security and social standing, but she also had a dream that someday she would find her one true love and be allowed to marry the man of her choosing. She knew it was a whimsical dream based on a silly childhood illusion she should have discarded long ago. It certainly wasn't grounded in the hard cold reality of being the chief's only sister, but it was still her dream. Her brothers, Michael and Duncan, had found love matches with their wives. Was she not allowed to wish the same for herself?

She turned to see the torchlight flickering in the great hall. Twilight was slipping away into the darkness of night. She knew she should be down there, arguing with her family, refusing to accept decisions made on her behalf without her consent. Instead, she was standing alone on the fortress walkway, on the verge of tears.

Shifting her gaze skyward, she blinked several times to clear the moisture pooling in her eyes. A lone star appeared in the darkening sky. Her eyes locked upon the tiny pinpoint of twinkling light.

"Kind fairies," she spoke aloud. "Whatever else fate may hold for me, please help me find my own true love."

The radiant star twinkled, as if it had winked at her. And then she felt it. She felt a presence and heard a voice softly whispering in the wind. "A wish expressed, a favor bestowed."

"Who's there?" she wondered aloud. She turned, looking anxiously around the walkway, but of course, she was alone.

Too many of Mother's stories, she thought, trying to reason away what her senses so ardently told her. Lady Lydia often told her stories about the fairies guarding the Isle of Skye, and she wanted to believe they were true. There was even a legend about her great-grandmother Sophie having descended from the fairies. But they were just stories, Kayla told herself, even as her heart and soul murmured the truth.

Turning her back on the lone twinkling star, she started to walk away, but her inner voice only spoke louder, refusing to dismiss what her senses were saying. She couldn't pretend it was simply her heightened imagination playing tricks on her. She knew a fairy was close by. She had heard her voice and felt her presence. For years, she'd been feeling the presence of an unseen fairy by her side, often at unexpected moments. Many times, she had wished that the fairy would appear, but each time, she had been disappointed. Now, more than ever, Kayla fervently hoped that when the time was right, she would finally meet her fairy.

Chapter 4

"*D*aniel, we've landed, time to wake up." Teressa's voice broke through the cushioned quiet of Daniel's slumber.

"What? Are we there yet?" Daniel jerked himself awake, aided by his sister's repeated jabs to his shoulders.

"Yes, we're here. We've landed. I can't believe you slept through it all." Teressa was gathering her belongings, including her travel journal, as fellow passengers made their way single file down the aisles. "I didn't want to wake you. I know how hard jet lag can be for a novice traveler, but we've got to get off the plane."

"I'm surprised I was able to sleep at all," Daniel said, pulling himself out of his sleep-induced stupor. "I didn't think I'd ever fall asleep when, all of a sudden, I closed my eyes for a moment, and I was out like a light." He expected to feel travel weary, but in truth, he felt like he had just awakened from a long winter's nap, totally refreshed.

"Yeah, well you were sleeping like a bear in winter when it's the middle of June," Teressa said.

"A bear with a shit-eating grin," Robert smirked.

Daniel ignored their comments, but he didn't try to deny it. Based on the few lingering memories from his fleeting dream, he had reason to believe Robert's observation was quite accurate.

After they collected their luggage and made their way through customs, Teressa pulled out her travel itinerary and checked her notes. "We've got a couple of hours before we have to catch the train to Inverness. Enough time for coffee and breakfast. Anyone interested?" She had assumed the role of travel guide, and Daniel had happily acquiesced. At this point, it wasn't as if he had much choice.

"Coffee sounds good to me, or maybe I should try some of that English breakfast tea. You know, when in London and all that rot. Do you have any Earl Grey?" Daniel joked, attempting to imitate an accent like the ones he was hearing around him.

"We're not in London, you goof. We're in Glasgow," Teressa corrected him.

"Earl Grey and some blueberry scones would do nicely right about now," Robert said, lending his support to Daniel's suggestion.

Teressa rolled her eyes. "Boys," she mumbled. "Come on." She led the way to the taxi stand. "We'll eat at the train station. It's cheaper than the airport."

As they followed her lead, dragging their suitcases, Daniel exchanged a knowing look with Robert. They could tell she was enjoying her role as a ringleader.

They barely had enough time to finish their breakfast before they were off and running to catch the train that would take them to Inverness. From there, they would travel to the Isle of Skye by car with Robert's mother.

Although reluctant to admit it to his little sister, Daniel found that the farther they traveled into Scotland, the more at ease he felt. The stress of travel, big cities, and workday tension was slowly but unmistakably being replaced by an inner calm settling into his soul. He could feel the weight and weariness of his life slipping away, leaving behind a feeling of well-being he hadn't experienced in years.

Being the youngest of three boys and the only one still living at the family ranch had forced him to spend most of his time helping his parents manage the place. Being on the ranch was a life he loved. He'd been happy working side by side with his dad, but his dad had passed away three years ago, and his mother had died earlier this year. All alone on the twelve-acre ranch, he was beginning to wonder if Over-Yonder was where he belonged. The ranch had been his parents' dream, and they had done it justice, but it wasn't necessarily his. He wanted to make his own mark in the world. He just wasn't sure where or what that mark would be.

As he relaxed onto the gentle massaging vibrations of the train, he felt a soothing sensation and a return to innocence that had long been lacking in his life. The smile growing inside him pushed to break free as he realized he needed to thank Teressa for this enforced leisure. He couldn't remember the last time he had been able to sit back and relax without duties to tend to or schedules to meet. And what a beautiful countryside it was, lush and green living side by side with raw and rugged.

This vacation was looking better than he had expected. Robert's cousins, Jack and Jenny, had moved into the ranch before he left, and they had immediately made themselves useful, feeling right at home. Jack especially was looking forward to becoming a modern ranch hand, learning all he could about tending to horses. Daniel had two full weeks to leave the cares of tending the home fires behind, and he intended to make the most of it.

His extended guardianship of the ranch was not one he regretted, but as he had recently told Teressa, he felt that it was time to move on and find a place where he belonged. He was about to lose his job with the mounted police, and he wondered what he should do next. He still had the ranch, but it was no longer self-supporting as it was when his dad was alive. It would take considerable changes and an infusion of cash to bring it back to full production. Maybe it was time to consider other options.

He had proved to himself that he was capable of earning a living; now he wondered if he was capable of creating a life, one that included his own home and family. The ranch was a great place to live in but was too big for a single man, and he had no prospects for a family anytime soon.

Chapter 5

*I*t was his second day on Skye, and already he was back in the saddle, riding free as the wind in the wide-open spaces. After an exhilarating all-out run that had taken man and beast to the brink of exhaustion, Daniel slowed his horse to a gentle walking pace. Leaning forward, he ran his hand along the stallion's neck, soothing the heated animal. The path they were on ran along a swift running river, and he directed the horse down to the water.

"Hey, Wilbur, I think we've earned a rest and a good long drink," he spoke to the animal in a cheery tone. *Yep, it's good to be back in the saddle again*, he thought as he hummed the old Western tune.

He dismounted near the water's edge and led Wilbur to drink his fill from the cool, clear stream flowing freely through the shallow valley. He'd been pleased with the selection of horseflesh available at the Skyeland Stables, and Garrett Riggs, the stable manager, had picked out a perfect mount. Once they had started swapping stories of life on a horse ranch, Garrett had quickly chosen Wilbur as exactly the right horse for Daniel.

"He's as loyal a dog, and as spirited as the day is long. He'll give you a good ride," Garrett had assured him.

The stable manager also provided him with a map of the established horse paths around the island and sent him on his way with plenty of snacks and a water canteen. It was shaping up to be a very good day.

Daniel knelt down and dipped his bandana into the running stream. He swiped the wet fabric across his face and over the back of his neck, feeling refreshed by the brisk slap of the cold cloth. Reaching into one of the saddlebags, he pulled out the canteen and took a long cool drink. He checked Garrett's map, examining the various horse trails, deciding which one he would take. He chose a route that followed the riverbed, then swung wide out of the valley toward Portree before heading back toward the Skyeland Stables. He figured it would give him a nice long ride and still get him back early in the evening, leaving plenty of time to get ready for the summer solstice party Teressa was planning.

He stowed the map and canteen back in the saddlebag and climbed back in the saddle. Spurring Wilbur forward at a leisurely walking pace, they moved along the wide flowing stream, heading for the next trail marker. Deeply breathing the brisk fresh air, he detected a hint of the nearby ocean carried along on the breeze. His gaze swept the horizon, taking in the bounty of the landscape. He was impressed by its rugged beauty. Lush green growth clashed with the abundance of rocky volcanic hills, each claiming their foothold in the rough rolling countryside. It wasn't a soft or easy land like the rolling pastures and fields he'd seen in the lowlands of Scotland. Skye presented its own unique challenges. He could see how the island continued to draw Robert back to his family's roots.

Filled with contentment, Daniel was reminded how grateful he was to Teressa for talking him into making this trip. Robert and Teressa had gone out of their way to ensure he didn't feel like a third wheel tagging along behind a newly married couple. Robert treated him like a brother, and Daniel easily returned the sentiment. He marveled at how well Robert and Teressa fit together, almost as if made for each other, and a part of him—make that a big part of him—envied their relationship.

Recently, he'd begun to feel as though he was reaching a place in his life where it would be a whole lot better if he had someone to share it with. He figured she'd have to be someone pretty special and a little out of the ordinary in this day and age. He was looking for a kind of old-fashioned girl who'd be committed to raising a family, rather like his mom. He wasn't interested in settling for less.

However, so far, his relationships with women left something to be desired. It seemed there were plenty of women who were satisfied with speed-dating their way into a relationship and then use instant text messaging as their primary form of communication. That type of courtship wasn't for him. He thought the idea of getting to know a person over time was much more appealing. He'd never experienced love at first sight and wasn't sure he believed in the phenomenon.

Lost in his thoughts, Daniel was enjoying the warmth of the sun shining through cotton-ball clouds gracing the bright blue sky.

Suddenly, the mild summer breeze turned violent. Without warning, the wind blowing in from the northwest increased ominously, spooking Wilbur as the horse shied away from the startling force of the rising storm. But it was unavoidable. Horse and rider were hit full-on by the hot fierce wind. It sprang up from nowhere, engulfing them in its wake.

The gale-force wind kicked up loose dirt, whipping twigs through the air like bits of straw and scattered leaves, sending the debris flying around his body. He raised his arms to protect his face from the stinging pricks of the flying rubble. His instinctive reaction caused him to lose his grip on the reins.

He felt the air being sucked from his lungs. He fought to catch his breath while struggling to maintain control over Wilbur. It was a losing battle. The combined force of the vicious wind and the bucking of the frightened animal threw Daniel off balance. He felt himself being ripped from the saddle.

Panic welled up inside him as he fought against the unnatural phenomenon. Rational thought eluded him. All he could think was *survival*. Being an experienced rider, he twisted his body into the fall as he fell toward the hard-packed ground, knowing it was going to hurt like the dickens. He landed on his backside with a painful thud. A second before he blacked out, he could have sworn he saw Wilbur suddenly disappear. Then everything went black.

Chapter 6

The next morning, Kayla rose with the sun. She had formulated a plan. It wasn't a very well-thought-out plan, and it was chockfull of risks, but her emotions were such that she knew she had to give it a try. While she wasn't comfortable confronting her mother about her marriage prospects, she believed it was perfectly acceptable to send a message to Arlin asking him to oppose the betrothal. Even if he was the youngest son of the MacDonald chief, since he was a man, they were much more likely to accept his decision on the matter. Maybe her own family wouldn't listen to her, but surely they would listen to Arlin.

There was the risk that Arlin was in favor of their betrothal, but she was fairly certain he was no more interested in an arranged marriage than she was. They had known each other since childhood, and he had never shown any interest in her, often treating her with a sense of superior disdain, as if being a MacDonald made him better than the rest of her family. She was counting on the possibility that his lack of interest in a betrothal was equal to hers.

It wasn't because she considered him to be truly ugly. He was fairly attractive, with a strong muscular body. Although she believed his nose was a tad too big for his face, many of her friends had claimed that Arlin wasn't a man they would kick out of a marriage bed. Unfortunately, she didn't share their sentiment.

Her only real concern was that Arlin might have developed an unknown fondness for her that she didn't return. It was unlikely, but she supposed it was possible. Choosing not to dwell on such a disparaging prospect, she clung to a pocket of hope that he would agree to oppose a betrothal.

After a restless night with not nearly enough sleep, Kayla knew she couldn't just sit around the keep for another day while her family plotted her future. She wanted to send a message to Arlin MacDonald, but she didn't feel right asking anyone at Scorrybreac to help her. What she needed was the help of an old friend, someone who would listen to her and support her without any questions. She believed Fern McLarkin was that type of friend.

Fern had married a few years earlier and lived with her husband and little boy in a cottage outside the village where they tended their sheep. Hopefully, Fern and her husband, Eldon, would agree to help her get a message to Arlin. Hopefully, Arlin would agree to oppose the betrothal. Hopefully, her plan would work out all right.

It was a long ride, and she wanted to get an early start. When the sun began making its appearance above the horizon, she was down at the stables preparing her brown mare for the ride. Gavin, the oldest of the boys who tended the stables, greeted her.

"Good morn', milady. Ye be here early. Do ye need any help with Sallie?" Gavin asked, referring to Kayla's horse.

"Nay, Gavin. I can manage by myself." Kayla gave another tug on the cinch belt holding the saddle in place.

"Is anyone else going riding with ye?" Gavin asked, taking a look down the row of stalls.

"I'm riding out to see Fern McLarkin. We're going up to the hills to enjoy the first day of summer. I expect to be gone all day."

"Do yer brothers know?" Gavin looked skeptical, and she knew he had good reason. It wasn't like her to leave Scorrybreac on her own.

"I don't need my brothers' permission to visit my friend. I can take care of myself," she spoke with greater confidence than she felt. "If any of them asks, you just tell my brothers what I told you. Do ye understand?"

"Aye, I think I do," Gavin answered, scratching his head. "I just hope they don't come asking."

As soon as Kayla was out of sight from the watchtowers, she spurred her horse into a spirited gallop, heading quickly across the rough countryside. She knew Sallie couldn't maintain this pace for long, but she was anxious to see Fern.

She had ridden a good distance, and all was going well. She allowed Sallie to slow to a walking pace. She felt invigorated with renewed confidence. However, as she crested the rise above the banks of the Glenmore River, her plan was once again thrown off course.

Her first reaction was gut-gripping fear when she came upon a foreign-looking man lying at the edge of the river flowing freely through the valley. She wasn't sure if he was alive or dead, but either way, it wasn't good to find him lying along on the trail. His mere presence created a problem she couldn't ignore.

She paused before approaching him, her eyes scanning the countryside while she listened for signs of anyone else in the area. For a brief moment, her fears almost got the better of her, and she considered riding on without investigating the stranger's condition. However, her growing curiosity, along with her natural tendency to offer healing whenever it was needed, finally won out. Convinced he was indeed alone and probably injured, she dismounted and cautiously approached the figure sprawled along the shallow running river. Her visit with Fern would have to wait.

She was certain she had never seen him before, and yet he looked vaguely familiar. His unusual style of clothing marked him as an outlander, probably English. He wore sturdy boots and a short leather jacket that looked expensive and well-made. Something about his boots looked familiar, but for the moment, she couldn't remember why. Perhaps she was too busy noticing his unusual indigo blue breeches and how extraordinarily good they looked on him.

Kneeling beside him, she paused for a moment to study her find. He was alive, of that she was certain. She could detect his breathing by the shallow rise and fall of his chest. He was also disarmingly handsome. His dark brown hair, cut short and neat, was brushed back from his forehead, highlighting the strength of his well-formed chin and sharply defined cheekbones. Her eyes paused a second longer at his mouth, taking in the fullness of his lips slightly parted as he breathed. Tentatively, she reached out her hand to lightly touch his face, softly running her fingers across his forehead and down his cheek as if to prove that he was real.

"Whatever shall I do with you?" she whispered, mesmerized by the unique situation this man presented.

Chapter 7

*D*aniel woke to the face of an angel. Backlit by the sun, she was framed by a halo of glowing red hair. Her pale white skin took on an iridescent glow. Innocent green eyes peered back at him. He smiled, thinking he'd gone to heaven.

Startled, the woman pulled back. "You're alive!"

His smile deepened. "Alive? You mean I'm not in heaven?"

The angelic vision shook her head. "Nay."

Of course, there was still the possibility he was dreaming. He was feeling dazed and light-headed. If this was a dream, he figured he could do whatever he wanted, and right now he wanted very much to kiss his angel. He attempted to lift his head toward the delicate face bending over him, but the painful protest of his muscles as he started to move confirmed he was both awake and alive.

"Oowww, what happened to me?" His hand came up to rub the back of his head.

"I don't know. I just found you here." She sat back on her heels, giving him room to move.

Daniel rolled gingerly to his side, straining to push himself up from the ground. The young woman reached out to help him sit upright. Looking around, he took stock of his situation. Apparently, he'd been knocked out when he fell from his horse. He didn't know how long he'd been unconscious, but he figured it couldn't have been for too long, as the sun was still climbing high in the sky.

He slowly moved his head from side to side, cautiously checking the extent of his injuries, softly groaning as his muscles rebelled. His back and neck were sore, but not too bad considering his fall. Other than suffering some aches and pains, nothing felt broken or out of joint.

"You didn't happen to see my horse hanging around, did you?" Daniel looked at the young woman sitting on the ground next to him.

"Nay, I've seen no horse in the area, just you." She watched his movements with curious large eyes.

Struggling to stand with her assistance, Daniel looked around and confirmed her statement. His horse was nowhere in sight. He was also struck by an uncanny feeling that something wasn't right. Maybe it was a result of his police training to always be aware of his surroundings, but somehow the area felt different. Everything looked pretty much the same, and yet somehow everything was different. Some trees seemed taller while others looked shorter, and the scrubby undergrowth appeared thicker than he remembered. It didn't make sense to think that the river, rocks, and trees could look different from one moment to the next, but they did. He shook his head to shake off the feeling. The sensation remained.

Choosing to ignore the anomaly for the moment, he directed his focus back to the woman by his side. Standing no taller than his shoulder, she looked up at him with those beautifully expressive pale green eyes. She was dressed in a long grey wool skirt and a white linen tunic belted at her waist with a thick leather cord. Unruly curls of red hair escaped the long braid hanging down to the middle of her back. He noticed she wore no cosmetics and had a real back-to-nature look about her. Her style looked like something he might see in the Haight-Ashby district of San Francisco, or maybe around Berkeley. It was a real throwback to the hippy era, but on her it looked good, better than good, and he liked the effect.

"I suppose introductions are in order. My name's Daniel." He flashed a friendly smile.

"I'm Kayla." Timidly, she returned his smile.

"It's a pleasure to meet you, Kayla. Do you live around here?" He hoped she was in a position to offer him a ride back to the stables or at least into town. He was pretty sure Wilbur had run off after being spooked by the sudden windstorm. He figured the horse had hightailed it back to the stables, leaving him with the option of walking back or catching a ride with his angel of mercy. Given his choices, he was hoping he could hitch a ride with the angel.

"I'm from Scorrybreac. It's not very far from here." She seemed reluctant to say more.

He remembered that Scorrybreac was the name of a local village. He'd seen it on his trail map. Expecting to find a phone there, Daniel made his request. "I know it's a bit much to ask, but do you think I could hitch a ride with you back to your village?"

She looked back over the hill and then down the river path as if deciding which way to go. Finally, a timid smile reached her lips. "My village? Aye, I think so. I mean, I can't very well leave you stranded out here."

"There are many who would. I'm glad you're not one of them. Thanks."

Kayla scurried to retrieve her horse and led it over to a boulder. Daniel immediately understood her intentions. The horse was large, and she was small, making it difficult to mount up without assistance. A step-up would make it easier.

He halted her movement. Lacing his fingers together, he leaned forward to offer his assistance. "Here, allow me."

"Oh nay, I couldn't." She resisted, stepping back from his gallant gesture.

"Please, allow me. I insist," he repeated his offer, maintaining his position.

Wide-eyed, she hesitated a moment before she timidly accepted his assistance. Gently placing one foot in his cupped hands, she pushed off to swing her leg across the wide backside of her horse. As soon as she was securely settled, Daniel braced his hands on the horse's backside, and in one powerful lunge, he mounted up behind her. It came easy from years of practice.

It was tempting to cuddle up close to Kayla's backside and embrace her in his arms, but he knew that would be too forward for this shy little lady. Instead, he opted for the more gentlemanly and prudent choice of leaving a few precious inches of space between them. Gently placing his hands at her waist, he indicated he was ready to go. He felt her momentarily flinch at his touch before she gave a firm kick to the horse's side.

Kayla held herself stiffly upright. Detecting her discomfort, he attempted to make small talk, hoping to put her more at ease. "You handle your horse well. Have you been riding long?"

"Aye, I've been around horses since I was a wee lass. My brothers took me riding even before I learned to walk. I've had my horse, Sallie, for a several years now." As she spoke, she seemed to relax a little. He was encouraged.

"I've been around horses my whole life. I grew up on a ranch. My dad raised horses. Do you go riding much?" He was thinking maybe they could have a riding date together on another day, preferably a day when he had his own horse and wasn't in need of a favor. Although riding in tandem with her did have its advantages.

"Not as often as I would like. More often, my duties keep me close to home." She hesitated a moment, then continued, "You're not from around here, are you?"

"I guess my accent gives me away. I'm from America, California. I've traveled for days to get here." He was about to say he was traveling with his sister, Teressa, and her husband, Robert MacNicol, but the thought slipped from his mind, replaced by a heightened awareness of his arousal as he detected the gap between them inching smaller and smaller as the rhythm of the horse slid him closer and closer.

"America, California?" she repeated slowly, looking puzzled. "That sounds interesting."

He couldn't blame her. She probably didn't encounter many American tourists on this remote Isle of Skye. "Yeah, well, it wasn't my idea, but now that I'm here, I'm liking it," he said.

"Will you be staying long on Skye?" she asked.

"I just arrived yesterday. We'll be here for a couple of weeks before we head back home."

"Oh, I see," was all she said.

Daniel felt her sink into silence. He understood. There was an aura of innocence about her. She probably wasn't interested in a vacation fling with a foreign tourist and saw no reason to encourage his attentions. Unfortunately for him, his attentions were already encouraged by her mere presence. He was itching to run his hands along her slender arms and massage her delicate shoulders. He was strongly aware of his desire to touch her, a desire so much greater than anything he'd experienced before. It was as if his whole being yearned to know the feel of her body against his. He didn't know how far it was to her village, but he was sure this would seem like one of the longest rides of his life. He was beginning to see the appeal this island and its people held for his sister.

Searching for something to say to break the awkward silence descending upon them, he opted for the safest topic he could think of. He asked about her family. "You said your brothers taught you to ride. Tell me about them." He found that most people felt more comfortable talking about their family than themselves.

"I have three older brothers, Duncan, Michael, and Roderick. I'm the youngest, and they rarely let me forget. They're very protective of me. They all ride well, of course, but it was Michael who taught me to ride. Of my brothers, he has the greatest patience."

"Your family sounds a lot like mine. I'm the youngest of three boys, and then there's my little sister. My older brothers, Brett and Conner, have moved away with families of their own, but I'm still close to my sister. Do you get to see your brothers often?" Her family sounded vaguely familiar to Daniel, and he was trying to remember why. He was hoping she wasn't offended when his hands slipped from her waist. They were now resting lightly on her hips. She had such a lovely curve to her hips.

"Of course, every day. We all live at Scorrybreac with our mother. My older brothers, Duncan and Michael, are married, but Rory and I are still unmatched."

"Did you say your brother, Rory?"

"Aye, Roderick. We all call him Rory."

"And your brother Duncan, you say he's married?"

"Aye, to Janet MacDonald. They have a wee bairn daughter, Amy. My brother Michael is married to Shannon. They have two young boys, Tanner and Torrin, and are expecting another bairn soon. Why do you ask?"

He realized that the description of her family sounded all too familiar in a bizarre sort of way. These were the names of the people in Teressa's journal, a journal that described traveling over seven hundred years into the past. He wondered if his sister had drawn on this local family to create her fantastic tale, or was it possible . . . ? No. He stopped his thoughts. It was far too unbelievable, and he certainly wasn't going to ask what year it was, like some dim-witted numbskull.

Daniel wanted to proceed with caution. It was probably all just one big coincidence. Rather than rushing to rash conclusions, he preferred to take it slow while he gathered more information.

"Umm, no reason. I just like hearing about your family. Do you think I'll be able to meet them sometime?" If Teressa had met these people, it might be interesting to swap stories with them. Perhaps he could find out why she had written a tale of fairies and time travel. He wondered if she had incorporated some of their local legends into her travel journal to add some spice.

"You'll meet them when we reach the keep. I'm sure Duncan will be able to help you get back to your friends. He always takes care of everything. We're almost there."

"That'll be great. I'd like to use your phone . . ." His words faltered abruptly. They had come to the crest of a ridge overlooking a low rolling plain. On the far side of the shallow valley, sitting high on the cliffs overlooking the sea, stood a large medieval fortress in all its glory.

"What were you saying? I'm sorry I didn't hear you." She twisted in the saddle to look at Daniel.

He didn't answer.

"What's wrong?" she asked.

He felt his blood drain from his face, and his mouth hung open in stark surprise as he stared off into the distance. Spread out before him was a village of humble ancient cottages. Curls of smoke rose from thatched roofs supported by walls of mud plaster. Some of them were painted in whitewash; most were dull grey. Farther up on the opposite bluff sat what he could only describe as a medieval fortress surrounding a castle. His mind struggled to understand what his eyes were seeing.

He figured it was either a perfectly well-preserved ancient castle or a recently built replica, and a darn convincing one at that. The village and castle looked like ancient Scottish dwellings, and everyone in sight looked dressed for the part. His guessed it was a living museum, rather like colonial Williamsburg in Virginia. No wonder Teressa had written about being in the thirteenth century. As he looked at the scene before them, it was easy to imagine such a far-fetched adventure.

He finally grabbed hold of his wits, setting aside his initial shock. He needed to get a grip.

"Wow, this place looks like a real medieval village. You say you live near here?"

"Aye. I live in the Scorrybreac keep." She pointed off toward the castle.

"In the castle? They let you live in the castle?" he questioned, disbelieving.

"Of course, we live there. 'Tis the home of the MacNicol clan. Have you no been listening to me?"

Chapter 8

*D*aniel continued to study his surroundings as an uneasy feeling churned in his gut.

"Are you all right?" Kayla asked, sounding concerned.

"Yeah, yeah, I'm fine. I'm just taking this all in," he answered. "This isn't quite what I had expected."

He took another look at the woman seated in front of him and realized she was suitably dressed for the time period. He wondered if she was a history buff, or one of those reenactment nuts who couldn't leave the past behind. His blunt reaction must have alerted her to his state of confusion, and he concentrated on regaining his composure. He didn't want to sound like some idiot tourist, rambling on about reenactment sites, living museums, or how bizarre the place looked, so he said nothing, keeping his thoughts to himself. Kayla followed his lead, and they rode the rest of the way to the castle in silence.

As they rode through the village, Daniel took it all in, noticing how the crude and ancient dwellings were sturdy but simply built. For the most part, they appeared to be in good repair rather than old and falling apart. Each showed signs of active habitation with a collection of men, women, and children engaged in what appeared to be normal daily routines. With unconcealed curiosity, several of them watched him pass.

Word of the approaching riders must have traveled quickly through the compound. When Kayla and Daniel emerged through the fortress gates, two large men in ancient costumes were standing at the center of the courtyard, ready to receive them. They wore long woolen tunics belted at the waist over knitted leggings with handmade leather boots held in place with straps.

Daniel slid off the back of the horse and reached up to help Kayla dismount. He left his hand resting possessively at her waist as he stood his ground beside her.

"Who do we have here?" the larger man asked. He stood with his arms folded across his chest, legs firmly planted. His face bore a dark expression. Daniel guessed him to be the man in charge.

Shooting a quick silencing glance at Daniel, Kayla rushed to explain, "This man is Daniel. I found him injured and alone near the river. He was thrown from his horse. It must have run off. He needed help, so I brought him here. I believe you would know what to do."

Turning to Daniel, she continued the introductions, "This is my brother, Duncan, chief of the MacNicols."

An uneasy silence consumed the small group as the two men openly assessed each other. Duncan fixed his steadfast gaze on Daniel, his rigid features clearly expressing his concern at encountering this unexpected intruder.

Daniel broke the standoff with a friendly half smile. "Duncan, chief of the MacNicols, is it? I believe it's my honor to meet you. I'm Daniel Ellers." A hint of macho arrogance leached into Daniel's voice as he addressed the clan leader. He stretched out his right hand in greeting.

Kayla stepped away from his side as if offended. "Daniel Ellers! Do you know of a woman named Teressa Ellers?"

Daniel broke his focus from Duncan, dropped his hand, and turned to look at Kayla. "Of course, she's my sister."

Kayla's eyes grew wide with amazement. "Your sister?"

Duncan stepped forward, taking control of the situation. "Kayla, go find Rory for me. Send him to my study. And say nothing of this."

Kayla turned to look at Duncan in disbelief, as if ready to voice her dissent.

"Go. Now," he firmly repeated his instructions. The stern look on his face let her know there was no room for argument.

She hesitated a moment longer, casting a sideways glance at Daniel before she turned away and stomped off toward the large stone structure dominating the fortress courtyard.

Duncan turned back to the stranger before him. "You, come with me." Not waiting for a response, he turned and headed back toward the keep.

The exchange between Kayla and her brother indicated something big was going on, and Daniel could tell he was definitely an outsider. Believing Duncan held the answers he needed, he willingly followed the MacNicol chief into the castle. As they crossed the courtyard, he kept an eye on Kayla. She was greeted by another woman, who turned to gape at him with trepidation before they hurried off together toward the far side of the building.

The authenticity of his surroundings continued to amaze him as he followed Duncan toward the main entrance of the large stone castle.

He noticed that the battlement wall of the fortress was guarded by very real-looking Scottish warriors, carrying very real-looking swords and longbows with quivers of arrows slung on their backs. Kayla's horse was being led to a nearby stable by a young boy clad in a rough woolen tunic and ill-fitting breeches. As he walked through the courtyard, many of the workers stopped their actions to turn and stare at him as if he was an alien and not just another lost tourist.

Daniel thought back to Teressa's travel journal. She had reported that it was the lack of modern technology that had finally convinced her that she had actually traveled back through time. Taking a close look around, he realized he was having the same experience. When he had first regained consciousness next to the stream, he had instinctively felt a change in his surroundings, but he hadn't been able to figure out what it was. Thinking about it now, he took into consideration the missing trail markers, the lack of paved roads or electrical wires, and the complete absence of mechanical or motorized sounds. It was getting harder and harder to believe this was just some kind of a staged historical village. It was as if everything modern had completely disappeared.

He continued to question his initial theory that this was simply a working replica of an ancient Scottish fortress. As disconcerting as the alternative might be, he was gradually, although reluctantly, considering the reality of the hard evidence being presented before him. As a policeman, he heavily relied on both gut feelings and hard evidence. From all appearances, this wasn't a working museum, and these people weren't historical actors. This was the real deal. That uneasy thought left him with a whole new set of questions regarding how and why.

Duncan led Daniel through the great hall and into a smaller room tucked into the far corner of the keep. Its furnishings were sparse. There was a table that served as a desk, two chairs, a stool, and a storage chest sitting below a cupboard carved into the thick stone wall. Motioning to one of the chairs near the small stone hearth, Duncan invited Daniel to take a seat.

"So, Daniel Ellers, why don't we begin with how you got here?"

If Duncan's expression was meant to intimidate him, he was doing a good job; however, Daniel detected an undertone of curiosity leaking through.

"I was out on a ride this morning when I suddenly got caught in a freak summer storm and was thrown from my horse. I must have passed out. When I woke up, I was looking at your sister, and my horse was gone. She was kind enough to bring me here for assistance. Like she said, it seemed like the best course of action at the time. I was hoping I could use your phone to call for a ride back to Skyeland Stables."

"That may be a problem. I don't know what a *phone* is, and I've never heard of Skyeland Stables," Duncan said.

Daniel sized up the man across from him. He wondered if Duncan was being honest or if he was so completely emerged into his historical role-playing that he refused to step out of character. Judging by the look on Duncan's face, Daniel opted for honest and figured this guy was his best shot at getting some valuable information.

"Okay then, if you don't mind me asking, and I know this might sound a bit strange, chalk it up to jet lag and the blow to my head, but can you tell me what day this is? More precisely, what year?" The idea that he was even asking such a question made Daniel uneasy, and he began to wonder if the blow to his head had caused more damage than he wanted to believe.

Unfortunately, it seemed that Duncan understood the question all too well. "'Tis the twenty-first day of September 1295. And let me guess, you're from the future."

Daniel stared at the man. "Are you pulling my leg?" His mind was racing, seeking answers before the questions could even be formed.

"Do I look like I'm pulling your leg?" Duncan eyed him with a mixture of wariness and disbelief as he returned Daniel's stare.

"You're telling me the truth? It's really the thirteenth century?" Daniel raised his brow in disbelief.

"Aye," Duncan confirmed.

"And this isn't some kind of historical reenactment?"

"Why the blaze would anyone do that?" Duncan looked at him as though he was a stark raving idiot, which was pretty much how he felt.

Daniel pressed the palm of his hand against his forehead. His head was starting to ache. It occurred to him that Duncan was looking pretty calm for a man speaking to someone from the future. "Does this type of thing happen often around here?"

"Nay, not often. You're only the second such visitor." Duncan emphasized the word *visitor*. "But I thought even once was highly unusual. Your sister visited us about three years ago. Did she no tell you about it?"

"Well, not directly. She never told me what happened to her here, but she kept a journal. Recently, I had an opportunity to read it, so yes, you could say I'm aware of the story, which up until now I didn't believe. I'm still not sure what to think about all this." He was struck by how amazingly prepared he was to deal with the situation, and all because he had inadvertently read Teressa's journal. As unbelievable as he had thought her story to be, without her validation that this was even possible, he might very well have gone stark raving mad from the unfathomable situation he was now facing. His logical mind, the one that placed such high value on hard evidence, might have deserted him when faced with such an improbable—no, make that impossible—situation, and yet here he was, talking to the chief of the MacNicol clan in the thirteenth century.

"So tell me, how is it that you Ellers keep showing up at my keep? Are ye cursed or am I?"

"Honestly, I don't know. According to Teressa's story, it has something to do with fairies, but I've never encountered any fairies." Daniel found it hard to believe he was having this conversation, but he was certain he was awake, and preferable as it might be, he was fairly certain this wasn't a hallucination.

There was a sharp knock on the door, followed by a man entering the study.

"Holy shit!" Daniel leaped to his feet. He suddenly believed he was the victim of an elaborate hoax. The man standing before him was Robert, Teressa's husband. "Robert, are you in on this? Is this some kind of weird joke? 'Cause if it is, I don't think it's funny."

"I am not Robert. I'm Rory. And I don't know anything about a *weird joke*." The man's stoic expression held no hint of a smile.

"You expect me to believe you're not Robert and this isn't a joke?" Daniel scoffed.

"I don't care what you believe. My name is not Robert." Robert's double turned to Duncan. "What's this about? Why have you sent for me?"

"Rory, this man claims he's Daniel Ellers." Duncan stood, pausing for only a second before adding, "Teressa's brother."

"Teressa's brother?" Rory repeated, his voice heavy with amazement.

"Aye, so he says, and I believe he speaks the truth," Duncan confirmed.

Rory stared at Daniel for a long moment, looking him over. "I've many unanswered questions, but there's only one that truly matters. How is Teressa? Did she return home safe?"

For a brief moment, Daniel remained silent. He needed time to digest the whole experience. His first reaction at seeing Rory was that he was seeing his brother-in-law, Robert, but on closer inspection, he could see the differences. This man wore his hair longer, and while he had nearly the same height and build as Robert, Rory was bulkier, more like a bodybuilder. He looked a lot like Robert, but his face was thinner and carried a weary sadness that made him appear older. Daniel could see this man wasn't his brother-in-law, and yet he felt an immediate connection to him, a sort of kinship.

One step at a time, Daniel told himself, *I can get through this if I just take it one step at a time.* Finally, gaining control of his thoughts, he answered Rory's question, "Teressa is well. She returned home safely."

"Does she speak of me?" Rory asked.

Daniel registered a flash of longing racing through Rory's eyes, and he instantly understood the man's concerns. He grappled with the idea that Teressa believed this man had reincarnated as Robert in the twenty-first century to be with her. He figured time travel by itself was strange enough to deal with; he didn't need to add reincarnation into the mix. A clear and resounding voice in his head screamed, *Do not tell.* His gut instincts told him it was one can of worms he didn't want to mess with. He immediately resolved not to say anything about Rory becoming Robert sometime in the future, regardless of whether it was true or not.

"Not a day goes by that I'm not aware of how much she loves you," Daniel answered. He felt it was a small act of kindness to give such reassurance to the man whom Teressa believed to be her future husband.

"What happened to her after she left here? Why has she not returned?"

"You know, I'm betting you've got a lot of questions, but I'm sorry to say I don't have a lot of answers. I can tell you she came home a changed woman. And I can tell you she's still very much in love with you. Right now, that's all I've got." Daniel wished he had more to offer the guy, but until a few days ago, he had been completely unaware of Teressa's deep dark secret.

Rory nodded, accepting Daniel's reply. "Thank you, brother." He offered his simple gratitude.

"Brother?" Daniel was taken aback by Rory's fitting use of the term.

"'Tis no secret. If Teressa had been able to stay here with me, I would have made her my wife. As far as I am concerned, that makes you my brother."

Yeah, well, maybe someday you'll get your wish, Daniel thought, awestruck by Rory's declaration.

"So what happens now?" Daniel questioned his hosts. He looked from Rory to Duncan.

"'Tis a good question. You say you haven't encountered any fairies?" As Duncan spoke, he went to the wooden cupboard set into the stone wall to retrieve a bottle of amber liquid. He motioned for Daniel and

Rory to sit down as he poured them each a drink. Judging by the fumes, Daniel guessed it to be old-fashioned Scottish whisky.

Settling back into the armchair he had so abruptly vacated, Daniel accepted the much–needed libation. "Nope, no fairies here," he said. *Just an angel*, he thought, thinking of Kayla.

"Other than to bring news of Teressa back to Rory, do you have any idea of why you're here?" Duncan asked, taking a generous swallow of whisky.

"No, not at all. I only recently discovered what happened to Teressa during her visit here, and I'm still finding this all pretty hard to accept. I've no clue as to why, much less how this is even possible." Daniel shook his head, perplexed. He took a drink of the strong liquor and nearly coughed, but held it back, his throat burning. He was determined not to look weak in the presence of these ancient warriors.

"From what Duncan and I were able to piece together, a powerful fairy named Moezell brought your sister here to secure a match between Duncan and Janet MacDonald. When her task was finished, she was sent back to her time," Rory informed Daniel.

"Yeah, that's pretty much the same information I have," Daniel confirmed. "But I have no idea why I'm here."

"Since she did it before, I'm thinking she did it again. 'Tis my guess that Moezell is behind all this. We'll just have to wait and see if she lets us in on her plans." Duncan shrugged. It was all he could offer for the moment.

"Isn't there anything else we can do? No other way to send me back?" Daniel asked. While it was pretty much in keeping with what Teressa had written in her journal, he found it hard to believe he was at the mercy of an unseen fairy.

"It's no in our hands. It's up to Moezell. We have to trust she knows what she's doing." Rory sounded hopeful. "My previous encounter with Moezell gives me a wee measure of reassurance."

"You want me to believe, much less trust, in a fairy I've never even seen?" Daniel was still finding it hard to believe they were talking about fairies as if they were an everyday occurrence. "Has either of you ever seen this fairy?"

"Aye, she appeared to me briefly after Teressa disappeared on the beach. She told me Teressa had to return to her own time. I've no seen any sign of her since," Rory explained.

"It's been a year since you've seen her?" Daniel asked.

"Nay, 'twas over three years ago," Rory said.

"Three years! In my time, Teressa's visit to Skye happened only a year ago."

"'Tis been three years and three months since I've last seen Teressa," Rory said.

"I wonder why she waited so long," Daniel asked, referring to the fairy.

"This suggests Moezell is working on her own schedule, for her own reasons. There's no much we can do until she makes herself known, except offer you our hospitality," Duncan said.

"We can do no more. You've been sent here by her magic," Rory added.

"By magic! You believe in magic?"

"Aye. What else would you call it?" Rory questioned.

"Honestly, I don't know what I believe, but I've never believed in magic." Daniel shook his head. Of course, before today, he hadn't believed time travel was possible either.

"Then I would say now is a good time to start," Rory said, flashing a mocking grin.

Chapter 9

*D*aniel held fast to the thought that his sister had returned back to their time as if she had never left. If Moezell, some unseen fairy, was behind all this, then hopefully, she would do the same for him. Granted, it wasn't much to hold on to, but if he really was at the mercy of Moezell, he felt better thinking that, sooner or later, she would return him to where he had been when this whole fiasco began.

Until then, as Teressa had written in her journal, he planned to make the most of his unusual experience. He figured it wasn't often that a man got to travel back in time, much less be met by such understanding and welcoming people. Most folks would probably try to kill someone who claimed they were from the future out of pure fearful ignorance, rather than be as accommodating as these MacNicol brothers. Thankfully, Duncan's fine Scottish whisky was helping to take the edge off an experience that could only be described as mind-boggling.

As unbelievable and bizarre as it was, Daniel realized he had been thrust unexpectedly into an elite league of gentlemen. Their membership was based on the shared (and very secret) knowledge of his and Teressa's origins, which included time travel and a powerful fairy. It ranked up there as being one of the strangest set of circumstances he could ever imagine, and yet it created an unspoken bond of loyalty that united them in a strong fraternal brotherhood. The feeling of belonging to this elite brotherhood provided a measure of security for Daniel. He knew he could trust these men with his life, and like his fellow police officers, he knew they had his back.

"Magic may be all well and good, and hopefully, it'll provide some answers sooner or later. But until then, if you don't mind, I'd like to return to the scene of my, um, accident to have a look around. I don't know what I expect to find, but I'll feel better if I can go take a look."

He had almost said the scene of the crime, but it was hard to say just what crime had been committed. Would being sucked back in time by a meddlesome fairy be considered kidnapping? This certainly was a new one on the books for him, and he had no other place to start than back at the beginning. Either way, whether he found something or nothing, he knew he'd feel better if he could take another look around.

"That seems reasonable. Before you go, you'll need to change out of those clothes. They look out of place, and you've already caused enough of a disturbance showing up as you have. We don't want more problems or people asking too many questions," Duncan said.

"What about Kayla? Does she know I'm from the future?"

"Probably not. We never told her about Teressa. We wanted to limit the number of people who knew. And we'd like to keep it that way with you." Duncan looked pointedly at Daniel, making his meaning clear.

"Rory, you should go with him," Duncan continued. "Help him find the place and make sure he makes it back here. We wouldn't want him to get lost now, would we?" Duncan shot Daniel an ominous grin and took another drink, finishing off the last of his whisky.

"Thanks. You know, I've got a lot to learn about how things are done around here, being from a different time and all. I'm hoping you'll be helping me out. What do you say?" Daniel addressed Rory. Of the two brothers, he felt he had better odds with Rory.

"Certainly, what are brothers for?" Rory grinned, swallowing the last of his drink.

"Great. Let's start with the toilet." Becoming uncomfortable, Daniel fought the nervous release of his bowels.

Rory scowled, indicating a lack of understanding.

"The head. The john. The shit house." Daniel kept trying until an amused recognition lit Rory's face.

"Aye, the shit house, we call it the garderobe. There's one outside. Come, I'll get you a change of clothes while you take a crap." Rory laughed out loud at Daniel's discomfort.

As Rory led him off toward the much-needed relief at the garderobe, Daniel took in every detail of his surroundings. They exited the great hall through a thick arched doorway and crossed to a small alcove built into the thick stone wall of the fortress. Along with the rather unavoidable dirt and grime, there was the strong scent of humans and animals and the sound of swords clanging as men trained in the nearby field. Seeing the ancient weapons and crude clothing along with the bad-ass fortress finally cemented the idea that he had stepped back in time. *Yep, amazing,* he though, *this is just freaking amazing. And it looks like I'm in for one hell of an adventure.*

After Daniel's rather primitive encounter with the ancient equivalent of an outhouse, Rory met him with a change of clothes. All he'd been able to find on such a short notice was a fresh linen shirt and a pair of funny-looking leggings he called trews. They didn't exactly fit, but they would have to do for now. At least he looked more like everyone else, even if he felt like an alien from Mars.

Following Daniel's description of where Kayla had found him, Rory was able to locate the site of Daniel's strange appearance along the river road. When the area he recognized as his "landing site" came into view, Daniel asked that they dismount and proceed on foot. This would prevent the horses from disrupting the original tracks. Retracing the hoof prints of Kayla's horse, both Rory and Daniel could clearly see where she had ridden in. Then, marked by the deeper indentations of the horse's hoofs, they could see where the two of them had ridden out together on Sallie. They found the crushed section of grass showing where Daniel had landed when he was thrown off Wilbur, but there weren't any fresh horse tracks leading up to the site from the opposite direction. From observable appearances, it looked as if he had simply dropped from the sky to land in this time and place.

Standing over the section of crushed grass, Rory shook his head, running a rough hand across his chin. "The only other time I've seen anything like this was when Teressa disappeared. She was running along the beach, trying to reach me. I saw her footsteps in the sand leading up to the where she disappeared, and then they just ended. If I hadn't seen her disappear right before my very eyes, I wouldn't have believed it. If nothing else, Moezell's warning allowed me to confirm that her disappearance was indeed magical."

"What do you mean, Moezell's warning?" Daniel asked, standing. He'd been crouched near his landing site looking for any clues left in the area. Other than the tracks leading away from the site, there was nothing to be found.

"Teressa had left the Isle Faire with my mother and sister, riding back to the keep with Duncan and his men. I was with the supply wagons. We were delayed getting back to the keep due to a fierce summer storm. That night, I had a vivid dream of Teressa slipping from my fingers, being pulled out of my grasp. Early the next morning, as soon as I woke, I knew something was wrong. I headed back to the keep as fast as Blazer could take me. When I reached the bluffs overlooking the beach, I saw Teressa. We were running down the beach towards each other, but before I reached her, she disappeared."

"Just like that? She disappeared?" Daniel snapped his fingers.

"Just like that. All that was left were her footprints in the sand. If I hadn't seen it, I'd find it mighty hard to believe. That's when I saw Moezell."

"What about Moezell? What did she do?"

"Looking back, I think she was trying to comfort me. I was mighty upset. She told me that someday we'd be reunited, if my soul desired. I've wanted nothing else since." Rory shot Daniel an appraising look. "The last time I saw your sister, she was wearing strange clothes, like yours. Duncan told me they were the clothes she'd been wearing when he found her, when she first arrived. He said she wore men's *trews*, like the ones you were wearing. Apparently, women in the future choose to dress like men."

Daniel laughed at Rory's comment. "Yea, I guess to your thirteenth-century way of thinking, modern women do dress like men, but their jeans fit so much nicer on their bodies."

The two men headed back up the slight incline to where they had left their horses. "Has it really been over three years since you last saw Teressa?" Daniel asked.

"Aye. Every year on the summer solstice, I've gone down to the beach to wait and watch for her return. And every year, for three summers, there has been no sign. Not until now, when you showed up. While it's encouraging to meet her brother, I can no deny it's a wee bit disappointing. I'd rather be seeing Teressa."

"No doubt," Daniel murmured as he mounted up beside Rory. "Three summers and you still keep watch?"

"Think of all the women who have passed through your life. Tell me, how often did any of them stirred feelings in ye beyond mere male lust?"

"I've had a few nice girlfriends." Daniel shrugged, defending his dating history. "None that stuck, but we've had some good times."

"Yea, I'm certain that many a lass has turned your head with her bonnie appearance, but how many have stirred your heart?" Rory tapped his chest. "If it's a common thing, I would be surprised, for you don't seem to be a man so free with his feelings. I've seen such men. They easily fall for the sway of a young woman's fine hips and just as readily seek another once their prey has satisfied their needs." Rory cast him a long hard look. "I know, I was once one of them."

That last bit of confession surprised Daniel. "Really? What changed?" They had reached the horses, but Daniel paused before mounting up.

"When I met your sister, I was consumed by a desire to know her, to claim her in a way I've no felt for another. Ever since her departure, no other woman has stirred my interest. Believe me, I have thought long on this subject. It seems I'm fated to love only her. What keeps my hope alive and my love strong is Moezell's word that we will be reunited if my soul desires. And thus far, I can tell ye, my soul does so desire."

"Moezell told you that you'd be reunited with Teressa?" Daniel realized he was staring. He blinked, shaking his head.

Rory nodded. "Aye." He mounted up onto his horse.

"Did she tell you how that would happen?" With practiced grace, Daniel swung his long legs astride his horse.

"Nay. Her only clue was that I would be the one to return to her, someday. She also said it was important that I live my life well. I don't know what it all means, but I can tell you, I intend to live a good life and stay true to Teressa if it means we have a chance to be together again."

Impressed, Daniel sat back on the saddle and gave a low, breathy whistle. To know such a love that transcended time was beyond anything he could imagine in his life.

Chapter 10

*K*ayla found Rory helping their mother, Lady Lydia, tend to her garden. Lady Lydia was busy amending the soil in preparation for next spring's new planting, and Rory was supervising some workers moving stones to section off a new herb garden. He worked right along with his men, making sure the planting beds were exactly as his mother requested. Being the youngest of the MacNicol brothers, Rory was known for his relaxed attitude toward life in general, but Kayla knew he took immense pride on a job well done.

She had delivered Duncan's request for Rory to meet him in his solar, telling him it was important, and as instructed by Duncan, she didn't tell him why. However, that didn't stop her from telling her mother as soon as Rory left the garden. She was bursting at the seams with the news and needed to tell someone.

"Mother, you'll never guess what happened to me." She was both agitated and excited by the morning's events.

"Nay, but I would guess you're going to tell me." Lady Lydia barely looked up from her garden bed. She was absorbed in turning over the soil of her herb garden, adding in handfuls of chopped-up vegetation that would enrich the soil as it decayed into the ground.

"I found a man injured along the road near the Glenmore River and brought him back to the keep. I just found out he's Daniel Ellers, Teressa's brother."

Lady Lydia stopped what she was doing, still holding a handful of ground greens, and gave her daughter her full attention. "You can't be serious."

"Aye, Mother, very serious. He's with Duncan in his study right now. That's why Duncan sent for Rory."

Lady Lydia stared at her daughter in disbelief. "Are you sure he's Teressa's brother? Could you be mistaken?"

"Nay, Mother. I'm sure. He told us so himself."

Lady Lydia dropped the mulch she was holding to the ground and stared off into the distance.

Kayla took advantage of her mother's silence and began to vent. "I can't believe he has the gall to show up here after all these years. Especially after his sister disappeared so suddenly without even so much as a fare thee well to Rory. He acted like he knows nothing about his sister's visit here, like he hadn't even heard of Scorrybreac until today. Why would he make the effort to travel so far unless his sister had sent him? Or would they have us believe it's just some strange family coincidence that they keep showing up at Scorrybreac?" She was angry over the exposed identity of their wayward stranger and was more focused on venting her rage than on questioning her mother's reaction.

"Aye, it does seem strange." Lady Lydia patted Kayla's hand, somewhat distracted. Finally, she looked over at Kayla. "Excuse me. I need to go to my chamber now. There's something I need to do there."

Without waiting for Kayla's response, Lady Lydia rose to her feet and headed toward the keep.

"But, Mother, aren't you even curious as to why Daniel Ellers is here? Aren't you going to talk to Duncan?" Kayla called after her, taken aback by her mother's apparent lack of interest.

"Of course. Perhaps. Maybe later." Lady Lydia waved off her daughter's concerns. She was already halfway to the garden gate.

Kayla sat back on her heels, stumped. What was happening to everyone? First, Duncan, and now her mother. Why weren't they more upset about Teressa's brother showing up unexpectedly? Regrettably, she acknowledged with a frown that he hadn't exactly shown up from nowhere. She was the one who had found him and brought him to their home.

When she found him lying alone on the side of the road, she had immediately assessed her predicament, running through her options one by one. Even after she was assured he was uninjured and fit enough to walk, she knew she couldn't simply leave him to find his own way. She had dismissed that option as being too unkind and unfriendly. She also knew she couldn't take him with her to see Fern. That would have raised far too many questions, putting her in the awkward position of having to explain his presence. In her mind, that had left her with only one option: take him back home to Scorrybreac and let Duncan deal with him as he always did with everything else.

A small corner of her mind was aware that this last option had granted her more time with the attractive man, but now she tried to dismiss such thoughts as being unimportant. Instead, she reassured herself that it was only due to the MacNicols' customary rule of hospitality that she had assisted the mysterious stranger and not because of her own personal interest.

42

Everything had changed when she learned he was Teressa Ellers' brother. She wondered why he acted as if he hadn't heard of Scorrybreac. Surely his sister must have told him about them. She had been lost and stranded at their keep for several days. She recalled with disdain how Teressa had called it "her unexpected detour," as if that somehow made it acceptable.

Kayla had been exceptionally angry when Teressa had simply disappeared one day, leaving Rory brokenhearted. As far as she knew, Teressa hadn't bothered to offer an excuse for her hasty departure, nor had she given her brother a proper farewell. She had simply left to return home, wherever that was. And Rory was so in love with her. Right from the start, when Teressa had first appeared at their keep, Kayla had worried that Rory's affections for Teressa would be abused. Unfortunately, she was right.

In the three years since Teressa's unexpected visit and abrupt departure, they had received no word from her or any of her family. At least not until now. She'd left without a trace, and Rory had been left brokenhearted for his lost love. Kayla, with her protective nature, had taken Rory's loss to heart, holding deep-seated resentment toward the woman who had hurt her brother. Now she had a tangible object at which to direct her resentment—Teressa's brother, Daniel Ellers.

♦ ♦ ♦

Lady Lydia had no doubt about *how* Daniel Ellers had suddenly appeared at their keep; she knew of only one person who could have arranged his appearance. What bothered her was that she had no knowledge as to *why* he'd been brought back in time. She needed to speak with her cousin—now. She just hoped her distant relative would make herself available. Lately, her cousin was becoming more and more independent, going so far as to create situations of her own. Now it appeared that her cousin, the little fairy Moezell, might have gone too far.

Lady Lydia hastened to the door of Duncan's study. She could hear the muffled voices of men speaking, at least two and possibly three. The thickness of the door prevented her from clearly hearing what was being said, but even if she could understand their words, she doubted it would yield the information she wanted.

After a moment of unproductive listening, she quickly proceeded to her chamber. Once securely behind the equally thick and private door of her bedchamber, she worked to calm herself, resting quietly in her favorite armchair and breathing deep, relaxing breaths. It would work against her if she allowed herself to be upset. When she felt her mind was sufficiently calm and under control, she closed her eyes and mentally reached out to her cousin, calling her name, requesting Moezell to make herself known. Nothing happened.

Lady Lydia called out again and waited.

In Lady Lydia's irritated state, it seemed that Moezell was taking far too long to make her appearance, and she began to wonder what could be delaying her little cousin. Just as she was reaching the end of her patience, a brilliant blue light filled the room.

"Ah, cousin Lydia, I heard your call. What a delight. Are you in need of my assistance?" The light dimmed, and a lovely young woman appeared in the chamber. She had long white blond hair, which hung freely to her waist, and ice blue eyes. A long, flowing, iridescent silver blue gown softly draped over her delicate body. There was a soft glow surrounding her, adding brightness to the room. As she moved to stand before Lydia, an impish smile lit her lovely oval face.

"I'm hoping you can tell me what has been occupying your attention lately. Are you working on anything of interest? Perhaps something that I should know about, little cousin?" Lady Lydia did not return the fairy's smile.

Moezell gave a look of concern as if she was in deep thought. "Nay, nothing out of the ordinary I would say, just your usual wish fulfillment." The smile returned to her face with the brightness of several candles. "You know how I love to indulge in wish fulfillment."

"Really, wish fulfillment is it?" Lady Lydia's expression remained calm, but she wasn't falling for her cousin's innocence. Her eyes narrowed. "Please, tell me more."

"Oh no, cousin, you know that wouldn't be right. I can't discuss the wishes of my humans. That could interfere with the outcome," Moezell stated innocently.

"Interfere with the outcome?" Lady Lydia raised her brows, tamping down her irritation. "Moezell, if this has something to do with my family, I believe I have a right to interfere."

"Nay, I don't think so." Moezell held her smile. "I am responsible for granting these wishes. And besides, who said they involve your family?"

Lady Lydia glared at her cousin for a long moment. It seemed that the younger fairy was growing some new wings. "All right, wishes are private, as you say. Let's approach this from another direction. Tell me what Daniel Ellers is doing in my keep." Lady Lydia resisted raising her voice. Being the elder fairy, although only half fey, such a lack of composure would be unseemly. She still held the ancient bloodline of the fey through her half-fey mother, even though her father was human. The fey bloodline was strong, dominating her human heritage.

"Daniel Ellers, you ask? Could he be the brother of Teressa Ellers, the woman you brought here three years ago to do your bidding to fulfill *your* wishes?" Moezell seemed to be testing her recently enhanced strength, and it appeared that she was enjoying the moment.

"You know very well she was brought here to secure the marriage between Janet MacDonald and my son. Do you call that fulfilling my wishes?"

"If not yours, then whose wishes could they be?" Moezell looked unreasonably calm in the wake of her cousin's ire.

"I did it for my family, to preserve our peaceful relations with the MacDonald clan."

"Admittedly, you had good intentions from the start. But was it also your intention to deny Roderick his one true love, his soul mate?"

"She was not brought here to become Rory's soul mate. And besides, arrangements have been made for them to be together again, if they truly are soul mates." Lady Lydia grew incredulous that her actions were being questioned. She could see that her greater experience no longer held sway over the younger fairy, and she didn't like it.

"What you arranged was for your son to give up his chance at happiness in this lifetime so you could keep him close." Moezell was no longer smiling.

"How dare you. I love my son." Anger flashed hot across Lydia's face.

"Apparently, not enough to set him free, to allow him to make his own choices. For years, I have heard Roderick's wish to be reunited with the woman he loves, but for now, that wish cannot be granted because of the solution you have so wisely chosen for him."

"You question my choices?"

"Yes, when I see the pain it inflects on another person's soul." Moezell maintained her calm composure.

Lady Lydia stewed. Of course, she was aware of her youngest son's discontent. She had hoped that over time, his sadness would fade, and he would once again regain his love of life, it was always such a large part of his character, but in recent years, it had grown small. His body and mind had remained true and loyal to his family, but Lady Lydia was aware that he'd given his whole heart and a piece of his soul to Teressa.

"What is done—is done. It cannot be changed. You still have not explained why Daniel Ellers is here at my keep." Lady Lydia hoped to gain control of the conversation.

"As I have said, I am granting wishes." There was more than a hint of mischief in Moezell's lovely ice blue eyes.

"Are you telling me Daniel Ellers wished to be sent back over seven hundred years in time?" Lady Lydia was highly doubtful of that idea.

"Nay, actually, I am not telling you anything about anyone's wishes, as I've already mentioned, but perhaps you weren't listening. That seems to happen a lot with you." It was Moezell's turn to lose her patience.

"I heard you just fine," Lady Lydia snapped.

"It is one thing to hear what is said. It's entirely another to listen. Now please excuse me. I have humans to watch over." With her final comment, Moezell vanished from the room.

"I'm not done with you." Lady Lydia struggled not to shout. Any louder and her voice would surely have been heard through her thick chamber door.

Lady Lydia quickly reviewed what Moezell had said, which, to the younger fairy's credit, had been very little. It seemed that Lady Lydia had taught her cousin too well in the fine art of purposeful evasion. All Lady Lydia had gotten from the fairy was that she was working on wishes, and she had implied the wishes involved more than one human. She still didn't know how these wishes concerned her family, but she was certain they did. Unfortunately, she had no way of knowing whom it involved, at least not yet. She wondered if Moezell had brought Daniel back to act as a messenger between Teressa and Rory. It was possible, and as good a guess as any.

Lydia had also learned that Moezell was still in a snit over the way she had handled their past encounter with Teressa Ellers. What had seemed like a good solution at the time was now proving to be packed with problems. Rory would be united with Teressa someday, if she proved to be his soul mate. He just had to wait seven hundred years and another lifetime for that to happen. Maybe it had been asking too much, but what was done was done; there was no turning back on her decision. Once circumstances were set in motion, results had to play themselves out. And that made her wonder what circumstances had Moezell set into motion.

Chapter 11

The smile plastered on Kayla's face was only a poor disguise for the rage brewing beneath the surface. It was one thing for Duncan to offer Daniel Ellers lodging in one of the chambers of the high tower where the druid Souyer lived, but to invite him to dine at their evening table was simply offensive. If it had been up to her, she would have handed him a crust of bread with some goat cheese and sent him on his way.

Instead, here he was, sitting across the table from her in all his frustratingly handsome glory. That was part of the problem, she reluctantly acknowledged. He was too good-looking, scary good, all sharp, neat, and very foreign-looking. Not at all like the men from around Skye. It only complicated her problem that she was drawn to his unique presence.

Kayla's intention to simply ignore the man was proving to be more difficult than she had anticipated. For most of the meal, she managed to focus her attention on her sister-in-law, Shannon, even though the conversation repeatedly centered on the joys of motherhood and the new babe Shannon was carrying. Her conversation with Shannon didn't mean she wasn't aware of what was being discussed with Daniel, only that she was choosing not to participate.

When Lady Janet politely asked why they had not received any word from Teressa for the past three years, Kayla's ears perked up. She was interested to hear Daniel's answer. Lady Janet had considered Teressa to be a dear friend, and Kayla knew she missed her.

"I believe Teressa would send her best wishes personally, if it was possible. Shortly after she returned home, our mother became seriously ill. Earlier this year, she passed away," Daniel said, honest regret darkening his gaze.

"I'm so sorry to hear of your loss. Please know that you and Teressa have our deepest sympathies. I hope you'll pass them on to your sister when you see her again," Lady Janet offered her heartfelt condolences.

"I certainly will. She spoke highly of you and Duncan. I'm sure your kind words will mean a great deal to her." Daniel gave Lady Janet a kind look in return.

Kayla felt small. She'd been harshly judging Teressa's absence only to discover that Daniel and Teressa had suffered through the loss of their mother. However, she still wasn't ready to completely forgive Teressa, not yet. The illness and passing of their mother went a long way toward explaining why Teressa hadn't returned, but it didn't excuse her untimely departure. Undeserving as it might be, Kayla felt a lingering need to hang on to her resentment. It had lived too long to die a quick death.

Kayla turned to look at Lady Lydia sitting next to her at the end of the table. The thought of losing her mother saddened her. Granted, in recent years, they weren't always close, and lately, it seemed as if their previously strong bond was growing thin, but she knew it would strike a blow to her heart if she lost her mother.

Kayla noticed that her mother was unusually quiet during their evening meal. Such silence was out of character for her. Although she usually held herself with perfect decorum, as matriarch of the clan, Lady Lydia had a way of letting her family know exactly how she felt on any given subject. Even though she was keeping her thoughts to herself, Kayla noticed that her mother was studying Daniel like a hawk stalking its prey. It made Kayla wonder if Daniel's presence was also causing her mother undue distress.

Kayla recalled how everyone had wanted to ignore Teressa's unexplained and very sudden departure from Scorrybreac. Although Teressa had always clearly stated that she was expected to return home, to just up and leave so suddenly seemed downright rude, especially since Kayla knew her brother had hoped to accompany Teressa back to her homeland. At the time, Rory had avoided discussing the matter with her, and she hadn't asked, but she could see the pain it caused him.

Duncan was more concerned with ensuring that Janet was happy and comfortable in her new home than worrying over Teressa's disappearance. Even their mother had shown no interest in pursuing the subject of her son's lost love. Now, whatever thoughts Lady Lydia had regarding Daniel's unexpected appearance at Scorrybreac, she was keeping them to herself. Once again, Kayla felt distanced from her family.

Misguided by the poisonous logic that anger often provokes, Kayla believed that holding on to her resentment of Teressa Ellers was a show of support for Rory. It was only natural that her ill-conceived logic extended out to resenting Teressa's brother as well. Unfortunately, she was finding the target of her resentment to be unfailingly charming and obviously attractive. The sun-bronzed skin of his finely formed face was starting to show a shadow of stubble, and she liked the way random streaks of auburn wove their way through his thick mass of dark brown hair. It was hard not to notice that his hazel eyes, with their swirls of dark green specks, created a hypnotic kaleidoscope effect when she stared at them for too long, which she tried to avoid doing. Unfair as it seemed, she was aware of the nervous tingling taking place in her belly, and she resented how her conflicted feelings were conspiring against her.

When she brought her thoughts back to the conversation, she realized her brother, Michael, was showing an interest in Daniel. Of her three brothers, Michael tended to be the quiet one. Being stuck in the middle between Duncan, the firstborn heir apparent, and Rory, his vivacious younger brother, Michael usually went about his business unnoticed. Kayla knew this was perfectly fine with him. It had allowed him to build a pleasant and quiet life with his wife, Shannon, with little interference from his family, particularly their mother. Instead, Lady Lydia had a tendency to direct her attention at Duncan and Rory, which suited Michael just fine. That didn't mean he wasn't aware of the happenings in the Scorrybreac keep, only that he picked his encounters well. Apparently, Kayla wasn't the only one concerned with the appearance of another Ellers at their keep. However, unlike her, Michael was letting it be known that Daniel had succeeded in catching his interest. And, she noted with interest, Daniel was proving to be quite capable of holding his own against Michael's frontal assault.

Daniel understood Michael's need to interrogate him and he was doing his best to give honest answers without saying more than was necessary.

"I'm wondering what has brought ye so far from your home. Have you business in these parts?" Michael asked.

"Actually, I traveled to the Isle of Skye at the request of my sister. She still speaks fondly of the time she spent here. She felt the adventure would be good for me after so much heartache at home," Daniel said. The jury was still out on how well his adventure was going, but the idea that world travel provided opportunities for unexpected adventures was most certainly accurate.

"And what is it ye do for your people at home?" Michael asked.

"I'm a police officer," Daniel answered. From the puzzled look on Michael's face, Daniel realized the term was foreign to him and went on to explain. "I patrol the streets of my city to ensure the safety of our citizens, to serve and protect."

"You're a guard," Michael clarified. He tore off a generous hunk of crusty bread and used it to sop up the gravy of his stew before chewing off an oversized mouthful.

"Yeah, something like that," Daniel agreed. He followed Michael's example, enjoying the thick lamb stew.

"Would ye be interested in training with my men in the lists tomorrow?"

"You know, that sounds like a good idea. I'd be very interested," Daniel replied. Michael's offer seemed friendly enough, and he'd been wondering what to do with his time while he was trapped in the past. The idea of sitting around twiddling his thumbs while he waited to be directed by the whim of some unseen fairy didn't exactly appeal to him. Exploring their ancient methods of self-defense would be interesting. All of the MacNicol men were built like trees—tall, sturdy, and muscular—and he wondered what training routine they used to produce such results.

"Good. We start right after the morning meal, if you're up for it." A snide smile slithered from Michael's lips.

Daniel quickly understood Michael's underlying intentions. The ancient warrior wanted to test the new kid on the block. That was fine with him. Bring it on. He was counting on his police training and extensive experience with martial arts to provide the fundamental skills needed for him to hold his own in ancient combat training.

"How well can you wield a sword?" Michael asked. He took a long swallow of ale, keeping an eye on Daniel as he drank.

"A sword?" Daniel questioned, stalling for time. He realized he hadn't fully considered their ancient methods of weapons training.

"Aye, swords, or do you have another weapon of choice?" Michael swiped the back of his hand across his mouth. His smirk grew deeper.

A gun would be nice, Daniel thought, but he was pretty certain they didn't have any of those around. Instead, he answered, "I have more experience in hand-to-hand combat"—he was thinking of his martial arts training—"but I'm also familiar with the baton, you know, a fighting staff." He'd take what he could get; he wasn't about to back down from the challenge. During his police training, he had qualified as an expert rifle and pistol marksman, but he didn't think those skills would be of much use to him here.

"So be it. I'm sure we can find a suitable method to test your skills." Michael's smile bordered on devious.

Yep, Daniel thought, *he's looking for a smackdown*. Eyeing the three MacNicol brothers sitting around the large plank table, he considered the odds. They were definitely stacked against him, and it didn't look good. He hoped he hadn't just set himself up for a brutal beating.

Long after the meal had ended, and the womenfolk had left the table, the four men lingered to drink their ale and exchange war stories. Daniel did his best to monitor the effects of the unfamiliar alcohol, trying to limit his intake of the heavy brew. In the company of the MacNicol brothers, it was a daunting task. Given the choice of matching their ale intake, becoming drunk and acting like a fool, or taking his time to nurse his drinks, he opted to nurse his drink with shallow sips instead of deep gulps. Too many times, he'd seen firsthand the ugly side of inebriation and what it could do to a man. However, even his best wasn't a fair match against the MacNicol brothers.

Daniel was fascinated to hear the tales of local feuds and battles the MacNicol brothers had encountered. These were tough times for the country of Scotland. After the death of their king, Alexander III, followed by his daughter, Margaret, Edward I of England had declared himself as feudal overlord of Scotland. All hell had been released, and the country was immersed in a political turmoil that threatened the lives of Scottish supporters. These days, as Daniel was quickly learning, it was hard to know your friends from your foes.

Duncan's first priority was the safety of his clan, and he was hoping the worst of the fighting would not reach Skye. Michael's first priority was to keep his men well trained and ready to do battle. Obviously, life in the thirteenth century wasn't for the faint of heart.

It was later than he had expected and Daniel was more intoxicated than he liked to admit when he finally made his way back to his bedchamber. He was staggering, but at least he was still standing. It was a challenge, but he was able to make it up the circular staircase of the high tower.

Stripping down to his boxers, he fell soundly into bed, mentally and physically exhausted. While he was fairly certain this wasn't all a dream, he wouldn't be at all surprised if he woke up and found himself back at Robert's cottage as if none of this had happened. Crazy as the day had been, he realized he had no way of knowing what to expect next.

Chapter 12

*K*ayla retired to her bedchamber, feeling more agitated than relieved. She was pleased to think she had made it through the evening meal without displaying undue interest in Daniel. A great help in her efforts had been the way Michael and her brothers had dominated the conversation. Which was as it should be, she told herself, for in truth she had no interest in the man. He could disappear tomorrow, and she wouldn't suffer at all for his absence.

Besides, she still had a bigger problem to deal with: the possibility of a betrothal to Arlin MacDonald. Unfortunately, she was no closer to solving that dilemma since her plan to send a message to Arlin had been interrupted by Daniel's unexpected appearance.

She wondered why she was the only one who found his presence so disturbing. The calm reactions of her mother and brothers rattled her nerves.

"Why do my brothers seem so intent on welcoming this stranger into our keep?" she wondered aloud as she paced her bedchamber. "Do they not see the threat of danger? He says he's from America, wherever that is, but for all we know, he could be an English spy."

There was a sudden flash of light, and Kayla heard a woman's soft voice. "Why do you see him as a stranger? After all, he is Teressa's brother."

Kayla raised her hands to shield her eyes against the brightness of the light. When it dimmed, she blinked several times, watching, as a beautiful woman stepped through the veil of the unseen. Kayla immediately realized that this ethereal woman was a fairy.

Startled, Kayla took two quick steps back before she bumped against her bed. If she hadn't been feeling their presence for so many years, she might have jumped right out of her skin. She only needed a moment to get the fright-induced pounding of her heart under control.

"Who are you?" she asked slowly, feeling somewhat overwhelmed by the appearance of a fairy.

"I'm Moezell, your fey cousin. I thought it was about time we met." The fairy smiled, and the room grew brighter.

"My fey cousin? You're a fairy?" Kayla's brows lifted in amazement.

"Aye. You are descended from a strong and proud family of fairies, on your mother's side, of course. Fey blood is always passed from mother to daughter, not that a few drops haven't mingled in with your brothers, but the lineage is most strongly passed through the females. Surely you know your great-grandmother Sophie was fey, born to a fairy in the fairy realm." Moezell spoke to Kayla as if it was a most natural thing in the world to be having a conversation with her half-human cousin.

"My great-grandmother Sophie. I thought she was a legend. I mean, I know Mother told me the stories, but I didn't know they were real, or I mean true," Kayla sputtered over her words.

"Aye, they're true enough to be sure. In her own way, perhaps a bit more slowly than necessary, cousin Lydia has been preparing you for your initiation into your heritage."

"My heritage? I'm descended from fairies? But what does that mean?" Kayla questioned, flustered by her lack of understanding.

"I know cousin Lydia has told you many of our stories. However, she failed to mention that you're half fey and a direct relation to our Queen, through her sister. Your great-grandmother Sophie is the daughter of Jeenie, the Fairy Queen's youngest sister. Jeenie, being a rather passionate fairy, had a fling with a human."

Seeing the look on Moezell's face, Kayla wondered whether the fairy approved of her ancestor's actions, or if she was envious.

"After the affair, Jeenie returned to the fairy realm and gave birth to Sophie. When Sophie was of age, Jeenie gave her the choice of living with the fairies or crossing over to the material world to live her life as a human. Sophie chose to live in the world of the humans. Not necessarily a bad choice. Less powers, but 'tis a far grander adventure. When she crossed over, she met your great-grandfather, Hubert, and well, I believe you know the rest."

Kayla nodded. She knew the story. And Moezell was definitely envious.

"Fey blood is always passed pure from mother to daughter and now runs through your veins. Have you no felt it through all these years, your connection to the fairies?"

"Aye, I have." Kayla was awed, remembering all the times she believed she had felt their presence. "I believed that someday, when the time was right, the fairies would show themselves to me."

"Well, here I am." Moezell spread her arms briefly, reconfirming her presence.

"But why now? Why not when I've asked for your help?"

"Such as when you wished to find your own true love?"

It was as if Moezell could read her thoughts. "You know about that?"

"Of course, I was there. It was me you felt and heard. You just could not see me. Like so many other times when I was by your side to watch over you." Moezell spoke with fond affection for her half-human, half-fey cousin.

"Is that why you're here now, because of my wish?" Kayla asked.

"In a manner, yes. When it comes to finding love, true love, there is little I can do. Fairies have no power to compel humans to fall in love. Humans have free will. 'Tis their greatest gift. All a fairy can do is provide opportunities, assistance, and resources. Falling in love is always the choice of the individual."

"Mother is trying to arrange my betrothal to Arlin MacDonald."

Moezell nodded. "Aye, I know."

"I know he's a fine man, but I feel no love for him." A spark of suspicion flickered through Kayla's mind. She wondered if her mother had sent their fey cousin to help convince her to accept the betrothal to Arlin. "Are you suggesting I should simply choose to love Arlin?"

"In matters of love, you should always follow your heart. I would suggest nothing less. But first, you must open your heart to find that which you seek. You claim you wish to find true love, but to find, you must seek with an open heart." A soft glow of loving affection radiated from Moezell.

Looking downcast, Kayla sat down on the edge of her bed. She stared at her hands clasped in her lap and contemplated Moezell's words. It wasn't a pleasant thought, but in a flash of self-honesty, she acknowledged that for years she had endeavored to keep her heart closed. She'd been hoping to keep herself safe from hurt.

When Kayla was still a young girl, she had seen Duncan's pain after he sent Janet MacDonald back to her family, and she had begun to build a defensive wall around her heart. Duncan had believed Janet would not be loyal to the MacNicol clan and had broken their betrothal. Years had passed before they were brought together again, in large part due to Teressa Ellers' matchmaking skills.

Then Kayla had watched as Rory gave his heart to Teressa. And she had seen how Teressa had deserted her brother, leaving him with a broken heart. So she built her wall a little higher, a little stronger, believing it made her stronger.

Kayla claimed she wanted to find her own true love, and yet she had done nothing to allow it to happen. Perhaps in some strange way, like the legend of her great-grandmother Sophie, she believed her true love would simply appear to her out of the morning mists.

Now, after asking the fairies to help her find her own true love, she was being told that she must seek him with an open heart. She understood the rightness of Moezell's words, and yet the leap of faith was too great for her to take all at once. She needed time to consider the consequences of such a possibility. She had reached the age of two and twenty without finding love largely because she had worked so hard to avoid letting love in. It was a bitter broth to swallow.

"An open heart, you say. I am no sure I know how that feels. It seems rather scary. As though I'm leaving myself open to a whole world of hurt that I don't want and have no way to control." Kayla's chest tightened with fear.

"Aha," said the fairy, "there's the rub. To lose yourself in love, you must let go of the fear that is holding you back. The greatest risk is to take no risk at all. You believe you can avoid pain if you avoid love, and yet I can clearly see the pain you feel from your lack of love. What you fail to see is the pleasure, the joy, yea, even the ecstasies that only love can provide. Rory understands that the love he has known with Teressa is worth any pain. And his pain is borne out, aye, even healed, by that same heartfelt love."

"The love of a woman who deserted him?" Kayla was angered by the thought.

"You judge that which you do not know. Teressa did not desert Rory. She was required to return home. The choice was not hers."

Kayla turned her gaze away from the fairy. She'd been holding such ill will toward the woman whom she believed had hurt her brother. She was remiss to learn it was unjustified. "I didn't know. Why didn't he tell me?"

"Why did you not ask?" Moezell's question was spoken without malice. "Your anger at Teressa and your compassion for Rory's pain drove you to see only what you wanted to see."

Kayla was silent again, feeling a heavy dose of remorse and a touch of self-pity as her past misjudgments were brought to bear. She returned her gaze to her entwined fingers. "He looked so sad, so lost after she left. I blamed it all on her." Her voice was small and wounded.

"He is sad over the loss of Teressa, but not for the love they shared. That is something he carries with him still. Have you no thought to ask Rory how he feels?"

"It seemed too personal, too painful to discuss," Kayla admitted.

"So you came to your own conclusions. So very human of you. Human imaginations seem to know no limits. 'Tis fascinating, but sometimes frustrating to observe."

Kayla didn't know how to respond to Moezell's observation, and yet she felt the truth of it. After an uncomfortable moment of silent reflection, she asked, "I'm still not sure what I should do. How can you help me?"

"I am here to be of assistance, to provide opportunities and resources to help you seek out your own true love. Have not my words of wisdom been of assistance to you?" Moezell asked, looking hopeful.

"Aye, your wise words have helped me greatly." Kayla brightened, encouraged by Moezell. Perhaps the fairy could help her solve her dilemma. "I've been thinking of asking Arlin to oppose the betrothal. Can you tell me, is that the right thing to do?"

"That choice is yours to make. I suggest you sleep on it, see where your heart leads you in the morn," Moezell offered. She stepped forward and stroked Kayla's long red hair.

"That doesn't seem like much help." Kayla pouted, retreating once again into her self-induced melancholy.

"Always so quick to judge." Moezell shook her head, frustrated. "Surely you can wait to see what the morrow will bring."

"I hope it will not bring another stranger such as Daniel Ellers. He ruined my whole day." Kayla spoke her mind without censor. She immediately felt the fairy's displeasure wash over her, but she'd been unable to stop her misguided words.

Moezell walked back to the center of the room; her gentle glow was not nearly as bright as when she had arrived. "Tsk, tsk, little one, be careful what you wish for. Fairies have ears." Moezell blew her cousin a kiss and stepped through the veil, returning to the unseen realm.

Kayla blinked once, then found herself staring at the empty space where Moezell had just stood. *Amazing*, she thought. The fairy's visit was an amazing ending to an already-exceedingly-strange day.

Kayla considered everything Moezell had told her as she prepared for bed. She felt as though she was no closer to knowing what to do about Arlin and her pending betrothal. The fairy had told her to sleep on it, but she didn't know how she was going to sleep with all this to think about.

Chapter 13

The day had been long, the night short. Daniel woke the next morning with wisps of a dream lingering at the edge of his mind. He was a knight, on a white steed, pursuing a quest. Surrounded by mists and dense green forests, he felt lost and unsure of what he was searching for. A woman in long pale blue robes and with silver blond hair and stunning ice blue eyes appeared. She had a surreal presence, rather like an angel. She handed him something. It looked like a map, but he couldn't read it. She gave him instructions, saying, "Seek and ye shall find, and when ye find, ye shall know her name." Then the angel disappeared, and he was thrown from his horse, unable to proceed, still surrounded by mists.

Breaking through the veil of slumber, he blinked several times, rubbing the sleep from his eyes. Dreams, he thought, never made any sense.

He stretched and lingered a moment longer in bed, appreciating how well he had slept. Of course, he was dog-tired when he fell into bed, and somewhat less than completely sober. Thankfully, the mattress he slept on was surprisingly comfortable, better than he had expected.

With the morning light filtering in through the window, he was able to get a better look at the chamber in which he slept. The bed was wide but barely long enough to hold his six-foot-three-inch body. Large wooden posts rose from each corner, supporting rods holding heavy wool drapes pushed back toward the posts. He wished he had noticed them the night before. They would have kept out the morning sun and kept in some warmth. He shivered, feeling the cold draft seeping in through the one window located in the chamber's thick stone walls. It held no glass, only a wooden shutter, which he had also failed to close. Obviously, he was still in the thirteenth century.

His first thoughts were of Kayla, the angel of mercy who found him and brought him to Scorrybreac. His morning member grew hard with the thought of her heavenly face. He imagined her greeting him with the dawn as she had the previous day down by the river. It was a most pleasant daydream to linger on while he rubbed his swollen member.

A single hard knock on the door announced Rory's entrance only a second before he entered the chamber. "Do you plan to laze the day away? Michael is expecting you in the lists for training, or have you forgotten?" He tossed a bundle of clothing down on the chest at the foot of the bed. "These are for you."

"I haven't forgotten. He said it was after breakfast." Daniel hastened to sit up, resting his back against the headboard, grateful for the cover the wool blankets provided while his daydream quickly deflated.

"Which has already been served in the great hall. You better hurry. The servants are the only ones still eating, and I can assure you, when they're done, they'll leave nothing for you," Rory informed him with a mocking grin.

Daniel picked through the clothes Rory had deposited at the foot of the bed. He found a serviceable pair of drawstring pants made of rough linen and pulled them on. Fumbling around, he found his socks and riding boots. Lacing up his boots, he noticed Rory eyeing them with a faraway look. "What?" Daniel asked.

Rory looked up. "Teressa had boots similar to yours. She was quite fond of them."

"That sounds like my sister. She has a thing for comfortable shoes, pretty much avoids wearing high heels." Daniel finished dressing, pulling a linen shirt over his head.

"I no understand. Why are your heels high?" Rory cocked his head, trying to understand the concept.

"Never mind, it's not important." Daniel had no desire to discuss women's footwear. "Let's just say she's a down-to-earth kind of woman." He stood ready to head out to breakfast, wishing he had a toothbrush.

"Aye, down to earth," Rory agreed.

On their way to the great hall, Daniel spied Kayla heading out of the keep on her way to the stables. "Hey, give me a minute, will ya? I'll be right back." Daniel clapped Rory on his shoulder.

"You're going to miss breakfast," Rory warned.

"Don't worry about me. I'll find something," Daniel yelled back. He was already halfway across the courtyard.

Rory shook his head at Daniel's impulsive actions and headed off to the lists, leaving Daniel to fend for himself.

"Hey, Kayla," Daniel called out as he jogged over to catch up with her. "Can I speak to you for a minute?"

Kayla glanced over her shoulder but continued walking toward the stables.

"Kayla," Daniel called her name again, coming up beside her, "I wanted to thank you."

She finally stopped and turned to face him. She wasn't smiling. In fact, judging by her frown, she looked a little annoyed.

"Thank me for what?" she asked, curtly.

Daniel maintained his friendly smile, hoping to win her over. "For everything. For being the one who found me. For bringing me here to Scorrybreac. But mostly, for being my angel of mercy."

His eyes feasted on the beauty of her face. Her unruly mass of autumn red curls was once again pulled back into its thick braid. Golden specks sprinkled throughout her dusty green eyes sparkled in the early morning sunlight. She was dessert for his hungry gaze.

"Your angel of mercy?" she questioned his choice of words, clearly curious.

"Yesterday, when I opened my eyes and saw your face, I thought I was in heaven seeing an angel."

For a moment, an unguarded smile lit her face. She was flattered, he could tell. Just as quickly, the smile faded, and she struck a poise of grim determination, lifting her chin and drawing her back a bit straighter. "You've no need to thank me. Anyone passing by would have offered you help."

"Maybe so, but it wasn't anyone else. It was you. And I'm grateful." He had lowered his voice to a husky whisper.

She anxiously looked away, searching the training field across the way. "Aren't you expected to train with Michael this morn?"

"I'll get there." He shrugged. Being a guest, he hoped the MacNicol brothers would cut him some slack. He figured that Michael wouldn't be happy, but maybe his delay wouldn't be too harshly criticized. Even if it was, there were worst things that could happen, like missing this chance to speak with Kayla, alone. "Are you going riding again today?" He motioned toward the stables.

"Aye. Why do you ask?"

"I was hoping I could join you, sometime, I mean, if that's all right with you." He hoped he didn't sound like a complete idiot. He had no idea how to go about asking a woman in the thirteenth century out for a date.

"Aye, well, perhaps later, but not now. I'm busy." She paused looking delightfully flustered, and then added, "You better go." She waved her hand off toward the lists.

"Okay, later then." He wanted to kiss her, to take a long, slow taste of her. She looked so cute standing there trying hard to present a face of grim determination. He detected more than a hint of interest from her. Yes, a full-blown kiss would be nice right about now, with her sweet pink lips looking so ripe for the picking. It would take her breath away, of that he was sure. From the look in her eyes, he figured that would be too much, and certainly too soon. Instead, he leaned in and gave her a brief brush of his lips upon her cheek, no more than a peck. Then he turned, heading off toward the keep.

His casual kiss must have taken her by surprise. She stood there for a long moment, her mouth gaping, watching him walk back toward the keep before calling out, "Where are you going now?"

"To the dining hall, I haven't had any breakfast yet." He paused, looking back.

"The cooks have stopped serving. There'll be nothing left." She took a deep breath, shaking her head in disgust. "My word, I can't let the poor man starve," she mumbled under her breath. "Are you always this helpless?" she grumbled louder.

She started after him and grabbed his hand as if he was a wayward child. "Come with me. We'll go find Bonnie. She'll find something for you to eat."

Daniel smiled a silly grin as he allowed himself to be led away by Kayla.

◆　◆　◆

"About time. I see ye've decided to grace us with your presence after all," Michael chided Daniel as he approached the training field. "I was beginning to think ye had decided to back out on the training."

"No, not at all. I just got a little delayed. I'm new here, remember. I'm still learning my way around." Daniel had willingly indulged in the opportunity to enjoy Kayla's hospitality before he finally managed to keep his appointment with Michael. Besides the benefit of being undeservedly pampered by Kayla, his delay had provided the additional benefit of being able to observe the training already in progress as he made his way to the lists.

The men training under Michael's direction were engaging in swordplay, wielding heavy swords as if they were mere extensions of their arms, which, for a true Scottish warrior, was a fairly accurate description. Daniel knew his lack of experience would make him no match for these men. They'd easily have him cut to ribbons and tied in a bow before he could get his game on.

Eyeing the layout of the lists, he saw the stockpile of weapons located at the outer edge of the training field. A bundle of fighting staffs stood among the various blades and bows ready for the warriors' use. He ambled over to pick up one of the long rods, checking its feel and balance. It weighed well in his hand, he noted, and it was well balanced at its center. He estimated the poles to be nearly seven feet in length, much longer than the practice batons he was familiar with, but he figured he could easily compensate for the difference. These practice poles were blunt at both ends, whereas a real fighting weapon would be outfitted with a blade. He nodded his approval. The hand-hewn fighting staffs appeared to be well made.

Michael walked over and picked up one the staffs, swinging it through the air with a whoosh of speed, barely concealing his snarky grin. His steel blue eyes glared at Daniel. "Ready?" he asked.

Daniel rotated his arms a few times, stretched, and loosened the muscles in his neck with a few twists and turns of his head. He would have preferred time to warm up, but it looked like he had missed that opportunity. "Yeah, I'm ready," he replied with confidence.

Michael led the way to a clear space in the lists. Duncan and Rory left their groups to watch the sparring match.

"Where's your coin?" Rory whispered to his eldest brother.

Duncan raised a quizzical brow, grinning. "Daniel's unproven. I'll place my coin on Michael."

"I'll take your bet, just to make it interesting." Rory returned his brother's grin.

Daniel knew he was in for trouble.

Michael and Daniel entered the training circle and faced off, each assuming a fighting stance. Their eyes burned with awareness of the other's slightest moves. Michael gave a sharp nod of his head, and they were off.

Thrusting and swinging their staffs, they each tested the other's defenses. Daniel knowingly held his skills in check, looking for the right opening to put them to use. For a while, he made a point of mimicking Michael's moves, testing his opponent's skills. Michael's brute force was greater than his talent, not that the warrior's stance or footwork was clumsy, just lacking skillful finesse. However, there was still much to be said for brute force. The two men circled and jabbed. With each thrust and counterthrust, their staffs clapped hard against the other. Daniel felt the vibrations of the forceful blows surge through the wooden pole, into his hands and up his arms.

After a few minutes of well-matched efforts, Michael faked a left swing, then charged forward, knocking Daniel backward. Daniel stumbled, struggling to hold his balance. He stepped back but lost his footing. Michael swung the staff hard right, taking advantage of the stumble, sending Daniel reeling toward the hard-packed ground.

Duncan elbowed Rory in his ribs.

Drawing on the momentum of the fall, Daniel rolled on his back as he hit the ground and somersaulted away from Michael. At the end of the roll, he threw his legs up and quickly back down, springing back to his feet. Michael didn't even have time to enjoy his momentary victory before Daniel recovered his footing. Using the staff for leverage, Daniel spiked the long rod into the ground. Adjusting his handhold, he twisted sideways to bring his feet up and out, delivering a staggering blow to Michael's chest. The quick action caught his opponent off guard and sent Michael stumbling backward, his arms flying. Daniel swiftly brought the staff around to knock Michael's feet out from under him. Quickly, too quick for Michael to react, Daniel had the staff twirled in his hands and poised at Michael's chest as the man lay splayed upon the ground. The pressure Daniel levied against Michael's chest was just enough to let him know Daniel had him pinned.

Michael instinctively grabbed for the weapon to yank it aside, but Daniel forced the blunt end of the rod under his chin. Daniel held his position a moment longer, allowing Michael to consider the possibility of a crushed esophagus, before he released the pressure.

Anger, fueled by a bruised ego, flared in Michael's eyes as he dropped his hands from the staff.

Daniel smiled. Not a gloating smile of victory, but one of friendly admiration. He backed it up with a genuine tribute. "It was a good fight. You gave me quite a run for my money. Almost had me."

Michael raised his hands in surrender, accepting defeat.

Rory got the last elbow jab at his eldest brother.

Pulling the staff back, Daniel offered his hand to Michael. The fallen warrior reluctantly accepted Daniel's assistance, overcoming his deflated ego. Knowing it was in his best interest to keep the peace, Daniel pulled Michael into a friendly man hug, clapping him firmly on the back.

"It's good to see ye can hold your own." Michael brushed the dust from his breeches. His comment fell just shy of being an outright compliment.

"Beginner's luck, I'm sure." Daniel modestly accepted the conservative accolade.

"Would ye like to try your luck again?"

"What I'd really like is for you to give me some training with those big-ass swords your men are using." Daniel's gaze was drawn in the direction of clanging swords coming from warriors training across the field.

"Claymores. Have ye no experience with them? Ye claim to be a guard for your people." Michael sounded surprised.

Mesmerized by the swordplay he was watching, Daniel answered without thinking, "Nope, can't say that I do. We don't have much use for them where I come from." As soon as he spoke the words, he realized his error.

"Where exactly do ye come from?" Michael's interest was piqued.

Daniel pulled his focus back to the men surrounding him. Duncan and Rory looked at him with blank expressions. He was on his own with this one. "A land far, far away across the sea called America. Have you ever heard of it?" The best defense was usually a good offense, and turning the question back on Michael gave him time to recover from his fumble.

Michael looked stumped. "Nay, I have no knowledge of such a place." He turned to his brothers. "Do ye know of this America?"

Duncan and Rory shook their heads. "Can't say that I do," Duncan replied.

"Must be a wee small place," said Michael.

Daniel jumped in to retrieve the ball. "Let's just say we do things differently there. So are you going to give me training with your claymores or not?" He shot Michael a look of defiance.

Michael took up the challenge. "Aye, let's see what ye've got."

Daniel grinned with relief and anticipation. He felt he had handled the situation well enough. There had been a moment when he thought Michael was going to get the best of him in the sparring match. Luckily, he had pulled off the final blow that landed the aggressive warrior on his back. It was shaping up to be a good day. It seemed that being misplaced in time presented all sorts of unexpected challenges, and for the moment, he was finding the experience very much to his liking.

Chapter 14

$\mathcal{K}$ ayla had planned to ride out to the hills to speak with her friend Fern. Her restless night had failed to produce a solution to her dilemma, and she was hoping to gain emotional support and some much-needed advice from her married friend. For the second day in a row, Kayla had failed to reach her intended destination, and once again, she had Daniel Ellers to thank for her failed mission.

He had delayed her departure before she had even reached the stables, stopping her so he could thank her for her valiant rescue. He had called her his angel of mercy. Reluctantly, she had to admit she appreciated the acknowledgement.

Then she had realized that he was going to miss his morning meal. After his declaration of gratitude for her assistance, the least she could do was to escort him to the kitchens. She was certain that without her help, he would have gone hungry, especially if he had approached the kitchens alone. Milly, the head cook of the keep, did not take kindly to strangers showing up at her door asking to be served after a meal had ended. Milly was already hard at work preparing for the midday meal, and morning leftovers were rare.

With Bonnie's help, she had grabbed two hunks of bread and some oatcakes just before the stable hands were set to finish them off. Those young boys were like bottomless pits and would lick the serving bowls dry if Milly let them. Thankfully, she did not.

"Here. Sit at this table, and stay out of Milly's way, or she'll skin you alive and serve you for the evening meal." Kayla directed Daniel to take a seat at the kitchen table where she placed the half-full platter of food.

Daniel complied, smiling at her display of frustration, which only served to irritate her more, even though she tried to remain in control.

"I'm mighty grateful. I'm sorry to take you away from your duties. I hope you know, you don't have to go to any trouble," Daniel said. That was an unlikely story. His seductive grin only served to contradict his polite words.

"Oh yea, I must, unless you wish to be sent away hungry," Kayla disagreed with him.

"If it's not too much more trouble, can I get a cup of coffee?" he asked.

"I've never heard of coffee. What is it?"

"It's a hot drink made from roasted ground coffee beans. It's strong and dark and a great way to kick-start your morning, or counter the effects of a hangover. Do you have anything like that?" he asked, still maintaining his silly grin and innocent puppy-dog eyes.

She eyed him with bewilderment, trying to think of a suitable substitute. She wondered why he persisted in frustrating her, and why she was trying to please him. She shook her head, more disgusted with herself than with him.

"I can brew a hot drink made from a mixture of dried herbs. Mayhap it will suffice. It's used to relieve nervous stomachs and ale-induced headaches," she offered, her voice sounding much kinder than she felt.

"Sounds good to me. Certainly worth a try."

She rummaged loudly through her selection of jars stored in a cool corner of the pantry until she found the selected blend of herbs she had in mind. She mixed the herbs into the kettle of hot water sitting at the hearth, and a comforting fragrance filled the room. The mere scent of it helped settle her nerves. After the herbs had seeped long enough, she poured the brew into a mug and set it in front of Daniel.

"I thank you kindly, ma'am," he said before taking a tentative sip of the hot drink. "Aahh, now that's good." He gave her a blissful smile. His short dark brown hair looked as though he had done no more than run his fingers through it to get it off his face, and the dark shadow of stubble gracing his jaw was unnervingly appealing. She didn't like it one bit.

Kayla tried to bear in mind her feelings of resentment toward Daniel, but a nervous fluttering running rampant throughout her body pushed harder to grab her attention. She wanted to be rid of him so she could regain control of her senses. It was unusual for her to feel this flustered, and she didn't find it appealing. She started to walk away.

"Won't you join me?" he asked. "It's not right for a man to eat alone." He looked up at her, all sweet-faced and innocent.

She didn't buy it for a moment. But she had to admit, that darn smile of his was charming. He had a funny way of speaking, and yet she enjoyed hearing his words. Alarm bells sounded in her brain, and the nervous flutter suddenly condensed, taking up residence low in her belly. Striving to overcome the uneasy feeling, she poured another mug of the steaming hot brew and sat down across from him. Obviously, her stomach could use a little of the soothing drink to calm the effect he was having on her.

She was a wee bit surprised when he lingered over the meal. Instead of gulping down his food as she had expected, he ate slowly, displaying unusually nice table manners. He didn't appear to be in much of a hurry to reach the lists for his scheduled training with Michael. Instead, he took time to politely engage her in a pleasant conversation, asking one question after another as he ate the oatcakes and bread, washing them down with the strong hot herbal brew.

He seemed to have a talent for gathering information, she noted, pouring on the charm and getting her to drop her well-developed defenses. Something in his manner made it all too easy to relax around him. She found herself telling him far more about herself than she had expected. He had asked in his well-mannered and charming way, and she had answered.

"So tell me, if you don't mind my asking, where did you learn the recipe for this tea?" he asked.

"Tea?" she asked, unfamiliar with the term.

"This brew," he said, lifting the mug. "I don't know what you call it, but I'd call it tea, herbal tea."

"From my mother. Since I was a child, she has schooled me in the healing arts. It's a legacy all MacNicol women share."

"I'm impressed. It hits the spot. Earlier, when you were on your way to the stables, were you planning to take a ride?"

"Aye, I was planning to visit my friend Fern. She's married, with a wee bairn. I thought the visit would do me good." She didn't know why she was explaining this all to him. She glanced over at Bonnie as she cut up chunks of vegetables for the midday meal. The serving woman seemed to be thoroughly enjoying her discomfort.

"Do you usually like to ride in the morning?" He seemed genuinely interested.

"Aye. I've always enjoyed the morning and watching the sunrise."

"Ahh, a morning person. It suits you." Again he flashed her that darn smile, as if he knew something he wasn't saying.

"I've always liked sunrises better than sunsets. Sunsets are beautiful to behold, if you've the time to sit for a spell, but there's nothing grander than the breaking dawn of each new day. Sunrises are more cheerful, more hopeful than sunsets." She wondered why she was babbling on like a foolish girl.

"You know, I never thought of it that way. But now that you mention it, yea, I'd have to agree." He looked at her as if she had just said the most amazing thing he had ever heard. She felt the color rise in her cheeks.

Seeing that he was almost finished with his meal, she rushed him along. "Ye best be heading out to the lists. Michael will be waiting for you."

"You're right. But you can't blame a fellow for waiting to enjoy the company of such charming women." He chugged down the last of his brew, then glanced over at Bonnie and gave her a wink. Bonnie nodded in return. Kayla felt a twinge of jealousy, as if they were sharing a silent communication to which she wasn't privy. The feeling churned in her stomach.

After Daniel finished his meager meal, he headed out to the lists, and Kayla breathed a sigh of relief.

"He's a right fine young man, is he not?" Bonnie offered her unsolicited opinion.

"He's a visitor to our keep and deserving of our hospitality. Nothing more," Kayla replied in a huff. She was in no mood to explain herself to her serving woman.

"I'm just saying . . . ," Bonnie began.

"There's no need for you to be saying anything," Kayla interrupted her. She refused to engage in such talk with Bonnie, even if she was her oldest and dearest servant. It wasn't right, and she was too flustered to discuss the matter further.

Bonnie held her thoughts, but the smile on her face was spread a mile long. Kayla ignored her, turning her focus on cleaning up after Daniel before she headed back to the stables.

As she was making her way across the courtyard, Kayla found herself slowing to watch the sparring match between Daniel and Michael. She told herself she was only going to watch for a moment. She thought it would be interesting to see his fighting technique, especially since he came from someplace strange and so very far away. Then she absolutely, positively had to be on her way. She needed to speak with Fern.

Watching him move with such powerful skill as he sparred with Michael, she had gotten caught up in the moment. She gasped when Michael got the upper hand and knocked Daniel off his feet, and she had very nearly cheered when Daniel quickly recovered to end the match with Michael pinned to the ground.

Silently she berated herself for her reaction. A wave of embarrassment washed over her as she realized she was standing in the middle of the courtyard gaping at the men in training. She quickly moved to the shadow of the stables, trying to collect her wits, hoping she hadn't been noticed.

She questioned her loyalties and what had prompted such an emotional response. Why would she cheer the victory of a man she hardly knew? When it came to her emotions regarding Daniel Ellers, there was much that didn't make sense. She was determined not to like the man, and yet she was finding that extremely hard to do.

Just as she was about to leave her hiding space and head into the stables, she was distracted by the sight of Daniel taking his claymore training from Michael. She could tell he was a novice with the weapon, and yet he took to the training with impressive zeal, quickly gaining skill under Michael's expert tutorage.

When she finally pulled herself away from the spying on the men, Bonnie had come looking for her. She informed her that Lady Lydia was looking for her. She was needed in the village to tend to a sick child. Her plan to visit Fern would have to wait for another day. It was as if the fates were conspiring against her.

Chapter 15

The morning of training was grueling. Michael was your typical fair-but-tough taskmaster, and Daniel couldn't remember the last time he had worked so hard or enjoyed himself more. By the time they reached a break in the training, the only thing demanding more attention than his hunger was the aching muscles developing in his arms and shoulders. A few hours of swinging a five-pound claymore added up to weary bones for an out-of-place citified cop like him.

He joined the MacNicol brothers and their warriors in the great hall for a hearty meal of mutton stew sopped up with crusty bread. After the meal, Michael and Rory were called away to deal with a broken door in the barracks. According to Rory, one of the guards had gotten a wee bit too drunk the night before and had used his foot to open the door to his room, breaking the latch. Michael needed to take a disciplinary action in the matter, and Rory went along for support, leaving Daniel to wander on his own.

Having some time on his hands, he was hoping to find Kayla and convince her to act as a tour guide to show him around the castle. The idea was vastly appealing and full of merit. Besides providing an opportunity to explore the ancient compound, it held the possibility of having time alone with her.

He was standing outside the large stone keep, considering where to start his search, when he spied Bonnie, the woman in charge of the serving staff. She was heading toward the building that housed the kitchens. He figured she would know where Kayla could be found.

Bonnie struck him as a woman who knew her way around the castle and the people who lived there. Maybe, if he got her talking, she would tell him more about Lady Lydia. From what he had read in Teressa's journal, he figured Lady Lydia knew a whole lot more about his time-travel adventure than she was saying.

He hurried over to catch up with Bonnie before she disappeared into the confines of the kitchens. His experience with the people who worked on the streets of San Francisco had taught him that acknowledgement of a person's services went a long ways toward opening doors of goodwill.

Unintentionally, but to his great fortune, it had been his gratitude expressed to Kayla earlier that morning that had secured him the meager leftovers from breakfast.

"Bonnie," he called out. "I wanted to thank you for getting me breakfast this morning. I don't know what I would have done without your help." He greeted her with his usual friendly smile.

"Oh goodness, sir, no thanks are needed. I was just doing my job, as Kayla asked of me. I could no let my mistress down. 'Tis Kayla you have to thank. You surely must be glad you've made a friend with her. She's a good one to have on your side," Bonnie gushed. She returned his friendly smile with one of her own.

"Speaking of Kayla, do you happen to know where she is? I haven't seen her since breakfast." He wasn't being completely truthful. He had caught a glimpse of Kayla as she stood near the stables watching the field training. Since it was apparent she was trying to conceal her observation, he kept that particular piece of information to himself. Not letting people know that you knew something they didn't want you to know usually proved to be a good idea. He had been flattered when he noticed her watching his training session, apparently forgoing her morning ride.

"The young mistress and her mother were called away to the village to see to a youngen down with a cough. They took some of Lady Lydia's herbs over to his ma and will do a healing for his chest. With their help, he'll be right as the sunrise by the morrow. 'Tis a blessing they are to provide such healing to our village folk."

Daniel noted that the head servant of the keep was not known for holding back on her thoughts or opinions. She was well on her way to middle age and had a well-rounded motherly image about her. She seemed like the type who would have served the MacNicol boys milk and cookies when they were younger and encouraged them to laugh away their hurts. Light chestnut brown hair haloed a cheerful face blessed with merry chocolate brown eyes and a constant warm smile.

"You speak well of Lady Lydia and Kayla. Have you known them long?" He joined Bonnie as she continued into the kitchens, not wanting to hold her back from her work while he attempted to pick her brain.

"Only all my life. I was born here in this keep. Raised to work for the clan chief and his family like my dear Ma before me, I am proud to say. I also have an elder sister, Anna. She lives in the village. She takes on the sewing, mending, and such. She's real fine with a needle and thread. Not something I ever took a liking to. I'd rather wash a floor or clean a chamber than sit still with needle and thread. But my sister, she's got a real talent for the work. Now it's nothing like the fine needlework Lady Lydia does. If you were to see her fancy work, I believe you'd be mighty impressed, even if you are a man. I believe you appreciate the finer things in life. I can just see that in you."

Daniel let his smile pour freely over Bonnie. She was a powerhouse of opinion, and he enjoyed her running commentary.

Bonnie's attention was diverted to one of the many young boys working in the kitchens. "Make sure you scrub them pots clean. Milly will throw a fit if a dirty pot messes with her soup for this evening's meal." She bent over to pick up a large basket of vegetables set just inside the kitchen door.

"Here, let me help you with that." Daniel reached out to help carry the large basket and move it over to the food prep table.

Bonnie nearly blushed at his offered assistance. "There's no need for you to be here working in the kitchens. This is women's work, and we've plenty of young lads to help. Shouldn't you be off training with the brothers?" Even as she spoke, she reluctantly accepted his assistance, letting him move the heavy basket for her.

"Michael and Rory are busy dealing with a drunken guard. Besides, where I come from, it's not unusual for men to work in the kitchens. Some of the best-known chefs are men. I'm just trying to help where I can, earn my keep, so to speak. I don't see this as woman's work, just something that needs to get done, so we can all eat. And Lord knows how I like to eat." He flashed her a winning smile. "I've spent all morning with the MacNicol brothers. I'm finding the pleasure of your company to be far more enjoyable."

Bonnie cast a skeptical eye at him. She might appear simple, but Daniel knew she was no fool. She knew better than to believe that a young buck like him was hanging at her skirts because he found her attractive, but as he was offering his services, she was able to overcome any qualms she had about putting him to work. "Well then, since you're here, you can help me get these vegetables cleaned and sorted for Milly. And while we're at it, you can tell me about your travels and what brings you to Scorrybreac." Bonnie's perpetual smile never left her face as she engaged in the friendly exchange of gossip.

Daniel's smile only deepened. Story swapping with Bonnie would definitely be a pleasant diversion. He began dunking and washing the fresh-picked vegetables. A basin of water had already been set up on the sturdy prep table that dominated the well-kept large kitchens. Racks holding an array of pots and pans lined the walls. The large open-face fireplace and built-in brick ovens had been fired up since before sunrise and would burn until well into the late evening hours doing service for the cook and her staff. Baskets of food had been brought up from the cold storage cellar, waiting for Milly's cooking talents to turn it all into tasty dishes for the MacNicol clan's evening meal.

"You could say I'm here at my sister's request. She was so impressed with Skye after her visit she wanted me to see Scorrybreac for myself. She spoke highly of you. She said you were a big help to her during her visit."

Bonnie shined under the unexpected compliment. "Your sister made a fairly large impression here as well. It was her matchmaking skills that brought Duncan and Janet together again after their broken betrothal. Cut right through all the bluster and pride of those two young folks like a hot knife in fresh churned butter, she did. But her leaving left Rory with a broken heart. Is she no expecting to return? We've heard nothing from her since her sudden disappearance some years ago."

Daniel did his best to answer truthfully while still evading Bonnie's search for answers he couldn't provide. "I'm fairly certain Rory will see Teressa again someday. It's just hard to say when that will be." Especially considering that, according to Teressa's journal, their reunion wouldn't happen for another seven hundred years. "But I can tell you Teressa shares Rory's feelings."

"Och, 'tis glad I am to be hearing that. I want nothing but the best for my lad, Rory, and if he thinks Teressa is what's best, then so be it."

Now it was his turn to dig for some dirt. "I thought Lady Lydia had something to do with Duncan and Janet's reunion. Wasn't she rather keen on them getting back together?"

"Aye, Lady Lydia always hoped that Duncan would fulfill his duty as chief by joining the two clans through marriage. Why, the two youngens had been expected to marry since they were wee bairns, and when Duncan sent Janet away, it caused a great disappointment for Lady Lydia. For certain, she knew she could no challenge Duncan's choice. She could no go against her own son and the chief of the clan. She was just waiting for the right opportunity to present itself." Bonnie moved the washed vegetables onto a clean basket lined with a drying cloth, ready for the kitchen lads to peel and slice under Milly's direction.

"And it looks like the right opportunity included Teressa." Daniel wiped his hands on the drying towel Bonnie offered to him.

"It would seem so. It was mighty convenient for a skilled matchmaker to show up just before the Gathering at the Isle Faire, especially since it was the first time in years that Lady Janet had been there. I believe Lady Lydia was right pleased to get those two together in such a quick fashion."

Yes, very convenient, Daniel thought, considering that Lady Lydia, with the help of Moezell, had been instrumental in bringing Teressa to Skye at exactly the right time. Hoping to gain further insight into any information that might be useful, Daniel gently guided the conversation along a different path. "Teressa mentioned something about legends of fairies and a great-grandmother of the MacNicol clan. Do you know anything about these stories?"

"Aye, 'tis true. The legend tells of the beautiful Sophie appearing from the morning mists to find Hubert, of the McLean clan. He was weary and wounded from battle, making his way back home. Sophie tended to his wounds and restored him to health with loving care. 'Tis said her healing powers came directly from the fairies." Bonnie gazed off to some distant point, as if playing out the vision in her mind's eye.

"Is that the same healing power that's been passed from mother to daughter over the years?" He hoped Bonnie would be caught off guard by his nonchalant question.

"Aye, 'tis the same. Lady Lydia learned from her mother and now passes the knowledge on to Kayla. 'Tis a gift they have, these daughters of Sophie."

"I wonder what other powers the fairies have passed along." Daniel watched Bonnie, evaluating her reaction.

"The MacNicol women are blessed by the fairies, 'tis true. Why they only need ask and the fairies . . ." Bonnie halted her words in midsentence and directed her focus back to Daniel. She must have sensed his desire for confidential information and realized she needed to be more cautious around him. "And well, you only need look at the bounty of the MacNicol keep to know the fates have smiled well upon this clan."

Milly walked in on the tail end of Bonnie's comment. She was followed by a boy carrying a basket of preserved meats they had retrieved from the smokehouse. "Aye, the fates have smiled well upon these MacNicols, but if we don't have the evening meal prepared on time, I doubt anyone will be smiling. Now off with you, lad." She waved a weathered old hand at Daniel, shooing him from the prep table, where she deposited the heavy load. "A busy kitchen is no place for a lazy warrior." Without missing a beat, she reached for her large meat cleaver, wielding the knife with well-honed precision. She cut into the raw meat with an amazing show of force for a woman of her age. Her hands, though aged from the daily chores of cooking, still held the strength of a younger maid.

Quickly stepping away from the prep table, and safely beyond the reach of Milly's blade, Daniel acknowledged it was time for him to go. He took his leave, wishing the kitchen servants well as they prepared the evening meal. He stepped out into the sunlit courtyard, whistling a happy tune, and headed back to the lists to finish out the day of training.

Chapter 16

*K*ayla and her mother approached a simple cottage at the far end of the lane. They'd been called to the village to tend to a sick boy. The cottage was one of the smaller ones in the village, and yet it housed a rather large family. There were seven children the last time she counted. One of the younger boys was down with a deep chest cough. Their biggest fear was that the ailment would spread to the rest of the family in the tightly cramped quarters.

Lady Lydia knocked on the battered wood door. For a moment, it looked as though the door was swinging open on its own accord, until a wee lass peeked around the opening. Her face and hands were clean, but her hair was uncombed, and her grey tunic was patched and dirty. The lass bid them to enter.

Kayla fought the urge to draw back from the odor escaping through the open cottage door. Smoke from the peat fire mixed with the smell of cooking and human sweat to create an unpleasant result. It was hard to evade the concentrated stench produced by so many bodies living so close together. The effect gave her pause to appreciate the airiness of her home in the large fortress keep. A glance at her mother showed she was less inclined to hide her reaction as Lady Lydia drew her headscarf across her nose and mouth.

Following her mother, Kayla ducked through the entrance and stepped into the central room of the cottage. It was dark and musty with all the shutters of the windows closed up tight. The young girl was just about to shut the door behind them when Lady Lydia stopped her. "Leave it open, child. We need the air and light."

The mistress of the cottage stepped forward. "My lady, my lad is ill. Is it no better to keep out the chill in the air from reaching him?" she asked. She was respectful, but Kayla could see that her first priority was her son.

"Nay. This stale air is far harder on him than a fresh cool breeze. Open the doors and windows. Let the air flow through," Lady Lydia commanded.

The mother complied, doing as Lady Lydia instructed. As her eyes became accustomed to the dimness of the room, Kayla could see the young boy huddled on a thin straw pallet near the rear of the room, his body clenched against another hacking cough. She glanced at her mother, who was still standing near the open door. Lady Lydia motioned her forward, and Kayla took to her task, kneeling next to the boy.

His one wool blanket was thin and too small to adequately cover his little body. Kayla pulled her wool cloak off her shoulders and draped it over the boy. He looked up at her in gratitude with eyes too large and fearful for one so young.

Kayla placed the palm of her one hand across his forehead. With the other, she reached beneath the makeshift covers and felt his chest. She could feel the rattle as he struggled to breathe. She gave him an encouraging smile. "Ye'll be all right, lad. Ye must believe."

He nodded, indicating his trust.

She turned to address the boy's mother. "I'll need a bowl of fresh water, and a clean washcloth."

"I can manage the fresh water. We've a rain barrel out back, but I'll be hard-pressed to produce a clean scrap o'cloth."

"The water will do fine then." Kayla pulled off her headscarf, bit at the edge, and tore the linen fabric in two.

The mother placed a bowl of water next to Kayla. She dipped a piece of the linen into the water and began washing the young boy's face and hands, cleaning off the spittle left behind by his coughing. After rinsing out the scrap of fabric, she folded it and placed it on his forehead, allowing it to cover his eyes. She felt him relax as he closed his eyes under the cool weight of the cloth.

Seeing that she had calmed the boy, she brought her hands near her face, blew on her palms, and then rubbed her hands together, reinforcing the energy held within. She placed both hands on the boy's chest, one near his throat and the other over his heart. She closed her eyes and let the healing warmth seep through her fingers.

At first, his breathing remained shallow and raspy, but as she continued to send her healing energy to his weakened body, she began to feel the results. His breathing became deeper, more relaxed, and the fluid-filled rattle abated.

She had sat with him for nearly half an hour before she felt the treatment was complete. In the course of the treatment, her energy had drained as she felt his return.

Sitting back on her hunches, she brought her awareness back into the room. She looked up and saw the boy's mother standing over her. Apparently, she had stood watch over her son the whole time. The open windows and door had helped clear out the stale air, blowing out the sour scents and replacing them with a fresh ocean breeze. The temperature of the cottage was invigorating, but not cold enough to cause her to worry.

"Ye may close the shutters in the eve before the sun sets, but allow them to remain open throughout the sunny time of the day. He'll still need a day or two of rest, but he'll be fine," Kayla addressed the mother.

"Have him drink this brew several times a day until he is well," Lady Lydia said, indicating a kettle of herbal brew she had prepared while Kayla had tended to the child.

"I can no thank you enough," the mother said.

"Your healthy boy will be thanks enough," Lady Lydia assured her. She turned toward the door, looking relieved to be leaving the cottage.

Feeling drained, Kayla walked beside her mother in silence as they returned from their work in the village. She had spent a good deal of energy tending to the sick boy, and the effort had worn her out. Possibly due to her fatigue, she slipped on the rocky pathway and twisted her ankle. Soon the injury began to throb.

Adding to her discomfort, her mind churned with thoughts from her previous late-night conversation with Moezell. Unable to stand the nagging disappointment a moment longer, and too exhausted to try, she gathered her courage and confronted her mother.

"I had a rather unexpected visitor in my chamber last night," Kayla began.

"You did?" From the look of shock on her mother's face, Kayla wondered if she had someone particular in mind.

"Aye, my cousin, Moezell, the fairy. I believe you know her."

Lady Lydia's expression changed, but she was still visibly dismayed. Apparently, Kayla's revelation was not what her mother had expected.

"Why have you no told me about our connection to the fairies?" Kayla asked.

"'Tis no a simple thing. I have been preparing you for the right time to reveal such essential knowledge. For years I have been training you in the healing arts. They are a significant gift of our fey heritage. And I have often told you stories about the fey and our great-grandmother Sophie."

"Mother, I am two and twenty. When were you thinking would be the right time to tell me I'm part fey? Did you plan to wait until I'm married and have children of my own? From what Moezell told me, this is something I should have been told years ago."

"Aye, well, Moezell. Apparently, she has started doing things on her own now. She did no consult me on this matter," Lady Lydia huffed.

"Why should she consult you?"

"She should respect my position as her elder cousin and the matriarch of this clan."

"What about your respect for me, your daughter? Have you no consideration for my feelings in this matter? Why must my fairy cousin be the one to tell me what you have always known?" Disappointment over her mother's lack of respect for her feelings surged through Kayla.

"As I said, I have been preparing you for the right time. Obviously, Moezell and I disagree on when that time should be," Lady Lydia continued to defend her position.

"Obviously. And in this matter, I believe Moezell is right."

"So now you know. Does it make you feel better to challenge your mother? Is this what your fairy cousin has been teaching you?"

"Nay, that's not what I mean." Kayla felt the sting of her mother's words.

"What else could you possibly mean?" Lady Lydia shot her a scornful look.

"I'm just saying you could have told me sooner."

"What would it have changed? I've been teaching you the healing arts. Look at how well you preformed today. Knowing you're half fey would no make you any better."

"You don't know that. Maybe knowing I'm half fey would strengthen my gift. Make me a better healer," Kayla tried to defend herself against her mother.

"It wouldn't have found you a husband. Soon, no one will want you. Will being half fey help you then?" Lady Lydia turned to focus on the path before them, refusing to look at her daughter.

Kayla bit her lip, holding back her tears. Her mother could have slapped her in the face; it wouldn't have hurt any more. Pain and anger swept through her, but she held her tongue. Her deeply ingrained respect for her mother kept her from voicing her true discontent. But she knew it wouldn't always be this way. Someday, when she was stronger, she'd be able to stand up for herself. She knew the day was coming.

Limping slightly from the increasing pain in her ankle, she walked beside her mother in stiff, stony silence.

◆ ◆ ◆

Daniel had spent hours testing out some of the fiercest weaponry available for ancient Scottish warfare. He rejected the battle-ax. It was too coarse and unmanageable for his taste. He was impressed by the quality of the smaller blades possessed by the MacNicol brothers; they called them dirks, but of course, they had limited uses. At the end of the day, it was the claymore that gave him the greatest satisfaction. There was something about the immense feeling of power that only the long broadsword could deliver. Unfortunately, he was remiss to admit that a hard day of training with the strange weaponry had taken a toll on his body. Even though he considered himself to be in good physical condition, the day of training had utilized a whole new set of muscles, and his limbs were strongly voicing their dissent.

After being dismissed by Michael, a ruthless but admirable taskmaster, Daniel stopped at the nearest rain barrel he could find to wash the sweat and grime of the training day from his body. He headed back to his chamber for what he considered to be a well-deserved rest before dinner, making considerable effort to ensure nothing about his gait or posture revealed the tentacles of pain snaking their presence throughout his body. The nagging discomfort had started at his shoulder blades and was now working its way toward his lower back.

As he approached the front of the courtyard, he spied Kayla and Lady Lydia returning to the keep. Choosing to ignore the rebellious cries of his muscles, he jogged to catch up with them. Coming closer, he noticed that Kayla was limping slightly, favoring her right foot.

"Hey there," he called out to the mother and daughter. "How you doing? Did your day in the village go well?"

"Good day, Daniel Ellers," Lady Lydia returned his greeting with formal politeness. "I believe our healing work will provide great comfort to the child and his mother."

Directing his concerns to Kayla, he noticed the pain reflected in her eyes. "Did you hurt your foot? You seem to be limping."

"Oh, 'tis nothing much. I stepped badly over some stones and turned my ankle. Some soothing salve and rest is all it needs." Regardless of her words, Daniel could hear the pain in her voice.

"Is there anything I can do to help?" he asked. Not waiting for her to respond, he reached out for her, wrapping his arm around her waist to help support her weight.

Lady Lydia took note of the bold gesture with a fair measure of disapproval. It was obvious she wasn't comfortable with Daniel's relaxed familiarity toward her daughter.

"Nay, no need to bother over me. I'm just going up to my chamber to rub some of Mother's salve on my ankle and rest a bit before the evening meal. I'm sure all will be well." Her steps were tentative as she continued walking, but at least she accepted his assistance.

Daniel didn't believe her. Her face bore the effect of her aches, belying her words. He tightened his grip, and Kayla shifted her weight, bracing an arm against his shoulder to alleviate some of the burden from her sore ankle.

"Please, let me help. I have experience with muscle injuries. I'd be happy to massage your ankle for you," Daniel offered as they limped along toward the steps of the keep. He welcomed the opportunity to massage her feet or any other sensitive body part that needed tending. He could already imagine starting at her ankles and working his way up from there.

"I'm perfectly capable of assisting my daughter." Lady Lydia stepped forward.

"Of course, I have no doubts. I was just offering to help." He quickly took stock of Lady Lydia's possessive disapproval. Pausing for only a moment, he looked for a way to turn the confrontation back to his favor. "You know I have a bit of soreness developing in my shoulders. Not used to training with a claymore, I guess. Do you think I could get some of that salve for my back?" He rolled his shoulders as a sign of the discomfort he felt, hoping to gain some sympathy votes from Lady Lydia.

"I will give you a supply of the salve. It will be up to you to find a willing servant to apply the medicine." Her curt answer left him with little doubt regarding her lack of sympathy for his alleged injury.

Daniel refused to be discouraged. He might be pushing the boundaries of Lady Lydia's tolerance, but he wouldn't back down. Ignoring the elder woman, he turned to Kayla. "You said you're a student of the healing arts. Perhaps if I rub your ankle, you could massage my back." He held her gaze.

Kayla appeared stunned by his bold suggestion. She didn't speak, but her expressive eyes widened in dismay. And she didn't look away. A slight gasp escaped her lips before an appreciative smile settled in.

Lady Lydia was quicker to respond. "I am quite capable of assisting my daughter. She is not a servant girl to be waiting on you and your aches."

"Hey, don't misunderstand me." Daniel held up a hand of peace. "It's not my intention to offend you, or your daughter. I just thought she'd be the best person for the job, being a healer and all."

It looked like he was going to lose the battle. At best, he hoped to minimize his losses. It wouldn't do him any good to really piss off Kayla's mother. He could already feel her animosity against him. He had no intention of creating an outright enemy, especially since his sister had reported that Lady Lydia was part fey and able to communicate with Moezell. He figured she was well aware that he came from the future. Not only that, her demeanor suggested she hadn't been involved in summoning him back in time, and she obviously wasn't pleased by his unexpected presence.

Kayla finally found her tongue, which for a moment had been lodged firmly between her teeth. "Mother, Daniel is right. I am quite able to see to his injuries." She lifted her chin a bit higher in a show of defiant determination.

"You are?" Lady Lydia looked amazed, obviously taken aback by her daughter's outspoken manner.

"I am!" Daniel's wide eyes focused on Kayla. No doubt he was as surprised as her mother that she had taken his side.

"Aye. And I know Janet is expecting you for a visit with Amy," Kayla spoke to her mother. "I'm confident Daniel's knowledge of muscle injuries will be sufficient to deal with my minor strain. If not, I am quite capable of directing his efforts."

Daniel and Lady Lydia took a moment to stare at Kayla, each displaying their individual response to her unexpected declaration. Her mother was struggling to conceal her blatant displeasure over Kayla's sudden assertiveness, while Daniel struggled to conceal his obvious delight.

Acting quickly to take advantage of her mother's shocked silence, Kayla continued her instructions, "Daniel, if you could assist me to my chamber, we can begin the healing treatments at once. I believe I have enough of the salve to serve both our needs."

"You will do no such thing," Lady Lydia said.

"Aye, I will. It's a reasonable solution. I'm tired and in pain. Daniel has offered to ease my pain. And as the clan healer, it's my duty to treat him." This time, Kayla was not backing down. Bolstered by the strength of Daniel's support, for the first time in her life she was standing up to her mother, and it felt good. Scary, but good.

"You would have him treat you, alone, in your chamber?" Lady Lydia nearly screeched her protest. "That can no be allowed. It is highly inappropriate."

"It seems far more appropriate than his chamber in the high tower. Or would you rather we tend to our pains in the middle of the great hall for all to see?"

"I do not approve." Lady Lydia glared at Kayla.

"I did not ask for your approval." Kayla returned her mother's stare.

She had expected her mother's reaction, well aware of the shocking implications of her suggested actions. At any other time, her mother's reaction would have been considered reasonable, even proper, but not this time. This time the tethering cord of compliance, which had recently been stretched to its breaking point, had finally snapped inside her. In a burst of confidence, she willfully challenged her mother's controlling ways.

This was the first time someone outside of her family had offered to tend to her pains, showing a real interest in her welfare, and it was simply unacceptable that her mother would try to deny her that satisfaction. After all, it was only a healing. She did them all the time.

This is why she didn't tell me I'm part fey, Kayla thought, *and why she believes I will marry Arlin. It never occurs to her to ask what I want. It's always what she thinks is best, always her way. Even the reunion of Duncan and Janet was as she wished. It was just good fortune that Teressa was there to help them rekindle their love for each other.*

Kayla realized her sudden surge of defiance was spurring a newfound appreciation for the strong and independent ways of Teressa, a woman she had once judged so harshly. She began to understand that the liberty of self-determination had its advantages.

She had never been one to question her family's requirements of her, much less her mother's requests. Always, she had been the dutiful daughter and sister to her family's demands, shying away from confrontations with her family. She had even thought to seek out her best friend Fern to request her assistance against the demands of the family rather than face them alone in her struggle for independence. She realized that was all about to change.

"I certainly hope you know what you're doing—and what you are risking." Lady Lydia's glaring eyes attempted to burn holes into Kayla's newly developed confidence.

"I believe I do." Kayla stood firm, returning her mother's glare. Nervous as she was, she felt her spirit soar as the full ramifications of her choices settled in. Not only was she being openly defiant of her mother, but if word got out about her being alone with Daniel—and she was sure it would—it could put a huge damper on her mother's plans to arrange the intended betrothal. It was one thing to think of disagreeing with her family, and even more precarious to voice her disagreement with them, but this open display of independence was a whole new level of risk for her.

Kayla knew her mother was furious, but thankfully, she refused to make a scene in front of Daniel. Delivering one final glare to each of them, Lady Lydia stomped off into the keep, doing her best to maintain her dignity.

A surge of excitement swept through Kayla. It had worked. It was scary, but it had worked. She had defied her mother. She knew her mother would be mad, but still, for the first time in her life she had stood up to her. She trembled with excitement over her minor victory, but there was also fear. Fear that she was stepping into uncharted waters, and she didn't know how to proceed. Feeling the strength of Daniel's arm supporting her around her waist, she felt stronger than she could ever remember.

Chapter 17

*D*aniel watched in amazement as Kayla stood up to her controlling mother, then watched Lady Lydia retreat into the depths of the great hall. As soon as her mother was out of sight, Kayla slumped against Daniel.

"Come, it's your turn to be my angel of mercy," she said. "Help me to my room. My ankle has begun to swell, and if I don't rest soon, I will be paying dearly tomorrow." She completely gave in to Daniel's support, dropping the pretense of strength she had been maintaining for Lady Lydia's benefit.

He reached an arm beneath her knees and scooped her off her feet. She gave a little squeak of protest, looking duly impressed, but offered no resistance. She was too tired.

"Why didn't you say something earlier?" He was grateful for the excuse to hold her near, regretting it was due to her injury, but not regretting the opportunity her injury provided. Moving up the narrow staircase leading into the keep, he could already picture massaging her aching feet in the privacy of her bedchamber.

"I didn't want Mother to know. She would fuss over me like a child, which I am not. I am not a child anymore. If only she would stop treating me as such," Kayla said with conviction. "And you need not fuss over me either. I need to get off my feet and let my ankle rest for a while, but you really don't need to carry me."

She claimed she didn't need his help, but the way she reached her arms around his neck and held on contradicted her words.

"Believe me, fussing over you is going to be my pleasure."

He walked through the great hall toward the narrow circular stairwell, holding her easily in his arms. She was strong and yet so fragile. It was as if she had no understanding of her own true value. He also noted it was nothing short of amazing how the mere act of carrying her, instead of adding to his aches, was relieving all the stress and strain he'd been feeling in his shoulders and back. In fact, he felt better than ever. He could feel comforting warmth pulsing through his body, delivering painkilling relief to his aching bones.

Kayla directed Daniel to her room, where he set her down on a chair near the hearth. He intentionally left the door to her chamber propped open, hoping to avoid the appearance of improper intimacy for her sake. He would have preferred to close the door, creating a private getaway, but his better judgment respected the precarious predicament they were creating. Even if she didn't, he understood the risk she was taking.

For him, the open door helped to lessen the opportunity, if not the temptation, to take advantage of the situation. It was something he thought best to avoid. He appreciated the faith and respect she had placed upon him, and he had no intention of letting her down. This way, they would be in plain view of anyone walking along the hallway seeking to spy on their activities. As a police officer, he'd seen firsthand how the mere act of closing a door could produce gossip and scandal with devastating results. Acting in plain sight made it much harder to spawn false accusations while helping him avoid inappropriate temptations.

Concerned for her warmth and comfort, he pulled a wool blanket from her bed and placed it on her lap. A sweet half smile lit her face as he tended to her needs.

Looking around the room, he began searching for the various items he needed. He found a water pitcher and a washbasin on the side table. He grabbed a drying cloth from the linen chest and pulled out the footstool she kept near her bed.

"Okay, tell me where this special ointment of yours is stashed," he asked, getting ready to settle into his task of attending to her injured ankle.

"It's kept there in the baskets near the window. The one on the far right." She pointed to the row of baskets. "That one, with the brown leather pouch."

After collecting the salve, he took the washbasin and water pitcher from the table, set them on the floor in front of Kayla, and poured some of the water from the pitcher into the basin. Settling his large frame on the diminutive footstool in front of her, he reached to remove her short leather boots, first the right and then the left.

Kayla began to protest, "Nay, only my right ankle is injured. You've no need to remove both boots."

"Trust me. I, ah, need to evaluate both ankles to determine the extent of the injury," he said, improvising. He gave her a look of confidence, hoping his explanation sounded reasonable. He had every intention of taking full advantage of the opportunity to not only soothe her aches and pains but also pamper her in a manner that exceeded anything she had experienced before. As far as he was concerned, such indulgence required nothing less than massaging both of her feet.

She hesitated, then nodded, accepting his actions.

He gently bathed her feet in the refreshingly cool water with all the care one might apply to a newborn babe, washing away the dust and dirt. He was careful to avoid creating any further discomfort to her swollen ankle. He wanted her to feel cherished.

It seemed to be working. She watched his every move, as if enthralled by his actions.

Laying the drying cloth across his broad thighs, he set the water aside and drew her feet into his lap, drying them before he began his massage. He began with her left foot and ankle, running his hands over her skin, testing the tension of the muscles that lay beneath the surface. Her feet were small and well formed, but not dainty. They'd been toughened by years of hard work and the freedom of going barefoot. He could feel the tension that had built up in her left ankle and calf as they took on the additional task of compensating for her injured right.

Looking into her eyes, he could see her apprehension. Her bravado was beginning to fade. "You're holding on to a lot of tension. You have to relax if this treatment is to be of much use."

Kayla nodded her acceptance, not trusting herself to speak. She was unaccustomed to the sensation created by the feel of a man's hands on her skin, and it was having a greater effect than she had anticipated, even though he was only touching her feet and ankles.

"Tell me if this hurts," he said.

He reached for her right ankle, and with gentle pressure, he walked his fingertips along the sole of her foot, beginning with her toes, which tickled at his touch. He pressed his fingers over the ball of her foot and across her arch. Moving slowly and methodically, he gradually inched his fingers toward the site of the injury. Her ankle was already showing signs of stress, becoming red and swollen. When his fingers reached the edge of the tender tissue, she winced ever so slightly, indicating he had reached his target, but she said nothing, waiting for him to explore further.

He stilled his hands. "Does this hurt?" he asked. It was spoken more as a confirmation than a question as he registered her reaction.

"Only a wee bit," she admitted. "Please proceed." She nibbled nervously on the inside of her bottom lip. Her rigid resolve melted away under the tender mercies of his touch.

He dipped his fingers into the salve and rubbed his hands together for a moment to warm the lanolin-infused lotion. With great care, he began to massage her foot, running his fingers over every inch of her now intensely sensitive skin. He began with her toes, and slowly, so very slowly, he moved along the muscles of her foot, constantly checking her reactions to the amount of pressure he applied, noting whenever she responded with pleasure or distress.

She was acutely aware of the effect his massage was having on her, and she didn't fight it. Instead, she gave into the care of his compassionate touch. By the time he reached the site of the injury, she had relaxed enough to allow him to continue the soothing massage and healing manipulations, releasing the stress and soreness from her overworked muscles. She was grateful when he continued to massage her calves, pulling the tension and stress from her legs.

Kayla felt herself drift into a state of dreamy relaxation, slipping into the role of a well-tended woman. It was a new experience for her, having a man fuss over her as if she was a person of value. Reluctantly at first, but then with increased self-assurance, she gave herself permission to enjoy the new sensation.

"I have never imagined such"—she paused, censoring her words—"such relief from the touch of another." Each word was weighed and measured as she endeavored to avoid the appearance of impropriety.

"But you're a healer. Surely you've provided such relief to others. Haven't you ever received healing in return?" His broad strong hands continued to rub soothing circles around her legs.

"Nay, none such as this. 'Tis my task to provide comfort, not receive."

"You need to be more generous with yourself. If you aren't, who will be?"

She sat in silence, digesting the thought.

"Is my massage helping to relieve your pain?" he asked.

"Aye, very much so. Where did you learn such a fine technique?" Her eyes were half-closed as she savored the pleasurable relief his hands were providing. There were times when the pressure of the massage reached the edge of pain, but it hurt so good as he dug deep into the muscle tissue of her feet, ankles, and calves, relieving the deposits of stress built up through the long hard day.

"I've never had any formal training, but I've experienced these types of treatments for myself."

"You must have been badly injured."

"No, not really. Massage therapy is usually more of a perk to fend off stiff muscles than to fix real injuries."

"I can't picture my brothers seeking out such relief from a healer, at least not for something as minor as an ankle sprain. They would rather disavow the pain than surrender to such pampering."

"This type of treatment is pretty common where I come. We're probably a bit soft by your standards."

"I believe I would have no problem embracing such healing arts. It must be grand. Tell me more about your home, the place where you come from."

His hands drew lazy circles on her feet. It felt so good, she didn't want him to stop.

He stared off for a moment, as if remembering. "I had a great childhood. I can't complain. I was born on a horse ranch. My dad bred and trained rodeo horses. He was damn good, and we worked hard.

"I've got two older brothers, and you already know Teressa, my little sister. My dad's name was Allen, and he named his three sons in alphabetical order, Brett, Conner, and me, Daniel. When Teressa was born, my mom, Francine, decided to stop with the alphabet game and chose to name her only daughter after our two grandmothers, Terrie Ellers and Ressa Withers."

Kayla cocked her head. "I don't understand."

"Terrie and Ressa, Teressa," he explained.

"How sweet. What a lovely way to honor both grandmothers. Was Teressa close to your mother?"

"Mom loved us all, with all her heart, but we all knew she loved Teressa best. They respected each other. I think you could say they were best friends. I'm told that's kinda rare between mother and daughter."

Kayla could agree with that. In recent years, her relationship with her mother had become strained, losing much of the comforting warmth she had known in her youth. She tried to tell herself it was to be expected. It was simply a part of growing up. She was no longer Mother's little girl.

"What about you, Daniel? Were you close to your parents?"

"Yeah, I was. Dad liked having boys. Being the youngest, I got more than my share of teasing, but I was able to hold my own. I'll have to admit, I think Mom had a tendency to favor me over my brothers, being the youngest boy and all. I remember she once said that if Teressa had been a boy, it would have been the death of her. She would have been outnumbered five to one, and it was more than she could handle. But we all knew that she was the one who had the best of us, what with four men to do her bidding. And believe me, she had us pups whipped into shape. There wasn't an Ellers boy who wouldn't give his best for her. But in the end, it was cancer that took her away to be with Dad. He passed a couple years ago. I think the only thing she wanted after Dad died was to be with him." Daniel paused a moment, dwelling on memories of his family.

"I'm sorry for you, to lose both your parents so close together." She felt genuine concern for him.

Daniel shrugged. "No need, it was their time. They lived good long lives, and I've never seen a more loving marriage. You could tell they belonged together."

"I like hearing your stories, listening to the way you speak. Please tell me more," she pleaded. She was thoroughly relaxed by the soothing sound of his voice and his foreign accent. She felt her eyelids grow heavy, lulled by his capable curative powers.

With relaxed fluency, he dove into the subject dearest to his heart. He told her about his life on the ranch and growing up around horses. He related some of the hellish pranks his brothers and he played on each other. All the while, he continued to lightly rub her feet, changing from deep tissue massage to gently soothing strokes. Kayla sat relaxed in the chair with her eyes nearly closed, quietly smiling.

Sometime along the way, Daniel stopped talking and noticed that Kayla had fallen asleep, overcome by her exhaustion. He took a moment to appreciate her peaceful appearance before he stood and gently placed her feet on the footstool. After tucking the edge of the blanket around her bare feet and ankles, he bent to place a chaste kiss on her forehead.

"Sleep well, my sweet angel," he whispered, brushing a stray curl from her cheek. Smiling, he took one last lingering glance at her angelic features before he exited the chamber, closing the door softly behind him.

Chapter 18

Early the next morning, Kayla paced around the great hall, waiting for Daniel to make his appearance, her anger building. What could he have been thinking to let her fall asleep so early in the evening? Hadn't they agreed that she would administer a massage treatment to ease his sore shoulders? She had every intention of soothing away his aches and pains, but instead, he had left her sleeping, causing her to shirk her duties as his healer.

Aye, it had all been so nice and relaxing, the way they had talked and laughed while he massaged her aching feet and ankles. In fact, it had been so very pleasant that she had fallen asleep. And then he had just left her there, in her chamber, alone, and sleeping. He had even thought to seek out Bonnie, telling her to send up a tray of food to her chamber, as if she was some kind of invalid, unable to carry herself down to the hall for the evening meal. She had to hear from Bonnie what a grand time Daniel and her brothers had at supper, exchanging stories about their day in the lists. She was sure she would have enjoyed hearing her brothers tell their tales about Daniel's introduction to Michael's training. But nay, she was left sleeping, alone in her room. What must her mother and the others have been thinking? That she was being lazy. Surely that's what they must have thought. Lazy and unkind to have let Daniel minister to her injury without returning the favor.

As she paced the great hall, checking first one entry for signs of his arrival and then the other, she considered how it had just gotten easier to resent the man, and not because he happened to be Teressa's brother. This time he had earned the resentment all on his own.

She was about to lose her patience and seek him out in his bedchamber when Daniel finally sauntered in through the wide front door of the keep.

Daniel flashed Kayla a warm welcoming smile. "Top of the morning to you, angel. I trust you slept well. How's that ankle holding up?"

It was a pleasure to see his little angel waiting for him. At least she appeared to be waiting for him, although from the look on her face, she appeared to be something less than happy. Maybe her ankle was still giving her pain this morning.

"My ankle's fine and I slept well, all thanks to you." For such kind words, her voice dripped of sarcasm laced with anger. "How could you do such a fine job of tending to my ankle and then just leave me sleeping like that?"

"Because I was trying to be nice?" he questioned with a shrug, his smile quickly fading from his face. Daniel knew she was upset; her displeasure was obvious. He just didn't know what he had done to earn her wrath.

"Nice! Do you think it's nice to leave a person sleeping alone in her chamber while the rest of the family gathers for the evening meal?" She stood with her hands on her hips, a storm brewing in her deep hazel eyes.

"Well, yes, when she looks as sweet and peaceful as you did when I left you." *Darn women*, he thought, *they're just as perplexing in the thirteenth century as they are in the future.*

"Did we no have an agreement that I would treat your sore shoulders after you tended to my ankle?"

"Yeah, sort of, but you fell asleep, and my shoulders felt fine. I forgot all about them being sore. Some beers with your brothers and a good night's rest was as all I needed." He shrugged his shoulders, which ironically enough were starting to tense.

"Aye. I fell asleep and you left me there, sleeping. You even had Bonnie send up a tray for my supper." She was beside herself with indignation.

Daniel could take no more of her talking in circles. He'd reached the end of his patience.

"Okay, Kayla, cut to the chase. Tell me what this is all about so I can make amends and we can go to breakfast." He tried to keep his frustration in check, keeping his voice calm, but he wasn't in the mood to placate her. He needed to know the reason for her anger. He was hungry, and breakfast was getting cold.

"You left me sleeping in my chamber after tending to my ankle. You didn't give me a chance to return the kindness, and besides that, I missed supper with my family. They must think me lazy, that I'm shirking my duties. Mother will think I took advantage of my injury. But I didn't, don't you understand? I didn't." Angry tears pooled in her eyes, threatening to spill down her cheeks.

The lightbulb finally came on. "Oh, I see. I really did let you down, didn't I?" His frustration washed away. He realized she had no prior experience with being pampered. A simple kindness that he took for granted was something new for her, and she was finding it difficult to accept. His frustration was replaced by a desire to reach out and hold her.

"Aye, you did," she said. The angry tears building up inside her finally spilled over, and she wiped away the wetness, embarrassed by their betrayal.

Drawing her aside to a nearby alcove, he gave in to his urge and gathered her into his arms. "I'm sorry, Kayla. Really, I am." He was glad that she didn't' resist, accepting his embrace. He held her firmly in his arms until he felt her breathe deep, relaxing against his chest. It was the clue he needed to know she was ready to talk.

Pulling back, he wiped away her tears, brushing his thumbs gently across her cheeks. "I get it. You're angry because you think I made you look like a fool to your family. Am I right?"

With reluctance, she agreed, "Aye." She nodded, her eyes downcast.

Not allowing her to cower, he raised her chin to look him in the eyes. "First, let me tell you, no one can make you look like a fool, because you're not. If someone even thinks that, then they are mistaken. It's not foolish to rest when your ankle has been injured and needs to mend. It's one of the reasons you're feeling better today. You are feeling better, aren't you?"

She nodded in agreement.

"It's because you got the rest you needed. Do you hear me, needed? Our bodies need rest to properly heal. You should know that."

"I do." She stood a little firmer, acknowledging the wisdom of his words.

"Let me ask you. If it was someone else, say Janet or Shannon, who came to you with a swollen and injured ankle, what advice would you have given her?"

A reluctant half grin escaped Kayla's lips. "I would have told her to stay off her feet and rest."

"Right, because you're a caring, compassionate healer, and you'd want what's best for anyone in pain. So why won't you give the same to yourself?"

"I can't . . . ," she began.

"Why not?"

"I, I don't know how." Her voice was small. This wasn't an easy thing for her to admit.

"Then it's time you start learning, and I'm going to help you. You can't keep giving to others and not give to yourself. Sooner or later, you'll experience burnout, and then you'll be no good to anyone, especially yourself."

She stared up at him with confusion. "Why are you being so nice to me?" she asked.

"How could I not, after all you've done for me? Besides, first impressions are hard to overcome. I think you'll always be my angel."

His fingers traced a path across her cheek and brushed her hair, hooking a wayward strand of red silken curl behind her ear. His eyes roamed across her face, trying to absorb every nuance. She remained quiet and still, as if frozen in place, not knowing how to respond.

Momentarily caught up in her beauty and the touch of his fingers on her skin, he leaned in to kiss her. When he felt her stiffen, he stopped and pulled back. What the hell was he thinking? One minute he was trying to comfort her and the next he was tempted to take advantage of her innocent trust. He felt like a cad. He was from the future; she was an inexperienced young woman from the past. He had no right to start something he couldn't finish.

Slowly becoming aware of the prolonged silence stretched out between them, he felt his lingering gaze turn into an awkward stare.

"Maybe we should go to breakfast. I'm mighty hungry, and while you're a feast for my eyes, you're doing nothing for my belly."

His stomach was rumbling, hungry for food, but an area just south of that was hungry for her, and perfectly ready to make itself known. He needed to create a distraction if he had any hopes of controlling his aroused hunger.

Kayla finally blinked, and he was rewarded with a glowing smile. "Breakfast, of course. You need to eat. What are we waiting for?" Stepping back, she turned on her heel and headed off toward the great hall, where the morning meal was being served.

Chapter 19

Daniel sat at one of the long plank tables, finishing off the last of his breakfast, watching the flurry of activity taking place around him. The great hall of the keep was a busy place. From across the great hall, Rory approached him, greeting him with a cheery nod.

"'Tis a grand summer's day. One of the last we shall see before the rain sets in. Let's go fishing." Rory clapped Daniel on his back.

"Shouldn't you be off doing warrior training with your brothers, or some such stuff?" Daniel drained the last of Kayla's herbal tea from his mug and stood to join Rory. The herbal tea was turning out to be a good substitute for coffee. He didn't know what she put in it, but it had a nice little kick, and it was a great way to start the day.

"Nay, brother. Today, I am no warrior, nor have I any wish to be my mother's servant. Today, I am a man who fishes."

"I see, a man of many talents." He liked Rory's attitude.

"I play well at work and work hard at play," Rory spoke with a relaxed manner, grinning broadly.

They tramped across the great hall toward the exit and headed out to the stables. The courtyard was buzzing with activity in spite of the early morning hour. *People sure do rise and shine early around here*, he observed. It reminded him of his younger days with his dad on the ranch when everything had been in full swing. Allen Ellers had rarely let his boys sleep past sunrise, and Daniel had learned early the value of a hard day's work. Seeing the bustle of the fortress, he missed those days and the feeling of home.

Before they reached the stables, Rory stepped into a storeroom to gather a few supplies, along with some woolen blankets and a couple of large leather bags to hold the sea creatures. He handed a set of the supplies to Daniel.

"I remember well another day I allowed for a day of play at the bay. I hope yer not as intimidated by a wee bit of cold water as your sister was."

"Couldn't get her in the water, could you?" Daniel scoffed, accepting the supplies Rory selected for him. He was well aware of Teressa's aversion to swimming in a cold ocean.

"Nay, she was stubborn in her attachment to the dry land." Rory paused. "'Tis hard to believe it's already been three years since she was here with me, laughing in the sunshine as we gathered sea critters for the evening meal." Sadness passed briefly through Rory's eyes as he reminisced on their time together.

"You miss her, don't you?" Daniel voiced the obvious.

"She is my love, my life, my soul mate. If she'd been able to stay, I would have made her my wife."

They entered the stables and Daniel inhaled the rich familiar scent of hay and horses. Rory led Blazer, his warhorse, from his stall, while Daniel readied a grey-and-white-spotted stallion. Aptly enough, the horse was called Spots. Out in the courtyard, Rory mounted Blazer, in one swift practiced movement. Daniel followed suit.

"Tell me something, if you had to leave this all behind, your home, your family, to be with her, would you still make that choice?" Sitting astride his mount, Daniel gestured toward the courtyard and the keep.

"In a heartbeat," Rory answered, deadpan serious.

"But you knew her for such a short period of time." Daniel was impressed, but he questioned Rory's unwavering conviction.

"Love is no about time. It's a feeling that goes beyond such constraints," Rory answered with calm assurance.

Daniel studied his friend's face. Apparently, Rory had given the matter a lot of thought over the years.

"You know, when Teressa came back, she told us she had met her soul mate, the man she wanted to marry. I'm guessing it's just a matter of time before the two of you are together again."

"Aye, time. That does seem to be the curse of this matter, doesn't it?" Rory clicked his heels against Blazer's, flanks spurring him off toward the castle gate.

More than you know, Daniel silently agreed as he followed Rory's lead, *more than you know*.

Daniel wanted to reassure Rory that everything would be okay, someday, but he had no idea how to begin. How could he tell Rory that his soul would be alive, and well, and married to Teressa seven hundred years in the future? Besides, how could he know if that was actually the truth, or just Teressa's outrageous imagination wanting to believe that Robert was the reincarnation of this man from the thirteenth century? And even if he did try to explain such a concept to Rory, what comfort could it possibly provide to him in this lifetime? It was all a bit too strange for Daniel's simple soul.

He was certainly no expert, but he'd heard about reincarnation, even done some reading on the subject. A lot had been written about it in recent years. There were reports of people having vivid memories of their past lives. Some were able to speak ancient languages they never learned in their current lives. Often they looked a lot like the person they claimed to have been in their past life. But it was difficult to know how much was truth and how much was a case of someone's overactive imagination creating dreams of things that never were, and were only wished for.

Daniel was willing to concede there was enough evidence to support a strong possibility for reincarnation, but it wasn't exactly proof. How could you really prove such a thing? Besides, it was one thing to read about other people's stories; it was quite another to encounter it firsthand, up close and personal.

As they approached the bay, Daniel was taken in by the raw rugged beauty of the coastline. The small bay sat in a protected crook of the island, intimately situated next to the commanding onslaught of the northern ocean. Beyond the shelter of the crescent beach, harsh waves battered the coast where the surging strength of the sea rushed against the encroaching land. The cliffs of Portree stood steadfast against the embrace of its powerful lover, firmly supporting the fortress of Scorrybreac castle.

"'Tis beautiful, this joining of the land and sea, it is no?" Rory breathed in the sight.

"Aye, 'tis beautiful," Daniel said, mimicking Rory's Scottish brogue.

Rory gave Daniel a long hard look. "Ye would do well here. This land suits you." He dismounted from Blazer and headed off down the beach.

"What makes you say that?" Daniel followed close behind, carrying their supplies.

"I can just feel it. And I always trust my feelings. 'Tis well-known the MacNicols carry a bit of the fey in our blood." Standing at the water's edge, Rory sent him a one-sided grin loaded with meaning.

"Yeah, so I hear." Daniel grinned and rolled his eyes with exasperation as he dropped the supplies on the sand.

"Really? What have ye heard?" Rory gave him a quizzical look.

Daniel hesitated, not knowing how much to reveal. "Well, I've heard the stories about your great-grandmother Sophie. They say she was half fairy when she married your great-grandfather."

"Aye, 'tis correct."

"Teressa told me your mother, Lady Lydia, is her direct descendant. If there's any truth to all that, wouldn't that make you a tad bit fairy too?" Daniel chuckled at the thought of the big Scottish warrior being part fairy.

"Why do I get the feeling ye know more than yer saying?" Rory's eyes narrowed into a scrutinizing glare.

Probably because I do, Daniel thought, but he wasn't about to open that can of worms. It wasn't his place to tell Rory that his mother had arranged to have Teressa brought back in time by Moezell, her fairy cousin, only to have her sent back home and away from Rory. There was no telling how much trouble it would stir up.

Daniel shrugged it off. "Couldn't say, maybe it's your fairy senses tingling." He wiggled his fingers in the air, laughing at the jest as he mimicked a modern comic book character.

"Aye, and how's this for tingling senses?" With one heave-ho, Rory knocked Daniel off his feet into an oncoming wave.

When Daniel came up for air, he was shuttering with cold. "Holy shit, dude, this makes the ocean back home seem like a freaking bathtub."

"You should see yer face." Rory fell to the sand in peals of laughter.

"You won't be laughing when I'm done with you." Daniel cupped his hand and shot a spray of ocean water at Rory. Rory side-stepped the worse of it and dove into a breaking wave, bringing the water play to an end.

Hours later, they headed back to the keep, tired but totally satisfied. It had been a splendid day of male bonding and seafood gathering once Daniel got past the initial shock of the frigid cold of the Atlantic Ocean, which actually wasn't much worse than the frigid cold of the Pacific Ocean back home.

Entering the kitchens, Rory and Daniel plopped their wet bloated bag of sea creatures on the prep table. Their fishing for the evening meal had served as a great excuse to avoid the ladies of the keep and any onerous chores that might have been inflicted on them.

"Hail Milly, I come bearing gifts," Rory greeted the head cook.

"'Tis best be gifts yer bringing me if yer going to come in here smelling of the sea and dripping with wet sand." Pushing the young warrior aside, Milly turned to examine the contents of the soggy pouch.

Daniel saw the mischievous look in Rory's eyes and knew this was a well-planned assault, one he had played out many times before. Daniel stood back and watched, enjoying the charade.

"'Tis only ye I could trust to turn these sea critters into a scrumptious meal. Can you no do that for me, my love?" With a wily grin, Rory teased the aging cook.

"Your love is for my good cooking, and don't I be knowing the right of that. I am nay an old fool." A slip of smile escaped the grouchy old woman's lips.

"Now, Milly, don't be speaking so. You'll break my heart." Mischievous humor played across Rory's face as he gathered the elderly cook into a hearty bear hug.

"'Tis your stomach me thinks that is in play here, no your heart." She accepted his squeeze of affection for a brief moment before she pounded against his broad chest with an ineffective thump from her large wooden spoon, pushing him away. "Now be off with you both before you turn this kitchen into a sodden salty mess."

As Daniel and Rory hightailed it out of the cookhouse, Rory slung a brotherly arm across Daniel's shoulders. "Ye must admit. 'Twas a grand day at the bay."

"Aye, a grand day indeed," Daniel agreed. "All that's missing is a nice cold brew."

"Ye mean ale?" Rory dropped his arm and raised a quizzical brow.
Daniel nodded.

"Then 'tis no a problem." Rory grinned. "I know how to fix that."

Chapter 20

*D*aniel had been hoping to carve out some alone time with Kayla, but he kept running into missed opportunities. There was plenty of work to keep her busy around the keep, and he was often being pulled away by one of the MacNicol brothers. One day he was training with Michael in the lists, and the next he was out foraging for seafood with Rory. Even when they gathered together for the evening meals, Kayla was always surrounded by her family, most notably her mother, Lady Lydia. The woman hovered around Kayla like an overly protective mother hen.

Daniel believed there was a way to get her out from under the watchful eyes of her protective family; he just needed to find it.

When he saw her crossing the courtyard toward the stables, he recalled that she had promised to take a ride with him. A ride out away from the keep offered the perfect opportunity for some alone time. Of course, his intentions were all on the up-and-up, he told himself. After all, he was a man of self-control and had no intention of seducing her or taking advantage of her innocence. He tried to convince himself it was just a friendly ride, even though he felt an undeniable surge of anticipation flowing through his gut.

He rushed to meet up with her just before she reached the entrance to the stables and launched into his plan of attack.

"It looks like you're headed out for another ride. My invitation to join you must have gotten lost along the way."

"Excuse me?" Kayla said, eyes blinking. "I've only come to check on Sallie and to give her a treat." She showed him the carrots she held in her hand.

"Mind if I join you?" Daniel asked.

She replied with a shrug.

He took it as a yes and walked with her into the stable. He was tempted to reach out in the dim of the building to grab her hand and pull her to his side. Instead, he kept his hands to himself, hitching his thumbs on his leather belt. When they reached Sallie's stall, he made a show of looking over the large brown mare, advancing his battle plan.

"It looks to me like she could use some exercise. She looks a little restless." He ran a hand along the mare's back and down her flank, while Kayla fed her the bunch of carrot tops.

99

"Really? How can you tell?" she asked, sounding concerned.

"I've been around horses all my life. Remember, I grew up on a horse ranch. It's important to keep your horses well exercised. Don't want them getting lazy or soft." He wanted to make it sound like he had her best interests in mind.

She glanced over her shoulder back toward the keep.

He saw her hesitation and moved in to advance his position. He gestured toward the spotted pony he rode to the beach with Rory. "Spots over there could also use a workout. I'd be happy to accompany you."

Before she could say no, he opened the tack box and started pulling out bridles and saddle blankets. "Here, I'll help you, and we can be on our way." He had her smiling. It was working.

Together they saddled the horses and led them out into the courtyard. After they mounted up, he asked, "Ready?"

"Aye, I'm ready." She gave him a curt nod.

"Then lead the way." He flashed her an easy smile.

She gave Sallie a tap with her heels, setting them off across the courtyard and out the main gate of the fortress. She headed them down the dirt road toward a gentle sloping hill lush with summer grasses.

"Ye know, I think Sallie's up for a good run, if you can handle Spots." She cast him a challenging look.

"Let's have at it," Daniel replied, still grinning.

With a brisk tap, she launched Sallie into a trot. Daniel came up beside her and matched her pace momentarily before spurring Spots into a full gallop. She in turn matched his pace. Together they soared over the ground in the late afternoon sun. The sky was a brilliant blue laced with large cotton-candy clouds, a perfect backdrop to the greenery spread out upon the land.

When he reached the rocky outcropping at the edge of the grassland, Daniel brought the pony to a halt, turning to watch Kayla come up behind him. Her face was flushed with pleasure, glowing with the exertion of the run. Her unleashed hair swirled about her face, dancing in the wind. The sight of her hit him square in his chest, just around the area of his pounding heart. Catching his breath, he absorbed the sheer pleasure of her company.

"Looks like you won," she said, gasping to catch her breath.

"Not by much. It was a good race." He was staring at her, enthralled by her beauty.

Dropping her eyes, she turned to look away. He followed her gaze, letting his eyes roam across the landscape. Thin soil clung to the volcanic landscape, blossoming with the green growth of spring turning into summer. A magnificent ridge of jagged stone dominated the distant view.

"It's pretty rugged out here," he said, making a rather lame attempt at small talk.

"Aye, rugged, harsh, and beautiful. 'Tis no a soft place." Her eyes glazed over with a look of uncensored affection for the land.

He understood her feelings. The Isle of Skye didn't offer an easy life, and yet he sensed her connection to the place. It supported her people and gave them sustenance.

"You should see it in winter," she continued. "When the land is covered in snow so white it hurts your eyes. Or the sky is so thick with grey it blocks the sun."

He doubted she had any idea how lovely she looked, completely absorbed in her appreciation of the countryside and the land she called home.

"Do you miss your home?" she questioned, turning to look at him. "Is it hard to be so far away?"

"You know, I really haven't thought about it too much. Too wrapped up in being here I guess." It stunned him to realize he really didn't miss his home, or his own time, at least not as much as he expected. He was displaced in a faraway land, in a long-ago time, and yet he didn't feel a need to dwell on home. His life in California seemed distant, even remote. It wasn't something he longed for. The here and now felt real, and surprisingly, even comfortable.

"Are you enjoying your time here?" she asked.

They began to walk the horses again, setting off at an easy gait, headed for nowhere in particular, allowing the landscape to take them where it pleased.

"Yeah, I am. This trip has turned out to be much more than I expected." A secretive grin tugged at his mouth as he thought how much of an understatement that was.

"Is that a good thing?" A hopeful smile curved on her lovely lips.

"I'd say it's a very good thing. This is the first time I've traveled so far. I've always been inclined to stay close to home. But this, yeah, this is a very good thing." And the best thing by far, he thought, was the opportunity to enjoy her company. Every time he came within five feet of her, he felt things he'd never felt before. He had the urge to grab her and ride off into the sunset. He guessed it was a case of too many Hollywood Westerns.

"I enjoyed hearing your stories, about your home and family," she said. "You've traveled so far. I've never been off the Isle of Skye. I'd love to hear more."

He could see that it wasn't feminine guile but a sincere interest in his life that provoked her questions. And in her innocence, she had no idea how appealing it was for a man to be asked to talk about himself.

"For years the ranch was all I knew. I lived, ate, and slept for the ranch, working with my dad and the horses. We raised horses for the rodeo circuit, barrel racers, and such. Quick, sure-footed breeds that respond well to their rider."

"I am not familiar with these things. Did you really race the barrels?" she asked hesitantly, looking totally confused. It was understandable, his words probably sounded like gibberish to her but she was doing her best to not let it show.

"Ride the rodeo? Yeah, I did. I had a good time, and I usually placed well, but it really wasn't my thing. I was more interested in the horses, seeing them excel in the hands of seasoned veterans. Those guys live for the sport. I took enough falls to know I don't want to risk my life and limb for an oversized trophy and a few bucks."

"A few bucks?" she asked.

"Reward money. It's paid out to the man who performs the best at the games."

"Ohhh." Her face brightened with understanding. "Your rodeo sounds much like our warrior games. Men seem to welcome the opportunity to display their talents for all to see. I'm sure you did well. You were very capable with the fighting staff against Michael."

Ah, so she admitted she had watched him that first morning in training. The candid confirmation brought a secret smile to his heart.

"My first love was always the horses." It was an unconscious gesture for him to reach out and stroke Spots along his velvety neck. "When it came time for me to branch out on my own, I was drawn into law enforcement, keeping the peace. But I wanted to do it from the back of a horse instead of . . . um you know, walking a beat."

He was about to say "ride around in a patrol car," but thankfully, he caught himself. There was no way he could explain an automobile, or that he had traveled through time without looking seriously deranged. It churned his gut that he had to monitor his words, withholding secrets from her, but he knew he wasn't ready to reveal such trust-shattering news. He didn't know how, but he figured he would cross that bridge when he got to it.

"That's where I learned to fight, to defend myself and others against the bad guys in the world. There are more than enough bad guys to go around. I wanted to play for the good guys' team."

That was one of the things that set him apart from his brothers. They were always the guys who wanted the glory and the big bucks, seeking to excel in every high school sport they could hook their fists into. He liked being a team player, the guy who defended the quarterback. Maybe it was a thankless job, but the way he saw it, someone had to do it, or the quarterback, usually one of his brothers, would have been ground meat at the hands of the other team. He didn't mind being the defender of the land, the one who kept the home fires burning. It was his choice to stay behind when his brothers left for college and careers in the aerospace industry. He just wished it hadn't become so lonely.

Now that his parents had passed, and Teressa was all grown-up and on her own, he wondered what new home fires he would find to defend.

"What about you?" he asked, returning to the reason he had whisked her away from the keep. "What's brought you to this place in your life?"

He'd like to know if there were any past or present boyfriends he should know about, but he didn't want to just blurt out the question. He was hoping a more subtle approach would get her to open up to him.

"Me? I have no tales to tell. I've lived my whole life here at Scorrybreac, the dutiful daughter of the MacNicol chief, never leaving the protection of my family."

"Nothing wrong with that in my book. It seems I have a liking for dutiful daughters."

"You do? What makes you say that?" Her shy smile brightened by a few degrees.

"In my line of work, rebels without a cause are a dime a dozen. It's the honest, hardworking folks like you and your family that give me a reason to get up each day and do my duty. Besides, I already know you're a healer. Tell me more about that."

She graced him with a beaming smile, pleased by his interest. "I learned from my mother, who learned from her mother. The healing arts are passed from mother to daughter. They've been a part of our family as far back as anyone can remember. Surely you've heard of our great-grandmother Sophie?"

"From what I hear, you have a talent for it."

"Who told you that?"

"Oh, I have my ways." He thought of the amusing hours he'd spent in Bonnie's company, plying the chatty woman with his probing questions.

103

"It was Bonnie, no doubt," Kayla guessed. "She's a great one for boasting of our clan's accomplishments. But tending to the needs of our clan has always come easy for me. It is not so much a talent but a gift I was born with."

"See there, you said it yourself, you have great accomplishments and a real gift." His grin turned devilish, happy to have caught her off guard.

"Nay, I no mean to boast," she protested.

"Kayla, when are you going to learn that it's not boasting to acknowledge your abilities?"

A delightful pink colored her cheeks. She looked away.

Daniel halted the horses. Reaching across to Kayla, he cupped her chin, turning her face toward his.

"You know what I see here?" he asked, looking deep into her eyes.

She remained quiet, holding his gaze.

"I see a woman full of compassion for her family and her people. I see a woman who seeks to serve those around her, forgetting to serve herself. I see you, Kayla, a woman full of innate talent and natural beauty." He also saw her struggling with her own sense of self and her desire to break free from the cocoon of her family. He could see the butterfly she was about to become.

"You do? You see all that?" she asked, looking wide-eyed and innocent.

"I wouldn't say it if it wasn't true." He paused for a moment and then asked, "So tell me, what do you see when you look at me?" He had no qualms against fishing for a compliment if it meant learning more about her feelings for him.

Her eyes brightened, still staring into his, while her lips curved upward into a shy smile. "Possibly the best man I have ever met," she stated softly.

The extent of her praise both pleased and flabbergasted him. "Ah, no, that's going too far. I'm just a hardworking stiff trying to find my place in life." He tried to shrug off the effects of the unexpected compliment. Clicking his tongue against his teeth, he nudged Spots on to continue their slow-paced journey. Kayla nudged Sallie to follow his cue, falling into step alongside him.

"It seems I am not the only one who has trouble accepting a compliment," she teased, gracing him with an unrestrained smile. "I wouldn't say it if it wasn't true." Mirth danced in her voice as she mimicked his words.

"Touché," he quipped. "It seems you have me there. Are you always this bold with the men in your life?"

"Me, bold? Sir, you must be mistaken. Why, I'm as gentle as a little lamb. The only men in my life are my brothers, and I can assure you, they do not encourage boldness in their little sister."

"I find it hard to believe you have not turned your considerable charms on another unsuspecting soul." *At last*, he thought, *an opportunity to hear of the men in her life*.

"I can assure you, no other has provoked me to the same degree as you, my fine sir." A nervous giggle escaped her lips.

"Really, I'd think a pretty woman like you would have a dozen boyfriends by now."

"Boyfriends?"

"You know, suitors, men seeking your attentions."

"I can make no such claim. There have been no others. 'Tis not been allowed," she confessed.

His shock to learn she was even more innocent, more inexperienced, than he had believed was accompanied by acute embarrassment over his offensive blunder. His jaw clamped closed on the proverbial foot he had just inserted firmly into his mouth.

"I can only wonder how many women you have back at your village vying for your charms." Her suggestive remark surprised him. His little butterfly had just gotten a little bolder.

"Right now, considering my recent track record, I'm thinking none." He was grateful for her kind words.

"Then I can only believe it's because you are too busy with your horses, or defending your village. From what I hear, you've made a very favorable impression with our serving women. Milly almost made it sound as if you were welcome in her kitchen."

"Milly barely tolerates me and my silly stories." He laughed, relieved to be back on solid ground.

"I could spend all day listening to your stories. Please tell me more."

"I would think you've heard it all from Teressa. I'm sure she had lots of stories to tell." He wondered how much his sister had shared with Kayla without revealing her twenty-first-century origins.

"Nay, not really. We didn't speak much," Kayla admitted.

"That surprises me, as I recall, she was here for several days before she had to return home." His own words sounded an alarm in his lust-driven brain. He was reminded that Teressa had been forced to return home; she had no choice. And someday, so would he, whenever Moezell decided to send him back. It surprised him how little he worried about not being able to return home. Instead, he realized his greater fear was that he would wake up one day and find this was nothing more than a dream.

"I must confess I wasn't very friendly to your sister. I didn't take the time to get to know her." She looked sad, regretful.

"Why not?"

"I knew she planned to leave, to return home, and when she did leave, she left Rory with a broken heart."

"She had no choice. I'm glad she came back home. I would have been worried sick if she didn't, but the choice wasn't hers." A heavy dose of frustration surged through him, chilling his blood. He knew he had no control over how long he'd be allowed to stay in this time and place. He also knew Rory was heartbroken over the loss of Teressa. Disappointing as it was, his own sense of honor demanded that he stop flirting with Kayla's tender emotions. It wasn't fair to risk putting her in the same position.

"I know that now, but I didn't understand it then," she tried to explain.

Mired deep in his own thoughts, he nodded, indicating he understood, but a dark shadow crossed his face.

"Daniel, are you feeling well?" Kayla asked.

"Yeah, I'm all right. I don't know what I was thinking. I'm sorry, Kayla. We need to go back," he stated bluntly. "I've kept you away from the keep for too long."

He wanted to kick himself for his irresponsible behavior. Instead, he kicked the horse's flanks, sending Spots into a gallop toward the fortress. How could he have been so selfish and thoughtless? He had no business pursuing this innocent young woman knowing he could disappear at any time without a moment's notice.

Chapter 21

*K*ayla wondered what had just happened. She wished she understood men better, especially this one.

His sudden appearance at the stables had caught her by surprise. She hadn't seen him alone since the morning after her foot massage, and she was beginning to believe he was purposely trying to avoid her. It wasn't her plan to take Sallie out for a ride. She had far too many chores waiting for her attention to indulge in such a frivolous use of her time. But when Daniel had asked her to go riding, all worries about chores flew from her mind.

She recalled her promise to go riding with him, but she had been putting it off, never finding the right time or enough nerve to approach him. It felt like avoidance to her, which didn't feel good. It was too closely akin to cowardice, and she was determined not to give in to cowardice where Daniel was concerned. For once in her life, she was determined to be brave, even bold.

Throwing off her usual caution and concerns, she had accepted his request to go riding, alone, just the two of them. If her mother had seen her leave alone with Daniel, there would have been hell to pay. Knowing she was taking such a risk made it all the more thrilling.

It had been pure joy as the horses raced across the land. It was exhilarating to feel the freedom of unrestrained movement if only for a while. She felt her heart race along with the horses as they moved with powerful grace across the rugged rolling hills she knew so well.

This was her home, her land, and she felt the pride of being able to share it with him. She had felt firsthand the cruel cold winters and the relentless storms that often battered the island, but she had also seen the blessing of each new spring's growth as it reclaimed its place on the land. It was the only land she had ever known. She couldn't imagine it any other way.

She felt comfortable with him, more comfortable than she had expected. His friendly smile filled her with a kind of self-confidence she'd not known before. The recent strain of her internal struggle against the restraints of her family, her mother in particular, had left her feeling disturbed by her churned-up emotions. In the carefree pleasure of his company, she had allowed herself to shed all her pent-up concerns. He was an easy man to be with. His pleasant manner made it so, and she enjoyed hearing him speak with his strange foreign accent.

Sometimes it sounded as though he was speaking a foreign language, but she enjoyed the sound of his voice too much to intervene. The lilt of his accent was so different from anyone she had ever encountered on Skye. Even his sister's speech didn't carry the same tuneful cadence. Teressa spoke with polish and refinement, as if she was well-bred and well-educated. Daniel's voice was friendly, as though it carried a smile. It made it easier to relax in his presence.

She liked that he put more value on doing the right thing than seeking the glory of the winner's circle. He was an honorable man who put his home and family before short-lived rewards and accolades. Whenever men gathered to compete for fame and recognition, there would always be another who would seek to knock the winner from the lofty perch of prominence; but a man who was confident in his own abilities, that type of man would always find sure footing in his life.

When he asked about her life and her healing arts, it was tempting to retreat behind her well-established wall of modesty and indifference, but he had persisted, drawing her out. She admitted her healing arts were not so much a talent as a gift she was born with, and apparently with good reason. Recalling her meeting with her cousin, Moezell, she was still adjusting to the knowledge that many of her abilities came from the benefit of her fey blood. She wanted to trust him, she wanted to tell him more, but she held back. It felt deceitful to withhold her recently gained knowledge, but it was scarier to think how he would react if she told him she was part fairy. She assured herself some secrets were necessary.

And then he had looked into her eyes and told her she was beautiful. No one had ever bothered to see so deeply into her soul, much less bless her with such a confirmation of her worth.

Boosted by his open show of support, she had even flirted with him a wee bit, spreading her wings and testing her ability to fly. For a moment, it felt good to play the role of being a lighthearted woman. Unfortunately, the moment didn't last. Instead, the effort had landed her on the ground with a painful thud.

It had all changed when he had asked about Teressa, and she had confessed her poor judgment of his sister. It hurt to know she had only herself to blame for shunning the woman. She had never asked Teressa about her home or family. She had not taken any time or shown any interest in getting to know her, and she was beginning to realize how selfish she had been. Teressa had become the love of Rory's life, and she was the reason Daniel had come to Skye, to meet Rory and his family. Now Kayla's harsh judgment and lack of interest was coming back to haunt her.

She had tried to explain her reasons to Daniel, telling him she didn't understand about Teressa's need to return home and leave Rory behind. But she had failed.

She had seen his disappointment and had felt the conversation take a sharp downward turn. She just didn't know how to stop it.

She had felt the change, felt him slipping away from her. Believing him to be angered by her admission that she had spurned his sister, her heart sank. But she couldn't blame him for his anger. Even now, as she recalled her disdain for Teressa and her presence in their keep, she felt the sting of how unfriendly she had been toward his sister. Knowing she had disappointed Daniel caused an ache in her chest that felt every bit as real as the pain in her ankle, only this time, she very much doubted he would willingly offer to soothe away her discomfort.

Chapter 22

*D*aniel didn't sleep well that night. His mind and heart were engaged in a fierce battle over thoughts of returning home to the future or staying in the past with Kayla. His head told him he needed to leave. He had no business being here, and he certainly had no right to pursue Kayla, an innocent young woman with no knowledge of his world. Especially when he knew that the risk of leaving and losing her was at the whim of some unseen fairy. But his heart told him to stay. He had no logical explanation on why or how he would be able to stay; but a piece of him persistently held on to the feeling, fighting to win his internal battle. His heart insisted that him he wanted to be with Kayla while his brain told him he must go.

The battle raged on, and his brain fought to take control. He told himself that such feelings were unreliable and illogical, and that he shouldn't listen to his heart. There was too much at stake. He told himself that he needed to forget about Kayla and get the hell out of Scorrybreac. It was best for everyone's sake.

According to Teressa's journal, she had been swept back to the future when she returned to the place on the beach where the time travel had first occurred. He wondered if that was the trick to getting back home. Maybe there were special, magical portals located around the island that allowed the fairy to move people through time. It was a crazy idea, but for the moment, it was the only clue he had. He figured that maybe, just maybe, by returning to the spot along the stream where his freaky accident had occurred, he could find some magical portal and go back to where he came from. Maybe he just needed to recreate his arrival in reverse to make the whole thing work. He knew it was a long shot, but his mind wouldn't let him rest until he at least gave it a try.

◆ ◆ ◆

Kayla headed out to the stables. She hadn't seen Daniel all morning, but she told herself she wasn't going there to look for him, even though she knew he liked to hang around the horses. She told herself she was only going to check on Sallie, but her instincts told her something was amiss.

As she approached the corral, she heard the guards talking.

"He raced out of here like a demon from hell, I tell you. You would think he had the devil chasing him," the first guard was saying.

"Ken ye where he was going?" the second guard asked.

"Nay, didn't have time to ask," the first guard replied. "I heard him say, 'I have to go back,' but it made no sense to me. Guess he's needed to return home sooner than he expected. I just hope the chief won't be missing the pony he rode out on over much."

"Who? Who raced out of here?" Kayla asked. She stepped up to the guards, fearful of the answer.

"'Twas that strange-speaking lad, the foreigner," the first guard replied.

"Which direction did he go?" Her gut tightened, and she felt her throat go dry. She could no longer dismiss her growing fear that something was terribly wrong.

"He headed out the gate and turned toward the river road. I lost sight of him soon after that. I dinna ken I needed to keep an eye on the wayward lad."

"Do you want us to go after him?" the second guard offered.

Kayla immediately decided on her course of action. "Nay, that's not necessary. I'm heading out that way. I'll track him myself. Just help me ready my horse." Though she tried to speak calmly, not wishing to reveal her worries to the guards, they felt her anxiety and rushed to do her bidding.

Within minutes, Kayla was heading out over the fields, past the village, along the river road. She feared that Daniel was leaving, heading back to where he had come from without even saying good-bye. *Just like his sister*, she thought, adding anger to her fear.

As she rode, she battled with herself. She wondered if she should be racing after him, in hopes of asking him to stay, or if it was better to just let him go. In truth, she knew she had no choice. She couldn't stand back and do nothing. She had to at least try.

Even as he rode toward the river road, Daniel continued to second-guess his choice. He believed it was his duty to return home, to leave this time, and yet a part of him hoped he would fail. It was his heart telling him he wanted to stay. He wanted to stay and explore the possibilities of this time and place, but most of all, it was his feelings for Kayla telling him to stay.

When he reached the incline above the river, Daniel paused. There it was, the area where his time-travel mishap had occurred. Spots pawed the ground, prancing to and fro, feeling the anxiety and uncertainty of his rider. Daniel hesitated a moment longer before he gave a swift kick to Spots's flanks, spurring the horse to gallop headlong toward the imaginary portal. He was surprised to feel tears stinging his eyes, blurring his vision as he raced toward his intended destination.

Horse and rider raced along the stream, heading toward his point of arrival. They passed the mark and galloped beyond.

Nothing happened. No gust of wind, not even the stirring of a breeze. He wasn't pulled from his mount and rendered unconscious. They passed through the area without incident. Nothing happened.

Daniel pulled Spots to a stop several yards past his point of reference. He turned and surveyed the area. According to his recollections, he was certain he was in the right place. Giving Spots another swift kick to his flanks, he headed back along the stream, this time slower, not wanting to risk missing the mark. Again they passed his point of reference without incident. His theory was being shot to hell.

Scratching his head, he dismounted from Spots and walked the pony back along the stream, stopping when he reached the matted grass indicating he was in the right place. He stared at the ground as if it held answers waiting to be revealed. It made no sense to him, but then again, he admitted, nothing about his situation made any sense. It had only been his wild imagination creating the theory of a magical portal.

"Are ye lost?" a man shouted from the top of the incline near the river.

Daniel nearly jumped out of his skin. "What the hell," he cursed under his breath. "Who are you?" he called back to the rider on the hill.

The rider leisurely walked his warhorse down to the stream. "Alec MacLeod," he answered as he drew near, towering over Daniel. "Who might ye be?"

Daniel eyed the large claymore hanging in a sling on the man's back and figured it was in his best interest to be friendly. "Daniel Ellers," he said. "I'm staying at Scorrybreac."

"Aye, Duncan's visitor. I've heard of ye."

"You have? How's that?"

"News travels fast on our isle. What are ye looking for? Ye seem lost." The warrior returned to his earlier question regarding Daniel's strange behavior.

Lost, Daniel thought. That seemed like an apt description. "I thought I left something here, but I guess I was wrong." He felt crazy stupid about his efforts to find some magical portal, but he had no intention of being crazy stupid enough to try to explain it all to someone else. "What brings you out this way?" he asked in a friendly manner, thinking he should be nice to a big man on a large warhorse with a big-ass sword.

"I'm chasing down stray cows," Alec answered.

"Having any luck?"

Alec looked at Daniel as if he was daft. "Do ye see any cows?"

"No, I guess not." He was feeling dumber by the minute.

Alec looked up, listening, and, in one swift motion, drew his sword from his back. Daniel heard it too. Both men turned to face the direction of an approaching rider. Daniel could kick himself for not bringing a weapon.

The horse and rider appeared over the ridge of the incline. It was Kayla, and the first thing Daniel noticed was her fear. Blatant fear was stamped large across her face, marring her natural beauty. He felt small thinking he was the one who put it there.

Alec turned to Daniel, giving him an appraising looking. Turning back to Kayla, he returned his broadsword to its sling and waved to her in greeting.

"Hail Kayla, you're looking fine this morn," Alec said.

"Good day to you, Alec," she returned the warrior's greeting as she approached them, then turned to Daniel. "Good day to you, Daniel Ellers. What brings you out here so early in the morn?" she asked, sounding calmer than she looked.

"Just looking around," Daniel answered with a shrug, grinning. It was strange how just seeing her filled him with joy.

"I found him here, looking a little lost, like one of my strays," Alec joked. "Maybe it would be best if ye took him home."

Kayla watched Daniel, silently conveying her fear. "Do you want to go back to Scorrybreac?" she asked, her voice small and hushed.

"Sure, that's probably best. I think I'm done here," Daniel answered, mounting up on Spots. He had given his theory a try, and it had failed. But knowing she had come looking for him somehow made the failure feel like a success.

"Will you be joining Duncan for the games?" she asked Alec, referring to an upcoming warriors' tournament that Duncan was planning.

"Wouldn't miss it. I'll be sailing in with some of my men. Someone's got to give ole Duncan a run for his money, and it surely won't be a MacDonald," Alec answered in good nature.

"I'm sure it'll be a grand time." Kayla turned Sallie around to face the direction of the keep.

"I'm looking forward to it," Alec replied, spurring his warhorse to head down a side path. "Fare thee well."

"It was a pleasure meeting you," Daniel called after the departing warrior, hoping he hadn't made a complete fool of himself.

Alec raised his hand in a final farewell salute but didn't look back.

Soon after they had traveled out of earshot from Alec, Kayla turned to Daniel. "The guards told me you had left. Where were you going?"

"Would you mind if I didn't try to explain it right now?" He was feeling too embarrassed about his actions to talk about it. Besides, it defied explanation.

"Were you thinking of leaving?" she asked.

He hesitated for a long moment before he answered. "I can't help but wonder if I belong here." It was the closest he could come to admitting the uncertainty of his situation.

"Of course, you belong here. You're welcome to stay as long as you wish," Kayla replied, apparently misunderstanding his meaning.

"Yeah, I guess so," Daniel replied, completely uncertain how long that would be.

They said little more as they rode back to the keep in near silence, each withdrawn into their own thoughts. Daniel seemed distant and moody. His actions and lack of words worried Kayla, and it chewed at her that she didn't know what to do. If he had an injured hand or a bleeding wound, she would know what to do, but she didn't know how to bring him out of his moody silence. She was practiced in the art of healing, not in the art of seduction.

When they returned to the stables, Daniel immediately began to tend to the horses. Kayla stayed by his side to help, hoping he would speak and tell her how he felt; but he said nothing, and they went about the task with quiet efficiency. He was still kind and considerate as before, but his lighthearted spirit had faded.

As they entered the great hall together, Kayla was greeted by her sister-in-law, Janet.

"Have you heard? My family is expected to visit. They'll be here in time for the games." She was obviously excited about seeing her mother and father again.

"Your family? Nay, I have not been told. I didn't expect them to visit so soon after the Isle Faire," Kayla answered with shocked surprise. She hadn't seen the MacDonald clan in nearly two years. Since Amy's birth, she hadn't gone to the Gathering at the Isle Faire, choosing instead to stay home with Rory to care for Janet's wee daughter. It had been her boon to

Janet and Duncan so they could attend the Gathering together. As chief of their clan, Duncan was expected to attend, and he wanted his wife by his side.

"The faire was months ago. My family hasn't seen Amy in nearly a year, and now she's almost two. The games are a perfect reason to visit. They agreed they could wait no longer."

A shudder of alarm raced through Kayla's body. It was also possible that the MacDonalds' visit had something to do with the betrothal her mother was attempting to arrange. "Who is expected?" she asked, trying to keep her voice calm.

"Mother and Father, of course, along with Angus and his wife. Arlin, Trey, and Beatrice are also coming. Farley is staying behind at the keep. There's so much to do before they arrive. Lady Lydia wants to ready the rooms in the high tower for them." Janet turned to address Daniel. "I'm sorry to impose on you, but I believe we need space in your chamber for Arlin and Trey. Would you mind doubling up with them?"

"That's no problem. Whatever works for you." Daniel shrugged. "If you have family visiting, I can just take a bed in the barracks."

Kayla spoke up, "Janet, there's no need to bother Daniel with our preparations. I'm sure we can handle this."

"It's no bother. I don't mind changing rooms," Daniel said.

"Daniel, could you excuse me? I need to speak with Janet."

"Sure. It looks like you ladies have your work cut out for you." Daniel gave them a parting nod and headed off toward the kitchens.

As soon as Daniel was out of hearing, Kayla pulled Janet toward the stairway leading to the family bedchambers. "Do you know why your family is coming? Does this have something to do with my mother's plan to have me betrothed to Arlin?"

"Duncan and Lady Lydia invited them here for the games, but I'm sure they'll want to discuss a marriage agreement. Why does that worry you?"

Stepping into her bedchamber, Kayla closed the door behind them. She was desperate to confide in someone. She hadn't been able to speak with Fern, and she needed the counsel of another woman. She believed she could trust Janet, and hopefully, her sister-in-law could keep a secret. But she was also Duncan's wife and, more importantly, Arlin's sister.

"Can I trust you?" she asked. "I need to speak to someone."

Janet reached for Kayla's hands, clasping them between hers. "Of course, you can. We're sisters. What has you so upset?"

"Please understand, I mean no offense to you, or your family, or your brother, but I don't want to marry Arlin. Don't take me wrong, he's a fine man. I just . . . I just don't want to marry him." The words rushed out of Kayla, propelled by a pent-up need to share the burden of her feelings with another.

"Do you no love him?" Janet's eyes showed no judgment, only tenderness.

Kayla shook her head. "Nay, I am sorry to say, I do not."

"Do you love another?" Janet asked.

It was a reasonable question.

"It's not like that." Kayla turned away to sit on her bed. She thought of Daniel and the way he made her feel, so special, needed, and valued. It was grand to think a man like him could love her. It was grand to think she could have a man like him to love in return. It was also impossible. A fanciful fairy tale made up of wild imaginings. She had only just met Daniel, and she knew so little about him; and after today's ride, she had even less reason to believe he cared for her. "Nay, I have no one else," Kayla said.

"Have you spoken to Duncan about this?" Janet took a seat beside her.

"Nay, I could never go against Mother. She wouldn't allow it." Not that she hadn't been thinking about it more and more lately. Her usually close bond to her mother was becoming stretched by the yoke of Lady Lydia's controlling ways. Before Daniel's arrival, she had never defied her mother. Now she was treading through new territory in their relationship.

"Why do you say that? 'Tis no your mother who is in charge here. Duncan is the chief of the MacNicols. He'll be the one to arrange your betrothal. He's the one you should talk to."

Kayla was touched to see Janet living up to her vow of loyalty to her husband. She knew Janet felt strongly about defending Duncan's position in the family. She was also well aware that Lady Lydia still believed she controlled the family. Sometimes it seemed to Kayla that Duncan didn't do enough to relieve their mother of that belief, preferring to honor her as the matriarch of the clan. However, when it came to matters affecting the clan's future, Kayla believed Duncan was in total control.

"What could I say? I'm a woman of two and twenty years. I should have married years ago and be raising children of my own. Instead, I follow my mother around like a little lamb and have no prospects for a love match."

"Kayla, you're a beautiful young woman, with great accomplishments. Surely there are any number of men who would be happy to make a match with you."

"There have been a few who have shown an interest, but Mother never found any of them to be acceptable. They were always sent away. Now she wants me to marry Arlin. I hate to think I'm passing up the only opportunity I'll have to be married. I've always hoped . . . I'm sure you understand, I've always hoped to marry someone I love. I know it's only a dream." *But it's my dream, and I'm not ready to let it go*, she added silently, casting her eyes downward with despair.

"What about Daniel? I believe Duncan approves of him. He seems to be fond of you. Have you no feelings for him?"

"It matters little what feelings I may have for Daniel. He is only here for a visit. Like his sister, he is expected to leave. You saw what happened to Rory when Teressa left. Nay, I've no desire to put myself in that situation. Besides, I can tell Mother doesn't like him. She would never approve."

While it was all true, Kayla wasn't sure if she was making the arguments more for Janet's benefit or her own. She couldn't bear to state her real concerns, that a man such as Daniel would have no real interest in her. Aye, he had been kind, but she found it difficult to believe his feelings went beyond gentle gratitude.

"'Tis is no about your mother's feelings. She is no going to marry the man. There was a time in my life when I almost lost being with the man I love because my mother didn't approve of him. It's only through the blessings of God and the help of Teressa that Duncan and I were reunited. When Mother saw how much I love him, she finally accepted the match, although I think Lady Lydia was always in favor of our betrothal. It has turned out well, and you can see how happy we are."

"But Daniel is expected to return home, just like Teressa. And we don't even know where that is," Kayla argued.

"Are you telling me you would no be willing to follow the man you love to be with him? Would you really make the same mistake I once made?"

Kayla shuddered. The idea of leaving Scorrybreac filled her with despair. "Wait, I never said I love Daniel. Aren't we getting a little ahead of ourselves here?" There was a defensive edge to Kayla's voice.

"I'm sorry. I didn't mean to imply . . . It's just that I thought . . ." Janet fell silent, embarrassed that she might have overstepped her bounds.

"I don't know how I feel about Daniel. At first, I resented him for just being here, but I do find him attractive." *Mother of God, I can't believe I am saying such a thing.* "Nay, Janet, I appreciate your concern, and your desire to help. I just don't see how I can get past Mother's desire to have me marry Arlin."

"'Tis why you need to speak to Duncan."

"And Mother's blatant dislike of Daniel?" Kayla asked.

"That might be a little harder. You know she means well. She loves her children. She just has a tendency to put her desires above all others."

"Maybe you could talk to Duncan or Arlin for me. Let them know how I feel," Kayla offered with hopeful enthusiasm. Janet was only a year older than Kayla, but right now, it felt as though she was far ahead of her in confidence.

"Nay. That is something you need to do. You need to stand up for yourself."

"I was afraid you would say something like that." Kayla's enthusiasm sank.

Janet laid her hand on Kayla's shoulder. "I can be there with you, to offer you moral support, if you'd like."

"Oh, would you? It would mean so much to me. I wouldn't feel like I was facing them all alone."

"Kayla, you're never alone. Your family loves you. In the end, they only want what's best for you. You just have to let them know what that is. And I recommend that you start with Duncan. Perhaps you should avoid confronting Lady Lydia until it becomes absolutely necessary."

"In that, you'll get no argument from me." A half smile returned to Kayla's face. Maybe there was hope after all. She was reminded of Moezell's advice. The fairy had told her she needed to set aside her fears and seek with an open heart.

Chapter 23

*K*ayla could hardly eat; her nerves buzzed with such intensity. She was about to take one of the biggest risks of her life, and it wasn't sitting well in the pit of her stomach. She had asked to speak with Duncan after supper. She planned to tell him that she did not wish to marry Arlin, and she feared it would not be easy. She realized there was much at stake. She could very well be passing on her last, if not best, chance for a suitable match.

What was even more disturbing were her conflicted feelings for Daniel. She'd been immediately attracted to him when she found him stranded along the river road, but her attraction was quickly tempered by strong resentment when she discovered that he was Teressa Ellers's brother, a woman whom she believed had hurt her brother, Rory, beyond measure. Now, having spent time with him, she realized that her attraction to Daniel far outweighed her resentment, and she found herself wondering if he also cared for her. He'd been kind and caring to her in a way that no man had ever been before, but as far as she knew, that was just his way. It didn't necessarily mean he was attracted to her. Bonnie had told her how nice he was to everyone in the kitchens. Even Milly had kind words for him.

Still, she'd been touched by the consideration he had displayed for her comfort when he had tended to her injured ankle. It was tempting to dream of a man such as him in her life, but it was more than she could hope for. Even if he was Teressa's brother, he was still a relative stranger, and he was expected to return home sometime soon.

Nonetheless, it was a tempting thought that picked at her brain. To believe he cared required a leap of faith on words not spoken, along with a courageous heart to pursue her deepest dreams and take an unknown risk. So much was based on her limited experience with Daniel, a man she hardly knew. A fearful voice in the back of her head told her she was making a grave mistake to pass on a suitable match with Arlin. She worried that she was looking for a white knight, a hero to rescue her from all her troubles. And that could be her biggest mistake of all, because as everyone knew such heroes only existed in fairy tales.

The evening meal passed with stomach-souring slowness as she steeled herself for the upcoming audience she had requested with

Duncan. She had little appetite and mostly picked at the hearty meal of mutton stew and crusty bread. She wished she had thought ahead to brew some of her herbal tea instead of the sweet spiced wine she sipped from her goblet. Her churning stomach would have benefited more from the calming warm brew.

Distracted by her thoughts, she tried not to focus overmuch on Daniel as he swapped stories with Rory and Michael. Casting an occasional fleeting glance his way, she was only dimly aware of their conversation as they spoke of prized horseflesh and the benefits of well-bred horses. Sometimes she would catch him watching her when she dared to sneak a peek from under her lashes, but just as often, he was too caught up in his conversation with her brothers to pay her any attention.

Departing from the dining table, Duncan motioned for Kayla and his wife to join him in his study. Kayla breathed a bit easier knowing her sister-in-law would be there for moral and emotional support.

Duncan poured himself a generous serving of his fine Scottish whisky, then took a seat in one of the large leather-padded armchairs near the hearth with its low-burning peat fire.

"I understand you wish to speak to me on a matter of some importance," Duncan said, casting an intimidating look at Kayla.

Kayla sat with Janet on the wooden bench. She forced herself to look at her brother and not down at her hands.

"Duncan, as my brother and chief of this clan, I think it's only right that you should know I have no wish to marry Arlin MacDonald," Kayla began with her well-rehearsed statement.

"Are you saying you're no longer interested in a betrothal to Arlin?"

"Nay. I never said I had an interest in marrying him." Kayla wondered if her brother was being difficult on purpose, even though his expression remained unreadable.

"Could it be you are still holding a torch for Murdock MacLeod?" Duncan asked. A slightly malicious grin indicated he was teasing her instead of taking her seriously.

Kayla drew a deep breath, swelling with indignation. "Nay, I am well past any fondness I may have felt for Murdock. We have both moved on from our childish affections." It was irritating to be reminded of her first experience with young love. She had not yet seen sixteen summers when she spent the whole week at the Isle Faire following the youngest son of the MacLeod chief like a lost little lamb. He was nearly five years her senior and had showed only a modicum of interest in Kennon MacNicol's only daughter. The following year, she had learned that Murdock had taken up with Merrie Lewis, putting a final damper on any desire she might have had for the handsome lad.

"What I am saying, if you will only listen, is that I wish to oppose an arranged betrothal with Arlin. I am aware that, as chief of this clan, you have the power to enforce such an arrangement. I can only hope that, as my loving brother, which I know you to be, you will see the greater benefit in allowing me to choose my own match." She hoped her case held merit, but she had very little experience with dissention. She seldom disagreed with her eldest brother, and she never argued. She feared she lacked the necessary skills.

"Pray tell, what would be the greater benefit in allowing you to choose your own mate?" His smile disappeared, and his expression became serious again as his jaw clenched.

"The benefit would be in seeing your sister well settled in a happy union that would bring honor, and, may I say, joy to this family." Even as she said the words, she felt how flimsy the argument appeared. What was she thinking? He had no reason to give in to her request. His primary goal was to see her wed as soon as possible to a suitable husband. There was very little to dispute that Arlin qualified as a suitable husband, except that he was not the man she wanted to spend the rest of her life with.

"Do you have a suitor in mind who can fill such a role?" he asked.

Color rose instantly to her cheeks. She had been dreading the possibility he would ask such a question. What could she say? That she hoped Daniel found her irresistible, or even acceptable, and would ask for her hand in marriage. What a load of sheep's wool was that? Too stunned to speak, she was relieved when Janet spoke up in her defense.

"My dear husband, I am doubtful that's a question Kayla is able to answer tonight. It seems the greater question is, do you choose to grant her request?"

"I can't very well let her leave off one horse until we know there's another to fill the stable," Duncan answered his wife.

"Duncan!" Janet was shocked.

"Brother!" Kayla was even more shocked. "How can you say such a thing, to compare my possible suitors to horseflesh? It's disgusting and indecent . . ."

"'Tis the truth," he stated firmly, interrupting her. "Kayla, I have a care for you, truly, I do. But as your brother and chief of this clan, I also have a responsibility to see you well wed. Two and twenty years on a woman does not sit well with a man. You may find my words to be harsh, but I only speak what we know to be true."

Feeling remiss, Kayla looked down at her hands twisting in her lap. Even though she knew he spoke the truth, she had been hoping for greater support from her brother. It was not her desire to remain indefinitely a single woman in his household, and yet if she rejected this chance for a match, she was woefully aware that might well be the unintended result.

Reacting to her silence, he asked, "Are ye telling me, lass, if Arlin comes to seek yer hand, I should refuse his request?"

Her eyes shot up to catch his. "Do you believe that is his intention?"

"'Tis quite possible. I believe Arlin seeks a family of his own. He is of an age when such is expected of him, and it may well be that his plans include you, fair sister."

She paused to consider Duncan's words. Was it truly possible that Arlin was in favor of a match with her? They had known each other for years, and yet she had never detected more than courteous indifference from him, and sometimes even less than that. She hadn't considered that he might pursue such a match. As she thought about it, she realized she had based her opinion solely on her feelings for him. If she had done that with Arlin, wasn't it also possible she had used the same reasoning in her attraction to Daniel, hoping he felt for her as she did for him? She began to seriously question her perceptions.

"Are you saying you will require my betrothal with Arlin, if he so requests?" Kayla worked to keep her voice calm, doing her best to hold back the tears constricting her throat and threatening to escape.

"I am saying, we will see what develops when the MacDonalds arrive. Until then, there are no promises to be made."

Kayla felt burning tears pooling in her eyes. She blinked them away, trying not to show her weakness.

"However"—Duncan held up a hand as if to ward off her tears— "since you have made your feelings known, I will take them into consideration."

Kayla nodded her acceptance, trying to take solace in his words. She couldn't help but feel as if she had been driven off course, as if the horse she'd been riding had been pulled from beneath her, and she was left to wander again on her own.

Chapter 24

The MacDonald family was due to arrive soon, and Daniel was doing his best to make himself scarce. At his own choosing, he had moved from the larger room in the high tower to a small cell-like room in the barracks. Still feeling like an outsider, he wanted to avoid the dinner celebration planned for the MacDonalds' arrival and went off on his own to explore more of the intriguing nooks and crannies located throughout the castle. The MacNicol clan was beginning to gather in the great hall, and he had no desire to hang around to observe the reunion of the two families.

After wondering through a maze of dimly lit corridors and narrow winding stairways, Daniel reached the top level of the high tower. He hoped to be rewarded with a spectacular view once he gained access to the rooftop. He wasn't disappointed. When he pushed open the heavy wooden door leading out to the tower's roof, he was greeted with a vast, sweeping vista of endless ocean.

Stepping out into the late afternoon sun shining across the rooftop, Daniel saw an elderly man dressed in long grey robes sitting on a bench overlooking the sea. He guessed him to be Souyer, the old master druid Teressa had mentioned in her journal. More than once, he had seen the old man watching him from afar, but this was his first personal encounter with the wizard. He had wondered why the druid was keeping his distance. It was obvious that Souyer had an interest in him, and yet the old man had made no attempt to approach him.

"So, finally we meet," Daniel greeted the druid, indicating his awareness of the subtle surveillance.

"I've been expecting you. 'Tis a fine day for contemplating life." Souyer remained seated on the bench with his eyes focused on the endless blue of the sea.

"It appears you know who I am, and I'm guessing you're Souyer, the master druid. Teressa mentioned you." Daniel crossed the tower roof and stood next to the old man.

"Did you enjoy learning about her time travels? I'm thinking her journal must have been very helpful for you, considering your unusual circumstances and such." His gaze didn't leave the sea, watching the constant ebb and flow of the ever-moving ocean.

"How do you know about that? Are you the one involved in this?" He had figured it was the infamous fairy, Moezell, who was behind his time-travel adventure, but perhaps the old wizard knew more than he'd expected.

Souyer finally turned his attention to Daniel. "Nay, 'tis not my doing. I am only an observer and an adviser. When the student is ready, the teacher will appear."

"What do you mean?" Daniel cocked a distrusting eye at Souyer. "Teressa has you pegged as a wizard wannabe, not a mentor."

Souyer gave Daniel an appraising look, looking slightly offended by his remark.

"Let's say I've evolved. I prefer being a wise, old, and somewhat mysterious sage. It's far more enjoyable than striving to be a powerful and respected wizard. Of course, I've still retained my position as master druid. 'Tis a title I've grown quite fond of, but it's much less tiresome being a sage. Playing the role of a wizard required a constant effort to demonstrate I was capable of supernatural abilities. It was a lot of bluster." Souyer waved a hand through the air. "Since Teressa's visit, I'm much more comfortable being a sage. Not getting any younger, you know. So, you have questions, have you not?"

Daniel was impressed. "Okay, let's start with the obvious one. Why am I here?" He folded his arms across his chest, doubtful that he would be given the answers he was hoping for.

"'Tis yet to be seen. I expect you have a task to do, much like Teressa. I'm sure you'll know when the time is right. For now, I recommend patience. Fate and the fairies have a way of revealing themselves in their own time."

"That's not a lot of help," Daniel scoffed.

"Don't be so quick to judge. Patience, remember. Certainly you have other questions?"

"Yeah, I have questions."

Souyer nodded.

For a moment, Daniel didn't speak. He stood next to the chest-high stone wall encircling the tower roof and gazed out to the ocean's horizon. Uncertainty churned through his gut, refusing to be ignored. He had resisted thinking too much about fate, and fairies, and mystical possibilities; but maybe it was time to accept the magic of Skye, as Rory had suggested. Maybe it was time to consider his fate and why he was here. He'd been thinking a lot about Kayla, thinking she was more than just another pretty face.

"I read once there are no coincidences. At the time, I wasn't sure what that meant. Now I'm thinking it wasn't a mere coincidence that Kayla was the one to find me lying along the road. It might have been a mean-spirited prank by a fairy that swept me back in time, but there must have been a reason I landed in that place, at exactly the right moment, so she could be the one to find me." He glanced over his shoulder to observe the druid-turned-sage. "Am I right?"

The master druid seemed impressed. "Aye, the world may appear random and chaotic, but it was no mere coincidence that brought you and Kayla together."

Daniel nodded, absorbing the druid's words. He turned to lean against the stone wall, his back to the ocean. "Okay, so tell me, do you think it's possible to fall in love at first sight—or something close to that?"

Souyer cast a sideways glance at Daniel. "That's one of the funny things about love. Usually, the best time to fall in love is at first sight."

The old man's answer surprised Daniel. "Really? You don't think there's some advantage in taking your time, getting to know a woman first to find out if she's right for you?" He voiced his concerns even though he found Souyer's comment curiously reassuring.

"Aye, and isn't the only reason you'd be taking that time is because she appealed to you from the moment you met? Oh, it may take some time before the realization settles in completely and makes itself known, but from my observations, as well as my own experience, either it's there or it's not. Wishful thinking will no make it happen—nor make it go away."

Daniel could see the logic of the druid's advice. Even a long, drawn-out romance was likely to start with the all-important first impression. Either the spark was there, or it wasn't. Still, he worried that his attraction to Kayla could just be a heavy dose of lust at first sight, an infatuation, or even a simple case of wanting what he couldn't have. The allure of the taboo was too strong not to be considered.

He thought about the moment he had first laid eyes on her as she was bending over him along the river road, backlit by the sun. He'd known even then that he felt an uncommon connection between them. A feeling of recognition stirred somewhere deep in his soul, as if he was aware he was meeting someone special. He had called her an angel.

He had already accepted that the why and how of his time-travel adventure was beyond his understanding, and surprisingly, that didn't seem to matter. The important thing was that he was here—in this time and this place with Kayla. The woman had slipped under his skin and into his dreams, her presence as comfortable as the well-worn jeans he had stashed in his chamber. There was a certain feeling of familiarity, but beyond that, there was a longing desire much stronger than the casual attraction to a beautiful woman.

And that was another thing that stood out to him. Kayla was a lovely woman in her own right, but he'd met many attractive women back home in San Francisco. California was loaded with more than its fair share of beautiful women, and yet none had captured his attention with the same degree of intensity as she did.

It was in her flaming red hair that framed her face like a halo, and glowed when struck by the sun. Her liquid green eyes with specks of gold that danced in tune to her emotions, flashing bright one moment and becoming dark and intense the next. They were a window to her soul, which she left open and unguarded for anyone who took the time to look deep enough. He was charmed by the smattering of freckles splashed across her pert little nose and dusty pink cheeks. She was a lovely little package, especially appealing to him. And besides all that was the alluring promise of her shapely and well-formed figure. He already had a clue as to the shapely curve of her backside. There was still the allure of well-formed breasts left to explore.

No, it might be a prank by a freakish fairy, but it wasn't dumb luck that had brought them together. There was a force of destiny at work here that went well beyond his comprehension. And in that moment, he realized he was eternally grateful, and totally confused.

Directing his thoughts back to Souyer, Daniel continued with his questions. "What can you tell me about this fairy, Moezell? Why haven't I met her like Teressa did? Why hasn't she shown herself to me?"

"From what I know of Moezell, she has her own way of doing things. As you know, there was a time when she worked with Lady Lydia, but recently, she has branched out on her own, taking more control of matters—or less as the case may be."

"How do you mean?"

"Lady Lydia, as you may have noticed, prefers to control the details, plans every step along the way. Moezell likes to set up situations and see how they play out. She has great fondness for humans and their volatile emotions. Her greatest joy is to watch them choose their destiny."

"No way, man. It wasn't my choice to be sent seven hundred years back in time." Daniel shook his head, folding his arms across his chest.

"Maybe you didn't pick the method directly, but there must be some need, some wish of yours that's longing to be fulfilled, or else, you could not be here. At some level, perhaps deeper than you are aware of, you were seeking this adventure, or it would no be happening. It was true with Teressa. 'Tis also true for you."

"You're saying I chose this mess I'm in?" The idea didn't sit well with Daniel, and he was ready to argue against such nonsense.

"Would you prefer dull and boring? Life is messy. If it wasn't, it wouldn't be any fun. All of life is a blessing, an answer to your prayers."

"I'm not a praying man," Daniel scoffed.

"Every thought you have, every word you speak, every choice you make is a prayer waiting to be heard, longing to be answered." A pleasant smile graced the old man's features. It appeared he rather enjoyed playing the role of a wise old sage.

"I never spoke a word about traveling back in time. The thought never occurred to me."

"Did you no find Teressa's journal to be intriguing?" A sly smile crossed Souyer's lips.

"Maybe, a little. But mostly, I found it to be unbelievable. Of course, that was before it happened to me."

"Think on it, what is the greatest risk, the one that scares you the most?" Souyer stared into Daniel's eyes, as if searching his very soul. "Every risk you take makes you stronger, and I no see you to be a weak man, Daniel Ellers."

Obstinate silence accompanied the steely gaze Daniel leveled at Souyer. He wanted to rail against the druid's words, claim them to be foolish, crazy ideas, not words of wisdom. But he realized the battle he was waging wasn't with Souyer. At some deeper level, one he wasn't yet ready to tap into, he felt the old man's words were true. As much as it irked him, he figured he'd just have to let it go—for now. Perhaps this wasn't the right time to understand it all.

Pushing off with his staff, Souyer slowly rose from his bench. "A storm is brewing off in the distance. It may take a few days to reach land, but it's out there gathering force."

Daniel looked out at the smattering of fluffy white clouds gracing the skyline of the setting sun, relieved to be speaking on a topic as benign as the weather instead of questioning his choices in life. "Looks fine enough to me," he countered.

"Summer storms can brew up suddenly, as if to appear out of nowhere. Watch for the signs." With that, Souyer turned toward the tower door, muttering under his breath something that sounded a lot like scripture verse as he shuffled off to return to his chamber. "I have planted my seeds in fertile soil. Now, we shall await the harvest."

Daniel shook his head, amused. *Silly old sage*, he thought.

Chapter 25

$\mathcal{I}$t wasn't possible for the arrival of Hugh MacDonald and his family to go unnoticed. The proud chief wouldn't allow it. The MacDonald chief and his wife, Lady Evelyn, rode through the main gate of Scorrybreac, crossed the courtyard, and stopped at the steps leading to the great hall of the keep on a pair of large dark warhorses. Following close behind came Hugh's sons, Angus, Trey, and Arlin. They were accompanied by Angus's wife, Elisa, and the MacDonalds' youngest daughter, Beatrice. Following at some distance, almost as if she was an afterthought, a petite young woman with chestnut brown hair and equally dark brown eyes tagged along behind the MacDonald clan on a far less impressive mule.

Having been alerted by his master-at-arms of their approach, Duncan stood at the top of the steps. Janet, holding their daughter, Amy, was at his side. At the bidding of her mother, Kayla was arranged to stand just behind Duncan with her brothers, Michael and Rory, on either side. When her mother wasn't looking, she stepped closer to Rory and clasped his hand for brotherly support. He gave her fingers a gentle squeeze of reassurance. Peering around the large frame of her eldest brother, she watched the arriving procession.

Hugh's staging was to be admired. Over the years, he had learned how to take advantage of most situations, using them to further his image as the right and mighty chief of the MacDonald clan. Kayla knew the MacDonald used his aggressive reputation to preserve the status of his clan, as was his duty. She noted how he tarried a moment astride his mount while his wife and children dismounted before he joined them to greet the awaiting MacNicols. This slight delay allowed his wife and children to be at the ready to follow close behind him, creating a show of strength in numbers as the collective troop of MacDonalds presented themselves at the Scorrybreac keep.

Hugh led the charge, climbing the steps of the keep with slow, regal determination. At a respectful distance of one step behind the chief was his wife, Lady Evelyn. She, in turn, was followed by their children, completing the grand presentation.

The MacDonald chief was not a quiet man. He preferred to make his presence well-known. After a nodding acknowledgement of Duncan, he greeted his daughter with an enveloping embrace before moving quickly to gather his granddaughter into his large burly arms.

"Janet, my dear daughter, you have found fit to grace us with a lovely granddaughter. She's the image of her mother." Hugh smacked his lips soundly upon Amy's rosy pink cheek before she squirmed and wiggled away, fleeing his embrace to return to her mother's arms. "'Tis a blessing for an old man already blessed with many fine sons and grandsons." The greeting was the mark of an old man well-schooled in the art of making a grand entrance.

Kayla didn't miss the backhanded jab aimed at Duncan and Janet. While she knew they loved their daughter completely, she understood all too well that the preferred objective for a chief was to produce male offspring to carry on the family name. Apparently, Duncan chose to ignore the rudeness of Janet's father for the sake of his wife and to keep peace in the family.

Rather than succumb to petty insults, Duncan greeted the elder chief with an appropriate level of respect for the father of his wife, even if it was undeserved. "I welcome the MacDonald chief and his clansmen into my keep. Yer looking to be in fine health. I trust your journey went well."

"Aye, well enough, thanks to my fine set of horses," Hugh boasted, motioning toward the dark stallions standing at the foot of the stairs.

Fulfilling her role as matriarch, Lady Lydia stepped forward to greet their guests, grasping Lady Evelyn's hands in hers. "Lady Evelyn, such a joy to see you again. It has been too long. Look how our granddaughter has grown." She motioned toward Amy. "And, Hugh, you're looking hale and hearty. 'Tis our pleasure to welcome you to our keep."

Kayla thought her mother's greeting bordered on disrespect, considering how she hadn't acknowledged Hugh until after she had greeted his wife.

Lady Lydia extended her hand to Hugh, who brought it to his lips for a slight brushing kiss. Upon his release, her mother returned her hand to her side, covertly rubbing her knuckles against the folds of her gown. With growing interest, Kayla noted the telling gesture.

From the edge of her vision, Kayla watched as the last rider dismounted at the foot of the steps with vivid relief. Judging by the younger woman's appearance, dressed she was in a plain brown wool skirt and muslin tunic, she guessed her to be Lady Evelyn's personal chambermaid. Nonetheless, something in the woman's expression and the way she carried herself brought questions to Kayla's mind. Even as she dismounted from the mule, she kept her eyes focused on the MacDonald men. Her mother must have noticed her also.

"Am I right in thinking you have found a replacement for Matilda?" Lady Lydia asked, referring to the young maid. She directed her question to Lady Evelyn, while her eyes tracked the younger woman's movements.

"Aye, and lucky for it. That's Becky, Matilda's niece, almost one of the family," Lady Evelyn replied.

"Really, how very fortunate for you." A half smile graced Lady Lydia's lips. "I'll have Bonnie see to her needs." She motioned to Bonnie waiting inside the great hall. "I can lodge her in the chamber with Beatrice, if you've a mind to keep her near. Otherwise, Bonnie will find space for her with the servants."

"Beatrice's chamber would be preferred," Lady Evelyn confirmed. As was her way, she continued on with a stream of chatter directed at Lady Lydia. "Becky has only recently taken on the position of my chambermaid. I'm sure you heard of Matilda's passing. She was my personal maid since I was a young woman. I miss her dearly. I couldn't bear the prospect of losing another chambermaid to old age. Thankfully, Arlin convinced me to enlist the services of Matilda's niece. She's the daughter of our blacksmith."

In Kayla's opinion, the young servant displayed an inordinate amount of pride and self-confidence for someone in her position. She was happy to see Bonnie take her off to the kitchens, where she would work with the other servants of the keep.

Duncan directed the gathering of travelers into his great hall. "Come, let us relax and refresh after your long journey. Food and ale await your arrival."

Duncan and Hugh led their families into the warmth of the great hall, which had been well prepared for their guests' arrival. Banquet tables laden with food and drink stood ready to provide for their pleasure. Duncan took his seat at the head table, flanked by his wife and mother on his right. To his left sat the MacDonald chief and Lady Evelyn. The respective family members followed in step around the long banquet table. Michael, Shannon, Rory, and Kayla sat on the MacNicol side of the table, with Angus, Elisa, Trey, Arlin, and Beatrice on the other.

Kayla surveyed the remains of the meal being cleared from the large plank tables. It appeared their guests had enjoyed the full bounty of the MacNicol hospitality. They had eaten their fill and then some. She noticed that barely a spoonful of the hearty seafood soup or a morsel of the mutton roast remained by the end of the banquet. Duncan's best ale and cider flowed freely to wash down the filling feast. Having enjoyed the abundance of the food to his fullest capacity, Hugh MacDonald motioned to a nearby servant for yet another refill on his tankard of ale before sitting back to relax.

"I am pleased to see the MacNicol chief is able to provide an adequate meal for your guests. I trust this has not overly taxed your provisions." It seemed as though the MacDonald chief had a natural ability to flavor every comment he made with a hearty dose of insult, often to the point where any hint of a compliment was effectively lost in the bitter spice.

"Aye, and I am equally pleased to see that you spared no effort in partaking of our hospitality." Duncan retorted, eyeing Hugh's platter as it was cleared from the table. It was all but licked clean.

Kayla could see that her brother was determined to be considerate to the elder chief for his wife's sake, even if the effort chafed mightily against his preference.

Hugh ignored the reference to his gluttony. "I'm a bit surprised to see Roderick still unattached." His gaze rested on Rory on the far side of the large table. "Last I recall, he was quite smitten by that saucy lass who accompanied you to the Isle Faire."

Kayla had no doubts that the MacDonald chief was well aware of Teressa's long-past departure from Skye. Their clan homes were not a far distance apart, and the island was too small for gossip to be confined to any clan's keep.

"Rory keeps his own counsel regarding his personal dealings. To my knowledge, he is satisfied with his current situation," Duncan said.

"And just what is his current situation?" Hugh inquired, his brows raised.

"You would be best served to ask Rory such a question," Duncan replied. Leaning back to relax, he accepted a refill to his tankard from an attentive servant.

Picking up the thread of the conversation, Lady Lydia broke in, directing her question to Lady Evelyn. "How fare your other children? 'Tis expected that not all were able to accompany you on this visit."

Kayla was glad for it. The visiting MacDonalds were already filling their limited number of guest chambers to their fullest, forcing Daniel to move into the barracks. The Scorrybreac keep was modest compared to the accommodations available at the MacDonalds' larger compound, but her mother had done all she could to ensure their comfort was well served. Lady Lydia would not have gossip spread about that the MacNicols lacked in providing hospitality to their guests.

Never one to miss an opportunity to boast of her family, Lady Evelyn readily gave an accounting of her children and their offspring. "Angus and Elisa have already been blessed with two fine sons, Hurley and Nevin. They, of course, remained back at the keep with their cousins. Farley and his wife have a brood of three to keep them busy, and Trey's dear young wife is already heavy with their first child."

"I'm so happy for them," Janet enthused, turning to catch her brother's eye. "They've been married far longer than us. I'm sure this is a welcome relief for them." She reached out to cover Duncan's hand, clearly proud of their young offspring, Amy, who had been born weeks shy of a full year after their marriage.

"We expect it to be another boy," Hugh broke in. "Our sons have proven to be successful in that area," he boasted once again.

Kayla rolled her eyes. Was there no end to his bluster?

"It appears only your youngest, Arlin and Beatrice, are without suitable matches," Lady Lydia said, ignoring Hugh's comment.

"I'm sure Arlin will have his pick of young lasses when he is of a mind to wed. And of course, Beatrice has only recently come into an age to make a match," Lady Evelyn said, quick to defend her youngest children.

Aware that Beatrice had reached her nineteenth summer, Kayla considered her to be a bit farther into the marriage market than Lady Evelyn wished to convey, but she couldn't very well argue such a point knowing that she was all of two and twenty.

"And what of your Kayla? Has she no suitors to grace your keep?" Lady Evelyn turned the topic back to Lady Lydia.

This was the moment Kayla had been dreading, becoming the subject of their conversation.

"Kayla has chosen to focus on learning the healing arts. She's well respected in our village for the talents she has developed. She's a great asset to our keep, as she will be to any clan she chooses to marry into."

For a moment, Kayla was surprised to hear her mother rush to her defense. She quickly realized it was only because Lady Lydia believed it was important for the MacDonald chief and his wife to see her as a desirable wife for their son.

"Thankfully, we have been well served for many years by our midwife, Astra. She has been there for the birth of each of our grandsons," Lady Evelyn said.

"As I recall, wasn't she also the midwife for the births of your children? Aye, one would expect her to be quite experienced by now. I wonder how much longer she can continue to be in your service," Lady Lydia rebutted.

"Actually, Clara, one of my younger maids, has begun her training with Astra. She's progressing well, and we expect when the time comes, she will be well able to take on Astra's duties."

"What a relief that must be for you, considering Astra's advancing years. As you may know, Kayla has not only assisted our midwife, Bettina, but has delivered a number of babes on her own. Aye, she'll be a welcome addition to any clan of her choosing," Lady Lydia reiterated.

"At her age, I'm surprised she hasn't already found a suitable match," Hugh mumbled into his tankard before taking a long deep draw of the amber brew.

Kayla was taken aback by the direct insult to her honor.

"I can assure you, Kayla has had her share of suitors," her mother retorted, her voice raising a notch higher than before. "We once considered a match with Murdock MacLeod, but we found him not to be in our favor."

"Murdock MacLeod joined with Merrie Lewis years ago. Surely there have been more recent suitors since him," Lady Evelyn remarked.

"Of course. You can no expect me to give a complete listing of all who have shown an interest in my dear sweet Kayla." Indignant, Lady Lydia held her ground.

Kayla was both grateful for her mother's arrogance and appalled by the nature of the conversation. She'd been watching the interplay between her mother and the MacDonalds long enough to realize that the MacDonald chief and Lady Evelyn had no intention of proposing a betrothal between her and Arlin. She could also see that her mother was only making matters worse with her blatant effort to promote her. If the conversation was allowed to continue much longer, she was apt to appear as damaged goods.

Kayla was glad Daniel had declined to join them for the evening meal. Having him watch her mother try to pawn her off to the MacDonalds would have been more embarrassment than she cared to endure. Surely it would have diminished any attraction he felt for her.

She wished she understood the twists of fate that repeatedly deposited Ellers on their doorstep, only to have them depart as quickly as they arrived. She wondered if it was a blessing or a curse bestowed upon her family. For Rory, she could see it had been some of each. She was beginning to understand that it had been a blessing for her brother to know such passion with Teressa, even if only for a limited time. But it had also been a curse when Rory experienced the heartbreak of their separation.

To his credit, Rory refused to view the separation as a curse. He had once said, "How could I feel such pain unless I had known such pleasure. One cannot exist without the other." At the time, she hadn't understood his remarks. Now they were taking on a new meaning.

"I have every faith in my sister's ability to attract a proper suitor," Duncan spoke up, interrupting his mother and Lady Evelyn. "In fact, she has spoken to me recently on where her interests lie."

"She has?" Lady Lydia asked, incredulous.

She wasn't the only one caught unaware by Duncan's announcement. Kayla hadn't exactly shared with Duncan whom she had in mind to replace Arlin as a possible suitor, but she figured her brother had a pretty good idea.

Catching Lady Evelyn's keen interest in her surprised reaction, Lady Lydia quickly amended her words. "I'm surprised she would speak to her brother of such intimate matters."

"I am the chief of this clan. I think it's only proper she share her preferences with me," Duncan said.

"Why, of course, Duncan, I only meant to convey . . ."

Before her mother could dig her hole any deeper, Janet broke in, "Mother, Lady Lydia and I are planning a picnic for Amy tomorrow. I'm sure you'll want to join us."

"Of course, my dear. Why wouldn't I?" Lady Evelyn responded to her daughter's invitation.

"I'm hoping if the weather holds, we can walk over to the meadow. It's well protected from the wind, and Amy can play in the wildflowers."

Silently, Kayla blessed Duncan's wife, relieved to be leaving the subject of her marriage prospects.

"I've arranged with Milly to have baskets of treats prepared for the outing," Lady Lydia chimed in, finally accepting the need to abandon the previous conversation. "We expect Elisa and Beatrice will join us, and of course, Kayla will be there."

Kayla sent a grateful glance at Janet, wishing she could melt into the floorboards, knowing it was impossibly impolite to leave the banquet table. Though she had remained silent throughout the ordeal, she was painfully aware of being the topic of their conversation. It was unsettling to know they were discussing her as if she wasn't even in the same room. It had the effect of making her feel more like a possession to be disposed of than a person with opinions and preferences. She understood it was her mother's desire to strengthen clan ties and provide for her well-being that was driving her to pursue a betrothal for her with Arlin, but she couldn't help but feel like a lamb being sold at market.

Hoping to engage Arlin in a pleasant conversation, Kayla directed her attention toward him. Much like his father, Arlin had been more focused on devouring the well-prepared feast than engaging in polite conversation.

"Did you fare well on your travels to Scorrybreac?" she asked.

"We arrived well enough, as you can see for yourself," Arlin answered, his tone anything but engaging. He immediately turned his attention back to his elder brother. "Angus, have you decided which games you'll be competing in tomorrow?"

"Archery, of course, is my strong suit. I expect to take the field," Angus replied.

"I expect to fare as well with the fighting staffs," Arlin boasted. "I doubt the MacNicol clan has a man who can best me."

Michael glanced over at the arrogant younger man. "I wouldn't be so sure if I was you. I've picked up a few new moves that may surprise you," he said with a knowing smirk.

Nothing would please Kayla more than to see Michael take down the loudmouthed Arlin. While the words nearly stuck in her throat, she tried one more time to draw Arlin's attention. "You sound rather confident. Have you trained long with the fighting staffs?" she asked.

"Of course, I'm confident. I'm the best in my clan," he answered gruffly. He dismissed her with a look of disdain, turning his attention back to his brother as they continued to discuss the upcoming games.

Kayla took a sip of wine to clear the bitter taste from her mouth and focused on keeping her face expressionless. She would not give Arlin or his siblings the satisfaction of seeing her cringe. Silently, she hoped Michael would do her the honor of knocking their rude guest on his backside tomorrow at the games, perhaps with a few ugly welts thrown in for good measure.

Looking away from Arlin, Kayla caught Beatrice's snide expression. The younger woman made no attempt to hide her condescending smirk. It was obvious she enjoyed watching Kayla flail in the wind.

"Which games will you be competing in, Rory?" Beatrice asked, her voice dripping with sweetness while her gaze focused on Kayla's brother.

"Nearly all of them," he answered, giving her his attention with a pleasant smile. It was just like her brother to be charming, as always. Kayla knew it was beneath his nature to mistreat any guest, especially a woman.

"I'm sure you'll do well in whatever games you play," Beatrice offered coyly, providing little chance for misunderstanding her innuendo.

"Aye, I'm sure I will." Rory nodded, grinning. He acknowledged her comment with elusive politeness, but he didn't offer more. Apparently, he had no desire to be pulled into her flirtations.

Beatrice looked as if she was about to say more, but Michael spoke first.

"Have you spoken to Alec MacLeod?" Michael asked Rory. "Do you know how many men he plans to bring to the games?"

"Nay, he has no given me an exact number, but if I know the MacLeods, we can expect them to come in full force."

This sparked a new round of male-centered discussions, and Kayla was again left to sit and observe in silence.

Throughout the evening, she kept an observant eye on Arlin and his siblings, hoping to detect his mood. For a man who was being sought by her mother as a possible suitor, it was evident that Arlin displayed a discouraging lack of interest in her.

However, there was an advantage to being thoroughly ignored. It gave her an opportunity to freely observe the interactions of those around her. She noticed that the younger generation of the MacDonald clan had formed a tight-knit alliance, slightly distancing themselves from their parents. The MacDonald siblings banded together, keeping close company to Angus, the hereditary chief, confirming his role as the anticipated chief of their clan and master. She wouldn't go so far as to say that Angus actually snubbed the hospitality of the MacNicol clan, but it was obvious he preferred to direct his attention toward his brothers and sister, who were never far from his side.

The one noticeable exception to their display of disinterest was Beatrice. In Kayla's opinion, Beatrice displayed an inordinate amount of interest in Rory, repeatedly trying to engage him in a conversation. While Beatrice was never far from the company of one or the other of her elder brothers, her eyes seemed to follow Rory wherever he was in the great hall. Rory, too occupied with his ale or the boisterous conversation of menfolk, did little or nothing to encourage the attentions of Beatrice, but Kayla noticed the younger woman's actions. Kayla noticed and took heed.

Chapter 26

*L*ady Lydia paced her chamber, barely able to contain her anger. Things were not going as she had planned, and she was not pleased. She didn't know whom to blame more: her cousin Moezell, for bringing Teressa's brother into their keep, or Daniel, for becoming such a thorn in her side. Not only was he encouraging Kayla's willfully independent behavior, but apparently, he was also becoming the focus of her attention. She wasn't accustomed to such blatant disrespect for her opinions, or failure in her manipulations of her family's affairs.

Wrapping her arms across her middle, Lady Lydia did her best to rein in her anger, refusing to allow it to get the best of her. She needed a plan. She needed to think, and anger would only muddle her thoughts. She had already tried confronting Moezell directly. That had proven nearly useless. Mayhap it was time to confront her unwelcome visitor. However, that idea, besides being distasteful to her, also carried considerable risks. While she didn't know why Moezell had brought him to their keep, she had no doubt her fey cousin was behind his appearance. A confrontation with Daniel had the potential of causing more problems than it fixed.

She had to consider the situation carefully. As long as he was under the protection of her cousin, a true fairy and the granddaughter of the Fairy Queen, she had no power over him. It was possible that Moezell had summoned him back in time to perform a specific task, as they had with his sister, Teressa. If that was the case, she wondered if Daniel knew what the task was and if he was willing to share such information with her.

It was highly unlikely, she acknowledged (they hadn't exactly become the best of friends), but hopefully, it wouldn't hurt to ask. If he was here to perform such a task, she could offer to help him along and speed his return to his own time. Perhaps such an arrangement would benefit them both. But it would take skill and a wee bit of luck to win him over to her way of thinking.

Regardless of his willingness to confide in her, there was one thing she needed to make perfectly clear. She had no intention of letting a time-traveling, short-term visitor disrupt her plans for her daughter. She needed to make a suitable match for Kayla with reputable kin from one of the neighboring clans to strengthen their alliances, and Daniel certainly did not fit those qualifications. However, even she couldn't overlook the fact that Arlin had shown a complete lack of interest in her daughter.

Lady Lydia returned to the great hall to search out Bonnie. She noticed that all of the MacDonalds, save Beatrice, had retired to their chambers. It was a disgraceful show of indecency. Even from across the room, she could see Beatrice was attempting to beguile Rory with her flirtations.

That suited her just fine. Let the young woman have at him. If she wanted him badly enough, she could have her dear father, the grand MacDonald chief, request a betrothal. Lady Lydia would welcome the opportunity to encourage such an arrangement. Maybe Beatrice's youthful beauty was just the thing Rory needed to get his mind off his long-gone Teressa and back among the present.

Focusing on her priorities, Lady Lydia pulled Bonnie aside as she was returning to the kitchens. "I know the hour grows late, but I'm concerned for Daniel. He was no seen at our evening meal," Lady Lydia said, even though she knew perfectly well he hadn't been invited or expected.

"Daniel took his supper in the kitchens with the servants," Bonnie explained. "He offered to help with all the extra work we had, and a real fine help he was, minding the roasting pits all eve. Many hands lighten the work, and Daniel says he is no against helping out where needed. Milly tried to shoo him away more than once. She told him it wasn't his place to work in the kitchens, him being a guest and all, but he would have none of it, claiming he was happy to be assisting wherever he was needed."

"Well now, Bonnie, that's all very interesting," Lady Lydia interrupted; she was well acquainted with her chambermaid's tendency to ramble on. "I would like you to find Daniel and tell him to meet me in Duncan's solar. I want to thank him personally for his troubles." She was pleased to be using Bonnie's information to her advantage.

Happy to do her bidding, Bonnie scurried away to find Daniel as requested while Lady Lydia went to wait in Duncan's solar. Thanks to Bonnie's diligent efforts, Lady Lydia didn't have to wait long.

Daniel had been wondering if he would get an opportunity to speak with Lady Lydia, alone, but he hadn't expected her to request a private meeting. It had seemed as though she was intentionally avoiding him, and he was highly doubtful that the MacNicol matriarch was suddenly interested in expressing her appreciation for his work in the kitchens. This was an intriguing turn of events and he was looking forward to hearing what she had to say.

He wiped his hands down the front of his trews. He looked pretty scruffy after a long evening manning the roasting ovens, but he doubted it mattered very much. He figured he was well past being able to make a favorable first impression. Taking a moment to gather his wits and composure, he drew a deep breath and knocked on the door.

"Enter," Lady Lydia spoke in a firm voice, loud enough to be heard through the thick wooden door.

"You called." Daniel bowed, greeting her in his best imitation of an on-screen butler.

Lady Lydia, of course, did not get the jest and ignored his strange tone of his voice.

"Aye, Daniel. Thank you for joining me. I hear you've been helping out in the kitchens, which is rather unusual, but I wanted to express my appreciation." Lady Lydia sat regally in one of the leather armchairs facing the large fireplace. Shadows flickered across her face. The faint glow from banked embers of the recent peat fire and a brace of candles on the sturdy wooden desk provided the only light in the room.

"No problem," he answered. "No thanks are necessary. I just like to help where needed."

"Aye, but typically, we do not ask our guests to earn their keep."

His brows drew back in surprise. Your guest! This was news to him. He had guessed he was more of an unwanted intruder in her life.

"I like to keep busy," he said. "And helping out in the kitchens is a lot better than mucking out horse stalls, not that I haven't done my fair share of that." It was also gossip central and, from a cop's point of view, one of the best places to gather information.

"Surely you have other *tasks* that deserve your attention." She looked at him pointedly.

"None that I know of, other than training with your sons in the lists. Michael's a fine taskmaster, but you know what they say, all work and no play." Daniel was still standing, evaluating the situation and wondering how to proceed. For the moment, it was to his advantage to let Lady Lydia take the lead.

"But if you do have a special task to perform, something that would speed you along your way, mayhap I can offer you my assistance."

Yeah, I bet you'd like to speed me along my way, he thought. "That's very kind of you to offer, but really, as far as I know, I'm just kinda hanging out. And let me say, it's a right fine place you've got here." Daniel was starting to enjoy her discomfort. She hadn't offered him a seat, but thinking this may take a while, he settled into an armchair near the hearth. He could see her cringe as she scooted back on her chair. It seemed she preferred to have him standing before her like one of her servants. He might be helping out in the kitchens, but he was no servant, and he wasn't about to play that role with her.

"Are you telling me you don't know why you're here?" she questioned his response. Obviously this wasn't what she expected, and it wasn't good news.

"Where would I be getting this information?" he asked.

"Have you no been informed? Has no one been sent to tell you?"

"You must have some idea who that would be." He stretched out, crossing his long legs in front of him.

She turned in her chair, moving her body away from him. "Surely you've heard of Moezell."

"I've heard a lot about the little lady, or should I say fairy, but I've never had the pleasure of meeting her." He held his hands near the glow of the banked embers, examining the dirt that had accumulated under his fingernails.

"You jest." She glared at him.

"No, I don't." He glared back at her.

"Do not deceive me. I want to know what you're doing here." Lady Lydia's eyes grew dark with anger.

"Yeah, well I'd like to know what I'm doing here too." Daniel sat forward in his chair. "Come on, Miss Lady Lydia, you can't fool me. I know you're half fey. I also know you have a meddlesome fairy for a cousin who goes around sticking her nose into other people's business, usually on your behalf."

"You have no proof of that." Lady Lydia shrank back into her chair, stunned.

"You think Teressa didn't tell me? I know everything. I know how you had Moezell bring her back here to hook up Duncan and Janet. I also know you had her sent back home when you were done with her, even though you knew she was in love with your son. Now she's gone and he's brokenhearted. He won't even look at another woman."

"I'd advise you to mind your manners. If you know all that, then you also know I have access to magic."

"What're you going to do? Turn me into a frog?"

"Fairies do not turn people into frogs," she huffed.

"No, you just send us whipping back and forth through time at your pleasure, as if we're your playthings. A regular cat with a mouse."

Lady Lydia assumed her most regal expression. "Let me tell you something, Mr. Daniel Ellers. Eventually, you will be sent away, just like your sister. Until then, I want you to have nothing to do with my daughter. You will stay away from her. Do I make myself clear?"

"And if I don't?" Daniel leaned forward, invading her space.

"If you don't, I will make it my personal *task* to make your life miserable," she stated.

"Oh, like being whipped through time and not knowing why isn't bad enough," he shot back at her.

"I wasn't the one who brought you here," she admitted in anger. She quickly looked away, thoroughly displeased.

He could tell she hadn't intended to let that one slip out. "Right. And if it was up to you, I'd already be gone. Which means it's not up to you," he gloated over her misspoken confession. "I wonder how much more is out of your control."

"Be gone. I have no more to say to you." Lady Lydia threw her hands up in frustration.

For a moment, Daniel thought he was going to go spinning back to the future. But nothing happened. No wind, not even a breeze. She just wanted him to leave the room, if not the keep. The latter part was out of his control, but he could do her the honor of leaving her presence, which suited him just fine.

Standing, he mocked her with a courtly bow. "As you wish, my lady," he taunted her and headed for the door. *Fairies my ass, that woman's a witch.*

◆ ◆ ◆

It had been a long day and an even longer evening spent in the company of the MacDonald clan. Kayla was filled with relief when she was finally able to return to the sanctuary of her bedchamber. She breathed deep, soaking up the calming quiet of her cozy room. Ah, blissful solitude, what a blessing.

Sinking into the chair next to the hearth, she willed herself to summon enough energy to stir up the fire and add another log to the blaze. Settling back to enjoy the warmth from the fireplace, her thoughts once again turned to Daniel. She noticed that this newly developing habit was occurring with increased frequency.

She had missed the pleasure of his company at the evening meal. She missed hearing the sound of his strangely unique voice. And she missed his kind manners. They stood in sharp contrast to the unpleasant display from Arlin and his kin. Time spent with Arlin and his family only served to increase her desire to avoid being married to the man. She saw no appeal in becoming one of the MacDonald clan.

"Oh Moezell," she spoke aloud to the empty room, "why does Daniel no want me? Why can't I have him instead of that beastly Arlin? Has my harsh judgment of his sister truly lost me any hope of gaining his affections?"

She was certain she could sense the fairy's presence, but Moezell remained silent and concealed.

Thinking back to the night the fairy had appeared in her chamber, Kayla began pacing, debating with herself.

"Moezell advised me to seek love with an open heart. I know she is right, but my fear of rejection holds me back. If I tell Daniel I care for him and he rejects me, what will I do? It would dash all my hopes, but I suppose it would also put an end to my fears." She stopped pacing, considering that possibility for a moment. Knowing the truth was a powerful but scary thought. It left no room for illusions. Moezell had advised her to take control of her fears and follow her heart. *Oh, if only I could,* she thought, *if only I could.*

Standing behind the veil of the unseen, Moezell watched Kayla struggle with her emotions. It was tempting to step through the veil and offer comfort to her cousin, but she knew Kayla needed to walk this path on her own. As difficult as it might be, Kayla needed to shed her old beliefs about herself if she was to fully realize her potential. She needed to be like the lowly caterpillar struggling within its cocoon to transform into a fully developed butterfly. Only then could she break free from her own restraints with enough strength to dazzle and delight, ready to take flight.

No, as tempting as it was, Moezell could not spare her that effort, nor would she deny her the thrill of her wondrous transformation.

$\mathcal{M}$ orning was giving way to midday when Daniel wandered over to the training fields to watch the games of the competition. Several warriors from the MacNicol keep and the surrounding villages were on hand to participate in the quest for bragging rights bestowed upon the winners. Earlier that morning, a group of men from the MacLeod clan had arrived by way of a fishing vessel. News of the games had spread to the Dunvegan keep, and they were anxious for the opportunity to compete. Among the MacLeod warriors was Alec, the second son of the MacLeod chief and a trusted friend to Duncan.

Officially, it was every man for himself, but Daniel could tell that the MacNicol clan was particularly intent on besting the MacDonald clan, and that the feeling was mutual.

While he was anxious to learn more about the various contests the medieval Scottish warriors would wage with each other, he didn't plan to participate. He'd already been asked and had respectfully declined Michael's requests for him join the games. Besides feeling like an outsider to the proceedings, he was intelligent enough to know he didn't have the experience or expertise to do the games justice. He also had no desire to look foolish competing against men far more experienced and skilled in their ancient contests. Rookie status didn't appeal to him.

Since the arrival of the MacDonald clan, he'd been giving the MacNicols and their visitors a wide berth, preferring to spend his time alone or hanging out in the kitchens with Bonnie and Milly. He plied them with friendly flattery and flirted with them in a way that reminded them of their younger days when they could still turn the heads of many a young warrior. In return, the elder serving women had taken him under their wing in a way not many had benefited from before. They fussed over him, plying him with special treats, and laughed at his easy humor.

It was there, in the kitchens, where he had met Becky, the young chambermaid accompanying Lady Evelyn. Daniel had offered his services to help Milly oversee the grilling of the roasted meats on the large indoor fire pit, drawing on his experience as a backyard barbeque chief. It wasn't hard to notice the shapely figure and pretty face of the new arrival while she toiled in the midst of the controlled confusion flowing through Milly's domain. Becky had barely stepped through the wide-open door of the kitchens before Milly put her to work refilling the heavy ceramic jugs used to serve the guests ale and spiced cider. Several times during the evening, Becky had returned to fill her jugs from the large storage barrels kept in the cool of the kitchen larder, and each time, Daniel had noticed that she lingered longer and longer in the great hall before returning to her duties.

As the night wore on, her pretty young face and shapely figure was undone when she demonstrated a sense of self-importance that went beyond anything he'd seen from the other serving staff he had encountered. All she could talk about was how important she was, being the only servant accompanying the MacDonalds. She claimed she was a valued assistant to Lady Evelyn and was loved by everyone in the family. She reminded him of a San Francisco socialite, struggling to prove her self-worth by putting on airs, but in the end, she failed to impress anyone with her attitude.

When Daniel passed through the kitchens early the next morning, he was informed by a none-too-happy Bonnie that Becky had hardly put in an appearance before she offered a flimsy excuse to head off to the training fields to deliver bread and ale to the menfolk. Bonnie was not one to be fooled by the young woman's antics. In fact, as she had informed Daniel, she knew very well that the lazy young maid was off gawking at the men participating in the games. Daniel did well to hide the smirk tugging at his lips. He had the distinct impression that Bonnie would welcome the opportunity to join the young lass for a pleasurable bit of male gawking, not that she would ever admit to such a thought.

As Daniel approached the edge of the training field, he spied Kayla returning to the keep with Shannon's two boys, Tanner and Torrin. They'd been out at the women's picnic and had decided to return before the others. When the boys saw Daniel heading toward the lists, they ran off ahead of Kayla, excited to be joining the men's games.

Torrin burst ahead of his younger brother to greet Daniel. "We're going to watch the games. Do you want to go with us?"

"I was headed there myself," Daniel informed him, rustling the young lad's russet hair.

"Are you going to compete?" Tanner wanted to know as he caught up with his brother.

"No, I'll leave that to the MacNicols and the MacDonalds. It's their party," he said.

"I'm sure you'd be welcomed if you wanted to join the games," Kayla offered as she joined the trio.

"Michael offered an invitation. I respectfully declined." Daniel flashed her a warm, welcoming smile. It was silently accompanied by heated blood racing toward his groin from the core of his body.

"Why is that?" she asked, looking surprised and slightly disappointed. "Don't you want to show your skills on the training fields?"

"It wouldn't be right. I'm an outsider here. Besides, I'm not familiar with these games. I'm content to be an observer and cheer for your brothers. Competitors always need a cheering section." Turning to the boys, he added, "Would you like to join me?"

Both boys shouted their agreement at once. "Can we, Aunt Kayla? Can we stay with Daniel? You can return to the picnic."

"It is no Daniel's job to be watching you two, young lads," Kayla began to admonish the boys.

Daniel interrupted her refusal to their request, "I don't mind. It would be my pleasure."

"But it's my job to be watching the boys," she argued. "And truly, I have no desire to return to the picnic."

"Well then, if they're in your charge, maybe you should join us and make sure I don't run off and sell them to pirates, or influence them to become black knights." He teased her with a provocative grin. For a moment, the boys fell silent with wide-eyed wonder. Before Kayla could answer, he added, "Seriously, it would be my pleasure to hang with the boys, and it would be nice if you wanted to join us."

He was being honest; he wanted her to stay. He wanted to spend time with her, to hear her laugh and see her smile. It didn't matter whether Lady Lydia approved of his actions or not; his affections for Kayla were real.

"Aye, it would be my pleasure also," she agreed, with a tentative smile.

"We don't need no silly girl to help us cheer," Tanner disagreed.

"Ah lad, you say that now, but someday you'll be proud as a peacock to have a woman cheering for you and your team. Besides, if your aunt joins us, maybe later I'll teach you some of my fighting moves." Daniel threw a couple of air jabs at the boys, who scurried to avoid the pulled punches. "Then I'll have a woman to show off to, and she can cheer for me. What do you say?" The last question was directed at the boys, but his eyes quickly darted to Kayla for her reaction. She graced him with a glowing smile. It settled warm on his heart. He could tell she was pleased by the idea.

"Look, they're starting the caber toss. Let's go." Torrin's attention was already distracted by the action on the field. Excited to see the competition, the boys ran ahead, racing toward the training fields.

"Now you boys stay back and don't get in the way. I don't want you getting hurt if one of those men should toss their long pole in the wrong direction," Kayla cautioned the boys.

Daniel held back a snicker at Kayla's inadvertent pun. She had no idea how easy it was for a man to "toss his long pole in the wrong direction." Placing a hand at the small of her back, Daniel escorted Kayla to the edge of the training field, where they could see the games and keep watch on the boys.

She fell into step beside him, turning for a moment to smile with approval at his actions.

He felt her reaction, how she relaxed as she walked beside him, registering his hand at her back. He felt how comfortable it was to be with her. And he felt his urge to hold her. He very much wanted to gather her into his arms. To pull her into a loving embrace and feel her soft, pliant body mold into his. He wanted to touch her soft auburn curls and run his fingers through her hair. His eyes dropped to her lips graced by her slight smile. How he would love to touch his lips upon hers, to taste her, to know the full pleasure those lips might hold.

But he resisted. Restraining himself, he waged his own private battle against his base desires. His body screamed with his craving. He wanted this woman. It tore at his innards how much he wanted her, and yet every reasonable thought in his head argued against getting involved with her.

He knew he could have her. With very little encouragement, he knew she would be his for the taking. But he couldn't do that. The "good cop" in him wouldn't let him.

It was temping to take whatever pleasure life offered him in the moment, accepting that they had very little time together. But he didn't know if he'd be here next week, next month, or even tomorrow; and he couldn't do that to her. She deserved better than a momentary lover passing through her time.

So he maintained his polite composure and continued to play the good cop, a role he knew well. He knew the rules. He knew how to act nice, how to treat a woman well; and while it wasn't easy, he also knew how to control the passion-driven fiend that crawled in his belly.

Daniel, Kayla, and the boys joined the rest of the spectators gathered to watch several rounds of caber tossing, stone throwing, and archery. Daniel was interested in seeing the types of games these ancient warriors would present. He knew the local fairgrounds back home held Scottish highland games each year, but he had never felt the need to check it out. Now he was getting a firsthand look at ancient warriors doing their best to strut their stuff. Regardless of the time or place, it was obvious these men liked to compete with each other.

Alec MacLeod and Duncan ended up very nearly tied in the caber toss. That event fascinated Daniel the most. It seemed rather crazy for men to hoist a long, skinny tree stripped of its branches to see who could land the darn thing the closest to the straight-up twelve- o'clock position. He figured it wasn't a skill he would be practicing anytime soon. He'd rather stick to martial arts or the fighting staff.

Hugh's eldest son, Angus, proved to be an excellent marksman during the archery competition, easily beating all other competitors in the field. That was a skill Daniel could see as useful in these times, and one he would seriously like to pursue. A bow and arrow seemed to him to be the next best thing as a replacement for the department-issued firearm he had carried on police duty.

During a break in the action, as the training field was being set up for the next event, the boys grew restless, as young boys often do.

"Aunt Kayla, I don't want to sit here anymore," Tanner began.

"Can we get closer to the warriors? I want to go out on the training field," Torrin requested.

"Yea, let's go out on the training field," Tanner cheered, supporting his older brother.

"Nay, you need to stay and watch from here. It is no safe for you out on the field. The men are too busy to be looking out for you," Kayla rebuked their attempt to leave her side.

"If you boys are tired of watching the games, how about a warrior game of your own?" Daniel offered.

"Yea, can we, Aunt Kayla, can we?" the boys sang in unison.

It looked like Kayla was going to deny the boys, but as she looked from one young lad to the other, she could see it would be a losing battle. "All right, Daniel, if you're sure it's no a problem for you."

"No problem at all, it'll be fun," he assured her. "I've got an idea. How about a game of defend the castle?"

"How do we do that?" Torrin asked.

"Follow me." Daniel led the boys and Kayla away from the training fields to a nearby grassy knoll. Along the way, he picked up a blunt-end fighting staff for him and a couple of wooden play swords of the boys to use.

147

"Okay, boys, see this group of boulders here? That's going to be your castle."

"Our castle?" Torrin asked. "Seems kinda small to be a castle."

"It can be as grand as your imagination. Think big. Now, Kayla, you stand back here behind the castle walls. You'll be the damsel in distress." Daniel grasped Kayla's hand and directed her where to stand. She readily followed his instructions.

Turning to the boys, Daniel continued, "Torrin and Tanner, it's your job to defend the castle and your lady from the clutches of the evil black knight."

"Who will be the black knight?" Tanner wanted to know.

"Me, of course," Daniel answered.

Torrin poked his younger brother in the ribs. "Who did ye think?"

It was only fitting that the boys should defend their aunt against the black knight, Daniel told himself, for truthfully, if given the chance, he would come and steal her heart away. But hers was a heart surrounded by beauty and grace and unblemished innocence, and to wound such a heart would truly be a grievous and unforgivable crime.

With all the props in place, he instructed the boys, "Okay, show me some of your fighting skills before I make my attack. But be careful not to really hurt each other."

Torrin and Tanner immediately took up fighting stances, raising their hands, holding their swords as their father and his warriors did during training. They clicked and hacked their play swords against each other, making all the right grunting noises one would expect to hear from men in training. Daniel had to chuckle at their natural ability to playact.

Watching from the sidelines, Kayla gently admonished the older boy, "Now, Torrin, you must be careful of Tanner. He's not as big and strong as you."

"I'm fine, Aunt Kayla," Tanner assured her. Although Tanner was younger, Daniel was sure he didn't want to appear weak, even as he backed away from his older brother's assault.

"Keep your guard up," Daniel coached him. "Look for an opening." He was enjoying their swordplay and the opportunity to mentor the boys.

Kayla stepped around the outcropping of boulders and headed toward the boys. Daniel raced over to her, bobbing and weaving back and forth to block her way. "Where do you think you're going?" he asked.

"I need to watch the boys," she gasped. A smile spread across her face, amused by his movements.

The boys stopped what they were doing to watch.

"Oh no, you don't." Daniel grabbed her around the waist, pulling her back up against him. "The boys are just fine."

Kayla started laughing, disarmed by his unexpected actions. Struggling, she made a halfhearted effort to wiggle away. When Daniel wiggled his hands across her belly, she broke into uncontrollable giggles as he tickled her sides. Squirming even harder, Kayla intensified her attempts to break away.

"I've got you, you feisty little thing," Daniel said, holding her fast in his arms, having no desire to let her go.

Kayla continued to squirm, causing Daniel to lose his balance. He wrestled her to the ground as he fell, rolling onto his back to break her fall.

"Feisty, you say? Aye, I can be feisty," she spoke with newfound determination, laughing as she continued to squirm in his arms.

Daniel used his weight to roll her onto her back as he pinned her to the ground. "I have you now," he laughed, caught up in the moment of play. "There's no escape."

Kayla gasped, trying to catch her breath. Her heaving chest pressed against Daniel. For a moment, time stood still as they each focused on the other. Staring into her eyes, Daniel brushed her disheveled hair from her face. He thought about kissing her. His eyes dropped to her lips. He began to lower his head.

Just as suddenly, the spell was broken when Torrin and Tanner jumped onto his back, beating him with their little fists in defense of their aunt, their damsel in distress.

"Stop, knave," Tanner yelled.

"We have you now, Black Knight," Torrin shouted, grabbing Daniel around his broad shoulders.

Their valiant efforts were enough to squash Daniel's desires and return him to his senses. It had been tempting, all so tempting to ravish her there on the grass, but thankfully, her nephews had done their duty to protect her innocence.

Daniel released Kayla and helped her to her feet. She brushed grass and dirt from her skirt as she returned to her place behind the boulders. Her breathing was labored, and her eyes shone with excitement from their tussle.

Brushing dirt from his clothes, Daniel turned his attention back to the boys, but his body was still vibrating from feeling Kayla lying beneath him. He wanted her, but now was not the time.

While they played, Daniel taught the boys some of the basics of martial arts, showing them how to take a fall and tumble correctly so they wouldn't get injured. They were able to master the skill fairly quickly, showing no fear. He also showed them how to fend off an assailant, using the momentum of the attacker to deflect his blows.

Next, he demonstrated how to spring back after an attack to catch an assailant off guard and how to use the proper kicks and punches from his martial arts training. Most of the moves were too advanced for the young boys, but they cheered at his display of skill, hoping someday he would teach them his impressive moves. Along the way, he cautioned them that, as true warriors, they were to only use their newly developing skills when it was necessary to protect themselves or their family.

"You are becoming fine young warriors," he told them. "It's important that you use your might to defend, not offend. Do you understand?"

"Aye, Sir Daniel," Torrin and Tanner responded in unison. In the course of the afternoon, Daniel had gained their youthful admiration for his fighting expertise, and they took his advice quite seriously.

Chapter 28

*D*uncan noticed Kayla and Daniel engaged in the playful warrior games with his nephews. It was obvious that she was enjoying his company. He couldn't recall when he had seen her so relaxed or laugh so easy with an outsider. *He'd be a good man for her*, he thought, *far better than Arlin*. He could no longer support his mother's efforts to marry off Kayla in a loveless match solely for the purpose of strengthening an alliance with the MacDonalds. It was true, they were a larger and stronger clan, but he was certain his sister deserved better than to serve as a bargaining chip against future battles.

Duncan knew that part of his obligation as chief of the clan, and more importantly as Kayla's elder brother, was to ensure his little sister was prepared to enter into a proper marriage with a proper suitor. Unlike his mother, it wasn't particularly important to him if she wed Arlin or another, only that she be wedded, and soon. He was well aware she was edging toward spinsterhood.

Duncan was still engrossed in his assessment of possible husbands for his sister when Michael took a bone-jarring fall during the final round of footraces. Seeing the pain etched across his brother's face when he hit the hard-packed dirt, Duncan raced to Michael's side along with Rory.

"What be the matter?" Duncan questioned when he reached his fallen brother. Michael's face was pinched with pain, his jaw was clenched, and his eyes were squeezed shut. Michael was not one to give in to pain, and the look of agony displayed in his face gave Duncan significant cause to worry.

"I twisted my knee. 'Tis a minor thing," Michael spat out through clenched teeth, holding the injured leg.

"'Tis no how it looks to me," Duncan contradicted his brother. "It looks like you'll need to sit out the rest of the competition."

"Nay, I cannot. I'm slated to compete with the fighting staff. 'Tis the last contest we need to ensure our win against those bloody MacDonalds, and I'll no be letting down my clan."

Duncan turned to look toward the direction of Daniel and the boys playing down in the grassy field. "Daniel can take your place. He's the only one we know who can best you," he offered, recalling Daniel's first day of training.

"Nay, Daniel has declined," Michael countered, sucking in breath.

Though pain was stamped across Michael's face, Duncan knew he'd resist admitting defeat.

"If he knows you are injured, I'm sure he'll reconsider. 'Tis only fitting we ask." Duncan placed a calming hand on his brother's shoulder. He understood the trepidation his brother felt about letting down his clan, but Michael's well-being was far more important than bragging rights. "Give him a chance," Duncan said. "Let him know he's one of us."

Michael hesitated a moment longer. "Aye, 'tis fitting," he finally acquiesced.

At Duncan's request, which was adamantly supported by Rory and Michael, Daniel found himself squared off against Arlin MacDonald as the last two competitors with the fighting staffs.

"Hah, I see they bring in the retainers to do their work. Just like the MacNicols, always picking up strays," Arlin scoffed at his opponent.

Arlin's pointed sneer left Daniel with little doubt that the "strays" he was referring to included his sister. He said nothing, knowing his disdain for his opponent only served to strengthen his resolve to kick his butt. He'd fight fair and square, but he definitely intended to do the man some serious damage.

The two men circled each other with their long blunted staffs in hand. Daniel felt the heat of the competition surging through his blood. He was pumped and primed, ready to put his energy into action. Watchful, he evaluated Arlin's strength.

"I saw you with Kayla. You know, they wanted to hand her off on me?" Arlin continued to badger Daniel, poking at him with verbal darts.

He'd overheard enough comments from the servants to know Arlin was referring to Lady Lydia's desire to arrange a betrothal. Kayla deserved so much better. He also knew Arlin was trying to bait him, looking for a weakness in his defenses. He refused to take the hook, drawing on an inner well of self-discipline to maintain his composure.

Daniel's eyes narrowed, his mind focused on Arlin's every move. Arlin danced around the ring, lunging and swinging his staff to test the strength of Daniel's defenses. Daniel parried, but held back, watching and waiting for the right moment to present itself. Knock, swing, jab, swing again, he emulated Arlin's moves, testing the other man's skills, letting his opponent show his hand before he took decisive action.

Arlin's blows were powerful, but he was letting his emotions and his desire to win overrule what little skill he possessed. Daniel felt strong. He wanted to beat Arlin, if only for Kayla's sake. He tried not to focus on clan honor or protecting his reputation. It was simply a matter of his skill against another's, and he felt confident in his abilities.

The parry and thrust wore on, blow against blow, each man giving little ground to the other. Arlin was able to deliver a bruising blow to Daniel's left shoulder. Daniel countered with a well-placed jab to Arlin's chest.

Finally, growing tired of the unproductive sparring, Daniel saw the opening he needed and jabbed at Arlin's left side before swiftly swinging his staff in a circular motion that caught Arlin off guard, delivering a breath-stealing blow to his rib cage, followed by a brutal pounding across the back of Arlin's shoulders. They were powerful hits, and highly effective.

Arlin gasped and shuddered, arching backward in pain. His loss of composure was all Daniel needed to finish him off. With one final swift swoop of the staff, Daniel knocked Arlin off his feet, his arms flailing helplessly as he fell backward.

Daniel spiked the long rod into Arlin's chest as the man lay splayed on the ground. The pressure he levied against the fallen man's chest was more than enough to let him know Daniel had him pinned and beaten. He was tempted to smack Arlin upside his head with the blunted staff for his earlier comments. He resisted, knowing it was a mark of poor sportsmanship, something he considered to be beneath him. But still, it was tempting, and he was only human.

Chapter 29

$\mathcal{K}$ayla cheered along with the rest of the MacNicols as she had never cheered before. As far as she was concerned, Daniel had just become her champion. She even allowed herself to laugh when she saw the MacDonalds' servant girl, Becky, trip over her skirts as she ran out on the field to assist the fallen Arlin.

Rory approached Kayla. "That was a fine thing Daniel did for us, agreeing to take Michael's place at the last minute." He draped his arm comfortably across Kayla's shoulders. "He really came through when we needed him." His smile was one of brotherly pride.

Kayla gazed across the training field to where Daniel stood talking to Duncan and Michael. The three men were exchanging congratulations in that boisterously happy way men did when they'd just bested another in competition, especially one so easily disliked.

"Aye, we're lucky he was here to take Michael's place." She was happy for her brothers as well as for Daniel. With his help, the MacNicols had won the day. He was one of them.

Feeling another thought tug at her heart, she turned to focus on Rory, a sad smile gracing her eyes. "How was it for you when Teressa went away? I mean, I've never really asked you about that and . . ." It was hard for her to ask such a personal question, even to her own brother.

Rory let his arm slip to his side and turned his gaze upon Kayla. "I'll no lie to you. It was heartbreaking."

"I was afraid of that." Kayla allowed her gaze to fall to the ground. She wasn't comfortable opening up old sores.

"And I would have been too if I had allowed myself to believe she would really go away. Even though she told me over and over how she had to return home, I never allowed myself to really believe she would leave me or that I wouldn't be allowed to follow. I wanted her to stay, and I believed I could make it happen. I may have been a fool in love, but at least I was a fearless fool." He flashed one of his signature sarcastic grins at Kayla.

"And now, are you still brokenhearted?" she asked, determined to learn the truth. She had allowed this matter to be ignored for too long, hoping to shield herself from his pain.

"Nay, sister. Now I'm simply a patient man waiting for my love to return." His smile faded, replaced by a longing look in his eyes.

"Return? Did Daniel say Teressa will return?" This was news to her.

"Nay, 'tis something my heart tells me. I just know we'll be together again, someday. It's the one thought I hold on to, the one holding me together. It allows me to face each day and do my duty."

"Is that why you're changed? I noticed Beatrice seeking your attentions. She's a pretty young lass, and yet you give her no mind. In your younger days, you would have encouraged her attentions, but now I see no interest in your eyes."

"I believe I have changed. It's called growing up." He chuckled, a roguish grin returning to his face.

"When did you become so wise?" she wondered.

Rory grew serious. "Teressa was a woman tied to her home and family. It was her anchorage. I see that clearly now. I have to tell you, Kayla, I no see Daniel as a man with an anchorage. For sure he has a love for his kin and home. You can hear it in the stories he tells, but he has no anchorage as Teressa did. He's a lone ship afloat in his life without a true rudder to steer his way or know where he's going. He has no anchorage to hold him where he's been, and I believe he's looking for a safe harbor. The question is, will he find it?"

She could see he was worried for her as well. Her feelings for Daniel were growing stronger day by day, and she understood he would not wish for her to suffer the same heartache he had known. She also knew, no matter how much he wanted to protect her, he could not protect her from her own heart.

Duncan and Daniel approached from the training field carrying Michael between them to spare him from the use of his injured knee. Following close behind was Duncan's friend, Alec MacLeod, with his troop of warriors. It appeared they had every intention of celebrating with the winning clan.

True to his nature, Rory quickly became boisterous and cheerful with the other men as they drew near. "Our hero approaches. Let us find some ale and do some drinking," Rory hailed the men. "MacLeod, I hope you brought some of that fine ale your clan is known for."

Kayla recalled many nights of celebration when Rory had overly appreciated the MacLeods' ale.

"I travel with nothing but our finest," Alec boasted.

"Aye, 'tis time for celebrating," Duncan announced. "Alec, I insist. You and your men must join us in the spirit of goodwill."

The men gave a rousing cheer of "haahraah" as they slapped large calloused hands on each other's shoulders.

"You know, Duncan, I've seen that wee lass of yours, and I believe your Amy will make a fine match for my nephew, Torquil, someday. What say you? 'Tis never too soon to make plans."

Kayla looked at her brother, hoping with all her heart he would agree. She believed that the MacNicols would be far better served by a clan alliance with the MacLeods than the MacDonalds. Even if the MacDonalds were known for being the larger and more powerful clan, the MacNicols had just proved they could get the best of them in a fair fight.

"Aye, 'tis something to think on—a dozen years from now," Duncan laughed. "Tonight we drink in celebration of games well won."

Carried away in the wave of excitement over their well-fought victory, Duncan clasped Rory with his free hand and led the men toward the keep. Of course, he would invite the MacDonalds to join in their wee drinking party, but Kayla believed they would probably keep their distance, preferring to find a dark and quiet corner where they could lick their wounds in private.

She watched as Daniel was swept up in the merriment of the moment, extremely happy for him. He turned to catch Kayla's eye for one quick glance, tossing off a wink to her. She had cheered for him when he had won the match against Arlin, and now, with the way he looked at her, she felt very much as though he was her knight in shining armor.

Chapter 30

After a long evening of drinking with Rory, Duncan, and the rest of the warriors, Daniel headed back to his room in the barracks, making a pit stop at the garderobe along the way. He stepped out of the primitive toilet facilities and adjusted his breeches, checking that everything was where it belonged. The clothes Rory had given him were comfortable enough, but the one-size-fits-most design required some minor nips and tucks to keep him looking presentable.

As he turned toward the barracks, a flash of brilliant blue light caught his eye. It came from the direction of the training field. Had he not known better, he would have sworn it was caused by an electrical light. Certainly, no candle or torchlight could have produced such a brilliant flash. Too curious to simply ignore the eerie image, Daniel headed off in its direction.

Cautiously, he stalked off across the shadowy courtyard with only the glow from the moon above and the sparsely spaced wall torches lighting his way. He reached the entrance to the training field, where he thought he had seen the flash of blue light, but no one and nothing was there. He wandered around the field, thinking a highly polished shield or a gleaming broadsword could have reflected a ray of moonlight in some freakishly bizarre manner, but he couldn't find anything that remotely explained the bright flash. There was nothing. He began to feel a bit foolish, wondering if the bright flash of light had only been a figment of his ale-enhanced imagination.

He was about to return to the barracks when another bright flash of blue light caught his eye, this time from the direction of the stables. Whatever it was, it was definitely signaling him, and it wanted him to follow. Not wanting to disappoint whoever was leading him on this wild-goose chase, he grabbed the only weapon he could find, a fighting staff that had been left propped up against one of the field posts, and continued on toward the stables.

As he neared the entrance, he could hear noises coming from inside. Most of them he could identify as typical animal sounds, but there was one noise, a kind of rustling, that indicated there were more than just animals lurking inside.

He held the fighting staff braced in front of his body with his back against the wooden frame of the building. He listened for a moment longer and heard the rustling again, this time muffled and farther away. Taking a deep breath, he quietly stepped in through the stable doorway and retreated into the shadows.

He gave his eyes time to adjust to the darkness of the stable. Soon he was able to detect the shadowy outline of a hooded figure hunched down in the straw at the far end of the shed row. It took him another good long moment, but he finally figured out what he was looking at.

It was Kayla, wrapped in her heavy wool cloak, huddled alone in the straw.

He straightened up and dropped his shoulders. *What the hell is she doing out here,* he wondered.

Setting aside the fighting staff, he started down the shed row, checking the gates at the front of each stall and softly calling out to the horses as he announced his presence.

"Hey, Spots, hey, Blazer, how you boys doing tonight?"

He kept an eye on the hooded figure of Kayla, checking her reaction. Did she want to remain hidden? Or would she accept his intrusion? If it looked like she was still trying to hide, he'd respect her desire for privacy and head back out, as if he hadn't seen her. Instead, he noticed that as he got closer, she sat up a little straighter and adjusted her cloak, dropping the hood away from her face. It looked as though she was sitting there waiting for him to see her.

He stepped up to the stall next to where she sat, made his inspection of Sallie, then looked over at her as if seeing her for the first time. "Hey, Kayla, is that you?"

"Aye, Daniel," she whispered.

"Uhmmm, have you been sitting in the dark this whole time?"

Kayla looked down at her hands. "Aye. It's quiet here."

"Mind if I join you?"

"I'd be pleased."

Daniel sat down on the hay beside her. "What're you doing out here?"

Kayla shrugged and sighed, "I've had enough of the celebration. I wanted to check on Sallie. 'Tis better than sitting in the great hall with my family and the MacDonalds."

"Won't they miss you?" Daniel picked up a blade of hay and stuck it between his teeth.

Kayla looked up at him as if he had two heads. "I doubt it. Why should they? They never notice me when I'm there. How can they notice me when I'm gone?" He could hear the pain in her voice.

"I can't believe that. It seems to me like your mother always has her eye on you, especially when I'm around. You know, I don't think she likes me very much," he spoke in a conspiratorial tone, as if sharing some great secret, trying to sound lighthearted. He was rewarded with her tinkling laughter. Unfortunately, it was short-lived.

"I'm sure you heard that she wants me to marry Arlin." Kayla glanced up at him but quickly looked away.

"Yeah, I've heard. How do you feel about that?"

She looked surprised that he would ask such a question. "I no believe Arlin wants to marry me. Have you seen the way he acts?"

"That's not what I asked. How do you feel?"

Kayla turned sullen again. "It doesn't matter how I feel. This is no about my feelings. This is about what's best for the clan."

"I beg to differ. This is all about how you feel."

"'Tis easy for you to say. You're a man. You do as you please. You've no one to tell you what to do or who to marry. Your life is your own. Mine is not."

He was tempted to argue with her. Lately, it didn't feel like his life was his own. But this wasn't about him. "You still haven't told me how you feel. What would you do if it was up to you?"

"I would no marry Arlin. I would send him and the whole MacDonald clan away tomorrow."

"Can't say that I blame you. I haven't found them to be all that grand myself." Daniel gave a lighthearted chuckle. In the dim moonlight, he could see her smile. Barely, but he had gotten a smile out of her.

"It doesn't matter. They no listen to me."

Daniel reached for her hand and brought it to his lips. "I'm listening."

She remained perfectly still, her eyes large and searching, her lips slightly parted. Holding her hand in his, he placed the palm of her hand to rest against his chest. Alone with her in the dark, it was too easy to give in to the temptation that had been plaguing him since the moment he met her. He dropped his head, placed his lips over hers, and kissed her. Ever so softly, he kissed her.

Dear Mother of God, she was sweet. He could feel her melting on his lips like warm milk chocolate, and dang if her taste wasn't every bit as delicious. He brought his free hand up to cup her cheek. Her lips parted, welcoming, inviting, and he delved deeper. He felt her fingers on his chest grab at his shirt, bunching the fabric in her fist, hanging on and pulling him close.

He pulled back for only a second to check her reaction. He saw longing and desire in her eyes. It was enough for him. He reached for her again, pulling her close. He could feel her reaction as she responded to his kiss, her body seeking his. He laid her down beside him as he rolled over on the hay, aligning their bodies in a lover's embrace.

Though she was innocent, and slightly awkward in her movements, he could feel the heated need in her response. He held her close, allowing his hand to roam freely over her body, exploring her lush curves, imagining the soft naked flesh concealed beneath the layers of her clothing. Thank God for her clothing. It was a thin but vital protection from his blatant desires. But it didn't protect her from his kisses. He smothered her with his kisses, and she yielded. Holding nothing back, she took as he gave.

He wondered when he had last made out with an innocent woman like her. Ten, maybe twelve, years ago. The sensation was unnerving. He wanted to pull the clothes from her body and ravish her right then and there. For one primordial moment, he nearly gave in to temptation. He buried his face in the softness of her neck and bosom, breathing in her scent, earthy, and fresh, and totally woman. He had to stop. He had to control himself. But it was too damn hard. He was too damn hard.

He had just reached a hand up under her skirt, seeking naked flesh, when suddenly he heard a noise. She heard it too. She stiffened. Almost as bad as being allowed to continue his ravishment of her body was the embarrassment of being interrupted. His first thought was for Kayla. He couldn't let anyone find her like this. The consequences would be too hard on her.

He motioned for her to be quiet. It was a rather needless gesture. She had no intention of making any noise. Softly, silently, he rolled away from her into the dark recesses of the narrow stall. He reached out to help straighten her clothing, pulling bits of straw from her hair and clothes. She understood. Pulling her close for one last kiss, he whispered into her ear, "You have to go."

She nodded.

She impressed him with her stealth. Moving with quiet efficiency, she made her way over to the next stall, holding her horse, and began to brush the animal's hide. She then began to whisper words of endearment, as if speaking for Sallie's ears only. Daniel appreciated her ingenuity. Within seconds, he heard a man's voice call out to her.

"Hey, Kayla, what are ye doing out here?" It was Rory.

Daniel breathed a little easier, but maintained his hiding place deep in the shadows of the last stall, his back against the wall. Rory was by far the more easygoing of the brothers, but Daniel had no doubts that Rory would obligingly kick his ass if he thought Daniel was trying to take advantage of his little sister.

"I couldn't sleep. I took a walk out here to check on Sallie," Kayla replied.

"Alone?" Rory questioned.

"Aye, alone." Daniel could hear the trepidation in Kayla's voice. He wondered if Rory heard it too.

"'Tis late. Ye should be up in your chamber, getting some sleep."

Kayla yawned. "I'll be going there now. Will ye walk with me?"

Good girl, Daniel thought.

"Aye, come along now."

Daniel could hear Kayla walk away, headed toward Rory. He crawled to the edge of the stall and very cautiously peered through a space in the boards. Rory wrapped an arm around Kayla, and they started walking away. Daniel let out the breath he'd been holding. A moment before they stepped out of the stables, Rory paused and turned to look over his shoulder. "Ye best get yourself to bed too, Daniel," Rory called out.

Kayla gasped, Rory laughed, and Daniel beat his fist against the wall. Dang, they were busted.

Chapter 31

*D*aniel had just finished training with Michael, and he was missing Kayla. He hadn't seen her all day. He'd heard that she was busy working with the women cleaning the keep from the previous day's revelry, and he'd been recruited to return to the lists to practice with the other warriors before he had even finished his breakfast. Duncan and his men had enjoyed the festive break the sporting games provided and the chance for some heated completion, but now, it was time to get back to work.

Immediately after the games, Daniel had offered to help bind and immobilize Michael's injured knee, but Michael had refused. Instead, after receiving a healing massage from Kayla, he claimed it no longer hurt, or at least not much. She had simply laid her hands on Michael's injured knee after rubbing it down with some of Lady Lydia's curative salve, and about twenty minutes later, he was up and walking with hardly a limp. It was almost as if he'd never been injured.

Daniel was skeptical about Michael's quick recovery. He wondered if the warrior's injury was really as bad as he'd been led to believe or if Michael had just used it as an excuse to get him to participate in the games. Michael and Duncan had both disclaimed such a notion, stating more than once how grateful they were that Daniel had stepped in to take Michael's place when he was no longer able to compete. When questioned about his quick recovery, Michael claimed it was simply due to Kayla's healing powers and soothing touch. Still skeptical, Daniel simply marveled at how quickly the allegedly wounded warrior had been able to recover.

After their night of revelry, many of the guards had wanted to sleep in, but by midmorning, Michael had his men back in the lists, training hard as always. He'd allow no rest, even if they were the momentary victors. There would always be challengers to take the champion's place if they were allowed to go soft. Besides, he argued, he could still direct his men through their drills even if he did have to lean on his fighting staff occasionally to relieve the strain. Injured or not, there were no excuses to miss a day of training.

By the time Daniel headed back to the barracks, he'd put in another hard day of training. It felt good to be out on the field once again, but now he was looking forward to a few hours of quiet relaxation. All day he'd done his best not to think about Kayla and how close he'd come to taking her innocence the night before. He was grateful for the mind-numbing distraction of a hard workout. At one point, Rory had made a sly comment about Daniel getting lost on his way back to his barracks room, but thankfully, nothing else was said.

Daniel was on his way back to his room when he ran into Souyer. The wizard greeted Daniel as they drew near. "So, my friend, I see Michael has put ye through another day of hard training. What do ye think of yer time here? It must be greatly different from the life ye once knew."

Daniel slowed his pace for the benefit of the old druid. "More different than I could have imagined. It's one thing to read about history. It's another to be physically forced to experience it." Daniel rubbed at a pain in his shoulder. "Don't get me wrong, I'm actually enjoying the hell out of this experience."

"Are ye now?" Souyer looked more pleased than surprised.

"Sometimes I catch myself feeling lost and confused, worried about when I'm going to pop back to my own time, but for now, I'm doing my best to just enjoy the whole darn thing." Daniel was grateful to have someone to share his thoughts with. Considering Souyer's unique understanding of Daniel's circumstance, the old wizard was turning out to be a respected confidant.

"Are ye no looking forward to returning home to yer family?" Souyer asked. He motioned for Daniel to stop so they could sit on a nearby bench and take advantage of the waning warmth of the late afternoon sun.

Taking a seat beside the old wizard, Daniel stretched out his legs and relaxed, welcoming the opportunity to speak his mind. "You know, truth be told, I really have little desire to go back and hang with my brothers. I rather like the camaraderie I'm enjoying with the MacNicols. Besides, my brothers have all moved away and have families of their own. I hardly ever see them anymore."

"Am I to believe yer no longer interested in going home?" Souyer sounded intrigued by Daniel's change of heart.

"Well, it's not so much that I'm not interested. It's just that I don't have very much to go back to. The family ranch is too big for me to run by myself, and I don't have anyone who wants to share the load. I'm about to lose my job. Pretty soon there won't be any more mounted police, and if I stay with the force, I'll just be another cop with a beat, chasing down the bad guys and rounding up the homeless off the streets." Daniel ran his hand across his forehead, wiping off beads of sweat, and turned his face toward the light afternoon breeze.

"So what is it ye want?" The old druid leaned on his staff, casting a sideways glance at Daniel.

"I want what everyone wants; a job I enjoy going to every day and a family to go home to every night. Isn't that what everybody wants?" Daniel stared off toward the horizon, picturing what a home and family might look like. A redheaded woman with dancing green eyes slid easily into the picture.

"How do ye see that happening?"

"That's a good question." Daniel shrugged and directed his attention back to the old druid. "I don't know the answer to that one. Not while I'm expecting to leave." And right now, it wasn't a question Daniel wanted to dwell on too long or too hard.

"Are ye certain yer going to leave here?" Souyer asked with pinched brows.

"Of course, I'm going to leave. Teressa returned home, and I expect I will too. The only difference is Teressa knew why she was here and what she needed to do before she was sent back. I don't have any idea why I'm here, or what I'm supposed to do. Lady Lydia thinks I have some task to perform."

"Did she say what it was?" The look on Souyer's face told Daniel the wizard was more than just interested. He was downright concerned.

"No, she didn't. But it sure would be nice if someone could clue me in before I have to leave." As much as he tried not to think about it, the frustration of not knowing was never far from his thoughts.

"Before ye 'have to leave'? That's an interesting thing to say."

"Well, it might be interesting, but it's not doing me any good. Not as long as some freaking fairy is in control of my life. If it wasn't for that unknowing part, I'd really like being here."

"How very interesting. What do ye find so enjoyable?" Souyer asked.

"Believe it or not, it's the unavoidable raw physical in-your-face kind of reality that's hitting me the hardest. I mean, I thought living on a ranch, raising horses, and doing chores with Dad was a physically demanding life, especially compared to the other boys who lived in town. The hardest part of their day was spent out on the sports field. Here, every day is a new challenge. There's no getting away from it. The only drawback is there's no hot shower at the end of a long, hard day." Privately, Daniel also knew Kayla was a big part of why he wanted to stay, but there was no use going down that dead end.

"What might a 'hot shower' be?" The druid gave him a quizzical look.

Daniel thought about how to describe a modern-day shower in a way that would do the experience justice for the old man. "Imagine a steaming hot waterfall being brought conveniently to a corner of your own bedchamber for you to enjoy."

"In the future, man learns how to control the flow of water?" Souyer was amazed by such a wondrous idea.

"That's only a minor feat of modern plumbing. It pales compared to the marvels man will accomplish. Someday we'll build castles that reach to the sky and fly across the land." Seeing the look of stark astonishment on Souyer's face, Daniel reined in his futuristic prophecies. "But today, I'm simply a man in search of a hot bath, even if I have to fetch and heat the water by myself."

"Well now, I believe a hot bath is something I can assist ye with. I know the whereabouts of a large wooden tub, often used for washing garments. I'm quite certain it could also support the cleansing of yer body. And I'm quite certain Bonnie would be happy to secure the necessary manpower to fill the tub with the heated water you require. I've observed she's quite taken with yer friendship. I believe she would deny ye little in the way creature comforts. All ye need to do is ask," Souyer informed him.

Within an hour, thanks to Souyer, and with Bonnie's help, Daniel found himself pleasantly ensconced in his cozy little barracks room confronted with a large tub of steaming hot water. "Finally," Daniel murmured as he relaxed into the comfort of the bath. It had taken a near-Herculean effort to secure the large wooden tub and heat enough water to facilitate his bath, but Bonnie had proven to be a champion in her efforts to provide the luxurious boon to her favored friend. The moment he slipped into the relaxing water, he felt their efforts had been well worth the results. Several days of sponge baths had forced his personal hygiene standards to be woefully compromised. Not to mention the good ole pleasure of soaking away one's aches and pains in a soothing tub of wonderfully hot water.

If I was stuck in this time, Daniel mused, *I'd get Duncan to build a communal bathhouse. It would be a blessing for the whole clan.* He could picture the structure and its components in his mind. It would have large wooden tubs, big enough to hold a full-sized man, with a fireplace to warm the building and heat the water. It would be best if it was located near a source of water.

Then his mind circled back on his words, *If I was stuck in this time.*

What if I am stuck in this time, he wondered? *How would I feel about that?*

He contemplated the idea as he scrubbed the grunge off his body, digging deep into his thoughts and feelings. Of course, he had considered the idea and had dismissed it, but that was before he got to know Kayla. Then it had felt like a curse, a dreaded outcome, but now it felt more like a choice. Unfortunately, it wasn't his choice to make.

In all honesty, he admitted to himself, the possibility had its appeal. Living in the thirteenth century on the Isle of Skye would never be dull. It would be a hard life, for sure, but it wouldn't be dull. He'd never have to worry about having a dead cell phone battery or falling behind on the latest electronic technology. But he'd also have to do without all the other modern conveniences he used to enjoy, like supermarkets, fast food, and fast cars.

And then there was Kayla. Always there was Kayla. The idea of being able to pursue a relationship with Kayla held the greatest appeal of all. He certainly wasn't fool enough to believe it was some idealistic notion of a warrior's life that appealed to him, at least not enough to hold him here. No, it was all about Kayla. She was the one who would make it all worthwhile.

He'd never met a woman he wanted to be with as much as he did Kayla. He really wanted to know her, talk to her, and understand what made her so unique. He wanted to learn more about her ability to heal with just her touch. He wanted to know what made her happy or sad.

He was enticed by her innocence. She wasn't jaded by the world around her, nor was she boastful or full of false pride. If anything, she suffered from a case of acute modesty, not only for her innate healing talents, but also regarding her natural beauty. Hers was a beauty that radiated from her soul.

He could understand her modesty, even her lack of self-confidence. She had grown up in the very daunting and loving protection of her three large, elder brothers. They cast rather daunting shadows, long and wide, which were only reinforced by Lady Lydia's mothering and smothering ways. He could see why Kayla had chosen to live in the comfortable shade of their love and protection rather than seek the limelight for herself. It was an easy place for her to dwell.

But he saw beyond all that, to the spirited woman deep within. She had the ability to take charge and know her own mind. He'd seen glimpses of it over and over. Yes, it was her spirit that resonated with him most. Something about her had grabbed his interest, and like an old dog with a bone or a miser with his money, it refused to let go.

A voice spoke in his head. *Right woman, right time.*

He shook his head, disheartened by the thought. It wasn't possible. How could she be the right woman if he was in the wrong time?

Chapter 32

Souyer sat alone on his bench, perched high atop the roof of his tower, watching the never-ending ebb and flow of the ocean below. He heard Duncan approach before he saw him, but then, he'd been expecting the chief. Over the past few years, as he progressed deeper into his new position as wise old sage, he and Duncan had grown closer. Souyer had to admit, he appreciated the transformation.

"I didn't see you at the games yesterday. Did our warrior contest no interest you?" Duncan asked as he approached the druid's favorite resting place.

"I watched yer games, and was quite pleased by the outcome. I just chose to watch from the comfort of the battlements. Better view from up there, and it didn't require me to mingle with yer horde of visitors." Souyer pointed with his staff to a prime spot along the fortress wall. It afforded a fine view of the whole bailey and training fields. From his perch above the crowds, he'd been able to see not only the warrior games, but he had a ringside seat for the courtship of Daniel and Kayla, even if they weren't admitting such intentions to themselves, at least not yet.

"Now that you mention it, you've made yourself even more scarce than usual since the arrival of the MacDonalds. Are you not missing the company of the MacDonald chief, especially after all you did to help him become my father-in-law?" There was a bold-faced smirk on Duncan's face.

"Don't be hanging me with that rope. It was Teressa's doing from start to finish. I was as much at her mercy as ye when it came to her ability to manipulate a situation. That woman has a true talent. I'll give her that."

Souyer thought back to the day Teressa talked him into playing his part to get the MacDonald chief to agree to Duncan's marriage to Janet. He could've kicked himself for not seeing through her little ploy, but her charm had worked its magic. He had fallen right into her plans to ensure Hugh MacDonald would not stand in the way of Duncan's marriage proposal and his daughter's happiness. But now, three years later, seeing the happiness of their union, he was more pleased than he was likely to admit at the success of Teressa's matchmaking skills.

"Aye, and apparently, it was her successful completion of the task that got her sent back to her time. I sometimes wonder if she sacrificed her happiness in exchange for mine." Duncan leaned against the battlement wall and folded his arms across his broad chest. "I've enjoyed these years of quiet happiness with Janet. Now I'm dealing with another time-traveling Ellers and a blotched betrothal between my sister and Arlin MacDonald."

"Nay, Duncan. From what I know, she had no choice in the matter. It wasn't part of Moezell's plan to have the lass stay in our time. She had a family that needed her back home, and home she had to return." Over the years, Souyer had learned of Lady Lydia's participation in Teressa's time-travel experience, but in loyalty to the matriarch of the clan, he had agreed to keep her involvement secret.

"And now her brother shows up, but we don't know why he's here," Duncan said.

"Ye would think a fairy wouldn't be displacing a person seven hundred years in time without a good reason." Souyer was fairly certain that, this time, Moezell was acting alone. His observations told him Lady Lydia wanted no part in Daniel's unexpected visit from the future.

"I wonder what it is. It's almost like he's searching for something."

Souyer gazed off over the churning blue of the ocean, his mind searching for the missing clues that continued to elude him. He recalled asking Teressa the same question, wondering what it was she was searching for. He was sure a person didn't travel halfway around the world and seven hundred years back in time if they weren't searching for something. The question was, did she find it?

A strange thought came to him, followed by a peculiar feeling in his chest. His instincts were telling him something, and he had learned to listen to his instincts. He had also learned to keep such feelings to himself until he knew more about them.

"Maybe it's time I paid the lad a visit." Slowly, Souyer stood up from the bench with the aid of his staff. His bones had grown stiffer with old age, and the chilly winds off the ocean, while refreshing, often added to his discomfort.

"From what I've seen, it looks to me as if the two of you have become fast friends." Duncan offered the elder man a hand, but Souyer declined his assistance with a wave of his hand.

"Aye, and now it's time for me to use that to my advantage." Souyer paused a moment to lean on his staff while he got his legs under control. His left knee had a nasty habit of giving out on him, and he would rather not have Duncan see him lose his balance, especially after he had declined the chief's assistance.

"What do you have in mind?" Duncan asked.

Even though Souyer had waved him off, the chief placed a firm hand on the druid's elbow, guiding him toward the rooftop doorway.

"Like I said, just a little friendly visit. By the by, what are ye going to do now that the plan for another marriage into the MacDonald clan seems to have failed?" Though he preferred not to show it, Souyer was pleased to be accepting Duncan's assistance.

"Mother was the one most in favor of their betrothal. No use beating a dead horse. It appears neither Kayla nor Arlin has any desire to be wedded to the other. As I see it, we've no need for another alliance with the MacDonalds. I've been talking with Alec MacLeod. His brother has a fine son, Torquil. The lad is nearly five years older than my Amy. I'm thinking, mayhap in a dozen years from now, we'll find a MacLeod alliance more to our liking."

"Aye, and a far smarter way to go, I would say. The MacLeods have always proved to be strong friends and allies to the MacNicols. Together, yer clans will have the strength ye need."

"And plenty-enough ale to service even Rory's needs." Duncan laughed.

"Aye, plenty-enough ale indeed," Souyer agreed.

Duncan and Souyer made their way down the long spiraling staircase of the high tower and entered the keep before parting ways. Duncan had guests to attend to, and Souyer had plans of his own.

Souyer's timing couldn't be better. As he approached the barracks where Daniel had taken a room, he saw the large washtub being removed by two of the stable lads. It took both of the lads to heft the large tub back to the laundry room. Daniel would be washed and refreshed from his day of training in the lists with Michael and the guards. A relaxed man was usually more open to a meaningful conversation, but just in case he needed reinforcements, Souyer had grabbed a jug of ale as he passed through the keep.

Daniel saw Souyer coming and held the door open for him.

"From the looks of ye, I would say the bath was a success," Souyer greeted Daniel as he entered the small cell-like room. He took a look around before setting the jug and pewter cups on the lone table.

"A fine success indeed. You have my debt of gratitude." Daniel smiled as he closed the door. "Here, take a seat. I don't have much to offer. You can choose from the bed or a stool, take your pick." Daniel's gesture took in the whole of the confined space.

Souyer chose the stool. It sat higher than the low rope-framed bed, and it would be easier to stand from when he was ready to leave. It also allowed Souyer to avoid sitting where another man slept.

"I brought ye some ale to aid in yer relaxation." Souyer pointed to the jug.

"Care to join me?" Daniel offered.

"I would be pleased."

Daniel retrieved the jug from the table and poured them both a drink.

Souyer accepted the offered mug with a nod. "Well then, let's drink to our health."

Both men took long deep swallows of the strong brew. It was one of the jugs left behind by the MacLeods, and it lived up to their reputation.

Daniel sat on the edge of the bed, and even though he stood a good five inches taller than Souyer, the resulting seating arrangement had him peering up at the wizard. He grabbed the meager bed pillow to stuff behind his head and leaned back to relax. He'd spent enough years being a cop to know when someone was looking for information. He figured the old druid had an agenda; he just needed to sit back, relax, and wait for the conversation to unfold.

"I understand ye've gotten the cold shoulder from Lady Lydia. From what I've seen, she's no happy to have ye here. Do ye know why?" Souyer jumped right into his inquiry. Daniel respected that.

"I think just showing up was enough to piss her off. I get the feeling she wasn't expecting me, if you know what I mean." Daniel took another deep swallow of ale. *They sure don't brew stuff like this in the future*, he thought.

"But she was expecting Teressa. She welcomed her with open arms," Souyer said.

"Yeah, and she also sent her away, and had Moezell take all the heat for her disappearance. How much do you know about that? Teressa wrote in her journal that Lady Lydia wanted her involvement kept secret."

"Aye, I don't think anyone else in the family knows. Teressa kept her word while she was here and respected Lady Lydia's request for secrecy."

"Professional courtesy for confidentiality. Teressa doesn't discuss her client's cases with anyone. I understand she didn't even tell Rory." Daniel respected his sister's professional integrity but wondered if she made the right choice.

"Which brings me to my next question. Rory and Teressa seem destined to be together. Moezell told Rory they'd be reunited. It's been three years, and instead of Teressa, Moezell brings ye back in time. I'm thinking ye know something. Am I right?"

Daniel figured that Souyer was probably better than most at reading people's thoughts. He also figured he was better than most at hiding his. He sat there stone-faced for a good long while, contemplating just how much he should share with the elder druid. To his mind, Souyer had proven to be a loyal friend and counselor, but best of all, he'd helped him organize his bath.

"Yeah, I know something, or at least I think I do. But let me ask you, why do you want to know?"

"I believe it may help me understand why yer here." Those were magical words. Souyer couldn't have picked a better incentive to get Daniel on his side.

"I've thought it over and over, and I don't know how it can help, but I'll tell you what I know. When Teressa came home from her vacation, she didn't come alone. She brought home a fiancé, the man she married."

Souyer nearly choked on his ale. "Teressa's married?"

"Yeah, to a Scottish sea captain from Skye. He transferred his job to San Francisco. They got married on New Year's Day. His name is Robert MacNicol, but she calls him Rory. And here's the kicker. These two guys, her husband Robert and Rory, they could be identical twins. When I first landed here and was introduced to Rory, your Rory, I thought he was Robert."

"What are ye saying?" Souyer stared at Daniel with wide eyes, mouth agape.

"I'm not saying anything. I'm just telling you what I know."

Souyer gave himself a shake and regained his composure. "Is Rory going to travel to the future?"

"No, I don't think so," Daniel said, shaking his head.

"I don't understand. Then how does he get there?"

Daniel peered into his cup of ale, as if searching for answers. "Well, we all die sooner or later," he said. He'd already been through the death of his parents and seen several fatalities as part of his job. Like it or not, he accepted death as a fact of life. "None of us get out of here alive. Maybe Rory just has something to look forward to when he goes. I'm not sure I agree, but Teressa believes Robert MacNicol is the reincarnation of Rory. As far as she's concerned, they have been reunited, in the twenty-first century."

Souyer drank his ale then rolled the empty cup between his hands. He gestured toward the jug, requesting a refill. Daniel jumped off the bed to oblige them both.

"Have you considered if this"—Souyer made a vague gesture with his hand, indicating the subject they'd been discussing—"if this could have something to do with the task ye need to perform?" The grave look on his face let Daniel know how seriously he viewed the idea.

"I don't like what you're saying. Makes it sound like I'm tied to his death, and I can tell you, that's not going to happen. I'd give my life to save his."

"Even if it meant ye could never go home?" Souyer's words hung heavy in the space between them.

"You don't know what you're saying." Anger bit at Daniel's words. "You're just making stuff up. Rory could live to be an old man. You don't know how any of this stuff works."

"If Moezell brought ye here, and if ye have a task to perform, and if Rory has to die . . ."

"Stop right there. Too many ifs and no probable cause. Doesn't hold up." Daniel didn't like what he was hearing.

"Ye think a fairy needs probable cause? Besides, if her goal is to reunite Rory and Teressa . . ."

"She wouldn't need me to do it. And if she does, she's going to be sorely disappointed."

Souyer took another long drink before he responded, "This puts a whole new light on yer situation."

"Now that I've shared, how's this information going to help me?" Daniel asked, feeling they were no farther along than when they had started this god-awful conversation.

"I told ye I feel a storm brewing. It's the kind of storm that will bring more than just rain. I'm no sure what it means. I'll have to give it some thought. But if I come up with anything, I'll be sure to let ye know." Souyer rubbed his head, already deep in thought.

"Yeah, you do that. Anything you can do that will help. But I'm telling you right now . . ."

"Aye, I know how ye feel." Souyer gave a shudder. "Aye, there's a storm coming. I can feel it in my bones." The old wizard hoisted himself up from the stool and headed for the door. He left the jug of ale on the table.

Daniel couldn't completely hide his disappointment. He'd been hoping for more, but he couldn't blame Souyer for being dazed by his revelation. He was finding it all pretty hard to believe himself.

Chapter 33

$\mathcal{K}$ ayla had retreated to the comfort and confines of her room to indulge in the rare pleasure of a long hot bath. It was a perfect excuse to avoid lingering in the great hall with the rest of her family and their guests. It had only been a few days since the arrival of the MacDonald clan, and Kayla was truly weary of their presence. It was Arlin in particular who wore on her nerves. The man had openly insulted her womanhood.

After she scrubbed her body clean with efficiency borne through years of habit, she took a moment to indulge in the still-warm water while she reviewed the events of the previous day.

She had seen how Beatrice MacDonald had blatantly cheered for Rory at the warrior games. Everyone noticed. Rory seemed flattered by the young woman's attentions, but he didn't appear to be unduly attracted to Beatrice, despite her best efforts to make her feelings known. Kayla understood that his heart still belonged to Teressa and probably always would.

Kayla recalled her brief conversation with Beatrice. It hadn't gone well.

"'Tis a wonder to see a MacDonald cheer for a MacNicol. Why do you show support for my brother and no your own?" Kayla had asked the younger woman.

"But of course, because Roderick would make a wondrous husband. Is that not obvious?" Beatrice had frankly admitted.

"Donna you feel you're rushing things a bit?" She was taken aback by Beatrice's aggressive manner.

"Nay, I am nineteen and wish to be married. I have no intention of waiting until I am too old to be desired." Her eyes swept over Kayla in a manner that spoke volumes.

Beatrice didn't have to say the hurtful words for Kayla to know what the younger woman was thinking. *Too old like me*, she silently added. She wondered if all of the MacDonalds shared her opinion. It would seem so, based on the way they treated her and their poor pretense of civility.

Brushing aside the stinging pain of her thoughts, she continued to question Beatrice. "And you believe Rory is the right man for you? The right choice for your husband?" Setting aside Beatrice's natural arrogance, it impressed her how the younger woman could make such a monumental choice so easily.

"How could he not be? He's strong and handsome, and he makes me laugh. I find Roderick to be a most pleasing prospect for a husband."

"Aye, as would most any other young lass he should encounter. What makes you think he will notice you above all others?" Kayla found her usual politeness slipping away.

"I'm the daughter of the MacDonald chief. An alliance with our clan carries great value. And I happen to know he has shown no interest in a match since his affair with that strange woman you brought to the Faire three years ago. Everyone knows she has disappeared from the isle, mayhap never to return." Beatrice directed her gaze back to the action taking place on the training field.

"She may have disappeared from the isle, but she has no disappeared from his thoughts. I know he still cares for Teressa." Kayla was highly pleased to share that wee piece of information with the MacDonald chief's daughter.

Scornfully, Beatrice turned her attention again to Kayla. "He may as well be in love with a ghost. He can no love a memory forever. When he seeks a real woman for his comfort, I plan to be the one he finds, ready and waiting for him."

"Your words prove you do not know my brother very well." Kayla enjoyed expressing her dismay with a sarcastic grin.

"And your words prove you do not know me very well. I always get what I want," Beatrice made her last spiteful remark before moving off toward her mother, turning her back on Kayla.

Kayla felt certain that such a smug display of superiority could only be expressed by one so young and so mistakenly sure of herself.

"Time will tell," Kayla quietly dismissed the younger woman. Time had a way of being a grand and arduous teacher. Her own experiences were teaching her that only too well.

Kayla had also noticed Becky, Lady Evelyn's chambermaid, at the games. In fact, everyone noticed her as she cheered for Arlin. And in return, he had made no effort to hide his affection for the serving girl, claiming to be her champion. Not much of a champion, Kayla thought, considering he had lost to Daniel. How ridiculous his antics appeared as he strutted about trying to impress the young maid.

He had even gone so far as to refer to her as "poor old Kayla." Not that she cared what he thought, but his words carried the stinging ring of truth. It had been a sweet victory indeed when Daniel had knocked the wind out of his overblown sails, defeating him with the fighting staff.

It had been such a pleasure to share the day with Daniel. The more time she spent in his company, the closer she felt to him, and yet she could tell he was holding something back. She sensed a part of him that was on guard, as if he feared to release everything he was feeling. She worried that it was just her imagination wanting to believe he really cared for her.

He was so polite and kind, treating her more like a well-respected friend than a lover, laughing and playing with her and the boys. But then, last night in the stable, the way he had kissed her. She had known there was something more. Something he wasn't saying that begged to burst free.

During their playtime with Torrin and Tanner, he had called her feisty. She thought about his use of the term. No one had ever called her feisty before. Hardworking and determined, aye, but never feisty. She realized she rather liked the idea. For a moment, she had believed he was going to kiss her; she had seen it in his eyes, but then her nephews had pounced upon his back and the moment had passed.

Kayla had watched how easily Daniel interacted with her nephews, and how quickly he had gained their respect and affection. He'd make a great father someday, and to some woman, a fine husband. A husband a woman would be pleased to build a life with. More and more, she knew she wanted to be his woman. She wished she could be the one he loved, but he insisted on maintaining a polite distance, pulling back at the slightest hint of affection. Even today, after their kisses in the stable, which more than hinted at affection, he had chosen to avoid her. He had trained with the men in the lists rather than seek out her company in the keep.

But for that one passionate moment in the stables, before Rory had found them, she had felt how much he wanted her. She had felt the way he had kissed her, the way he had touched her. Their stolen kisses in the dark had awakened something that could no longer be denied.

Rising from the cooling water of her bath, she stepped out and rubbed a drying cloth over her body before she wrapped her long wet curls with the fabric. Pausing as she reached for her night shift, she took a moment to appraise her appearance in the small mirror on her table.

The sight that greeted her was not unpleasant. Her honest assessment acknowledged that she was no longer a blushing young beauty, but she believed her face still held some appeal. Standing naked in the warming glow of the fireplace, she continued her personal evaluation, her critical eyes examining the length of her body. The flames of the fire cast a golden light dancing over her skin. It was true she no longer carried the slender young body of an adolescent girl. In its place, she now boasted the lush curves of a well-formed woman. Her breasts sat ample and firm on her chest. She believed her backside and hips were not overly large and added a pleasant roundness to her appearance. She had a body ripe for bearing children.

I can still be attractive to a man, she thought as she ran her hands along the curves of her body. In truth, the only man she truly hoped to attract was Daniel. She wondered what it would be like to have a man like Daniel make love to her, take possession of her body and soul.

Standing naked as she was, she felt the temperature of the chamber drop rapidly as the wind rustled at her window. Pulling aside the heavy fabric draped across the opening, she gazed out upon an approaching summer storm. Thick grey thunderclouds led the storm front. Off in the distance she could see the downpour of rain over the ocean as it treaded its way toward land. It was a fascinating sight to see the wide storm column moving across the ocean.

Suddenly, filled with determination and a bold plan, she dropped the drying cloth where she stood. She pulled the thin nightdress over her head and grabbed her heavy grey wool mantle. Wrapping the cloak over her shoulders, she quietly slipped from her chamber. Her destination was Daniel's room.

If she hurried, she could make it to the barracks before the downpour of the storm hit the cliffs of Portree. In silence, she made her way down the stairs and out the back passages to the barracks. Pulling the hood of the mantle over her still-damp hair, she dashed across the final few yards to the wooden building, quickly locating the door to Daniel's room.

Her heart thumped boldly in her chest as she knocked upon his door with three quick taps. Daniel greeted her naked to the waist, wearing only loose drawstring breeches. Her pulse raced as she took in the sight of him. His startled expression left her unsure if he was surprised or pleased by her visit.

"Kayla, what are you doing here so late?" he asked, pulling her into the warmth of his narrow cell-like room and out of the cold of the night.

She brushed the hood of her cloak back from her face as she stepped in from the cold. It fell to her shoulders, revealing the curling ringlets of damp hair, indicating she had just finished her bath. It would only take a fleeting look for him to see that beneath her cloak, she was dressed for bed.

"I need to speak with you. I know this is impulsive of me, but I waited all day and I didn't see you. We never seem to have any time alone. I mean except . . ." She paced the short length of the barracks cell, fearful of his reaction or that her nerves would desert her.

"Is this about last night? Because, you know, I really need to apologize. I shouldn't have taken advantage of you." His usually cheerful expression had faded, replaced by remorseful hangdog eyes.

"You don't understand. I mean, you don't need to apologize," she stammered.

"Yes, I do. What I did wasn't right."

Her mind nearly froze. Had she misunderstood his desire? Had his kisses been fueled merely by lust and not true affection? Her boldness slipped a notch as she fumbled with her excuse. "Nay, it's that I—uhmm, I need a favor from you, Daniel. I need a defender." *Aye, a defender,* she thought. Hopefully, he wouldn't refuse to defend her honor, even if she had misread his intentions.

"A defender? What do you mean? Has someone hurt you?" He took a protective step toward her, and then stopped.

"Arlin has insulted my virtue. Well, maybe not my virtue, but certainly my honor. He called me an old maid, not worthy to be wed. I need someone to defend my reputation." She worried that if he refused her, Arlin's claim might very well be true.

"You can't believe that. You know it isn't true. What does Duncan say about this?"

"Nay, I cannot go to my brothers. It would be expected for my family to defend me, and that would only reinforce Arlin's claim that I'm too old to find a proper suitor."

"Kayla, it's not that easy." He ran his fingers through his hair, looking sadly frustrated, as if she was placing an excessive burden on him.

"I'm not asking for much, just some of your time."

"My time? What do you mean, my time?"

Realizing the horrendous mistake she was making, she became defensive. She tilted up her chin. "It shouldn't cause you undue delay. I know you'll be leaving soon."

It was stupid of her to make the same mistake as Rory, wanting him to stay when she knew he would leave. At best, all she could hope for was a brief moment of his affection, and then he would be gone. But she would gladly take whatever he had to offer, without regrets.

Daniel's eyes narrowed, focusing on hers. "Why do you say that?" he asked.

177

She met his eyes. "When we first met, you said you were just visiting, that you would only be here for a few weeks." She remembered well the first day they had met along the road. So much had changed since then.

"Oh. Well, that was before." He shrugged, looking away.

"Before what?" she questioned.

"I mean, I don't know when I'll be leaving. I kinda like it here, and I want to work with Michael for more training."

Her heart soared. All she heard was that he liked it here and he was staying. It was enough to give her hope.

She suddenly recalled Moezell's words. "The greatest risk is to take no risk at all," the fairy had told her. Now Kayla found herself contemplating an idea holding great possibilities, but it also held great risks for her self-esteem and emotional well-being. The mere idea of it made her tremble.

She nearly gave in to her long-held fears, but the greater part of her, the part that already loved him, needed to know. If his answer was nay, she reasoned with herself, (fearful as it was to consider) she'd be no worse off than she was now. She would merely be aware of his true feelings for her and perhaps better prepared to deal with the results. But if his feelings were anywhere near to her own, it would give her something to hope for. Hope that he would stay at Scorrybreac. Hope that her prayers had been heard and her wish would be granted. Hope that he could someday love her.

Searching for just the right words to say, she took a deep breath. Slipping her cloak from her shoulders, she dropped it to drape across the bed. "Daniel, do you no find me attractive?" she asked. Rushing on, she added, "Perhaps I speak too boldly, but you—you did kiss me. Do you not care, even a little?"

"Of course I do. More than you seem to know." His voice came out husky, laden with desire.

The light of the single candle burned from the bedside table. Surely it revealed her curves through the thin fabric of her nightgown. His eyes bore into her skin, but he didn't move.

"I mean, are you interested in me as more than a friend . . . mayhap as a lover?" This was proving to be harder than she had expected. Her emotions were so strong, so close to the surface. Her nerves felt raw with anticipation, so much depended on his answer. She risked a great and painful fall, and yet she knew she could not hold back from seeking the answer.

Stepping forward, he framed her face with his hands and rested his forehead against hers, still holding her at bay. He closed his eyes for a long, hard moment.

She could feel the heat of his naked torso so close to hers. Giving in to her newfound sensuality, her hands instinctively rose to touch the hardened muscles of his chest.

"Kayla, you need to sit down." He grabbed her shoulders and turned her toward his bed. Then he stepped away from her, putting distance between them.

"On your bed?" It wasn't proper, but then again, being alone with him in his room dressed in her nightgown and him half naked was already highly improper.

"Sit anywhere you want. There's something I need to tell you, things you need to know, and I'll feel better if you're sitting down."

Oh my, this must be serious, she thought, taking a seat on the stool. What could he possibly need to tell her that would make him so somber? He had just said he was planning to stay, that he liked it here, but he didn't say he wanted her. He'd spoken no words of love or affection. Had she read too much into his attentions? Had his kisses been no more than a momentary pleasure? Perhaps he had another woman back home, someone waiting for him. She dammed herself for her rash actions, her mind racing with all the fearful possibilities she could imagine.

He began to pace the length of the small room. "I want you, Kayla. I won't deny it, but I won't compromise you to get what I want."

After being nearly frozen with fear, her heart once again sprang into action. *He wants me,* her mind shouted with joy. *He wants me.* Holding her emotions in check as best she could, she fought to maintain an appearance of composure.

"That's quite respectable of you, Daniel, but will you allow me to compromise you to get what I want?"

He stopped pacing. "Now, Kayla, just what do you have in mind?" Daniel took a step back, a nervous look on his face.

She smiled, fully aware of the effect she was having on him. This was a first for her, this feeling of power over a man, and she was finding it to be a heady experience.

She stood and took a step toward him. "You said you want me. Is that true?"

"God, yes, it's true."

She grew bolder and took another step forward. "Have you another to whom you are matched?"

"No. There's no one else, Kayla. There's no one but you."

"Then kiss me, Daniel. I want you so much. Just kiss me."

In an instant, his resistance was shattered, and she was in his arms, feeling the strength of his passion fueled by her own. *The force of it,* she thought, *oh my god, the amazing force.* It was so powerful, like nothing she could imagine. It went beyond her wildest dreams, taking her to the moon and the stars on dazzling sparks of light.

His mouth was warm and fierce upon hers as she melted into his embrace. How could she have waited so long for this passion? The days and nights of wanting, the sensation of their first kiss—they had only created a warehouse of unspent energy that ignited the moment their lips touched. His hands blazed a hot trail across her skin, fueled by the energy that surged between them. This was no mistake, no deception of desire. They shared a passion and desire that could not be denied. It burned too bright.

Chapter 34

*I*t didn't happen often, but it happened enough to be greatly feared and deeply dreaded. Fire was a devastating foe. Once it gained control, it viciously destroyed without discretion.

It happened at the stables. Crowded conditions caused by too many horses, coupled with an approaching storm, were a formula for disaster. Rory had gone to the stables just for that reason, to check on Blaze and the other horses as the storm gathered its forces. The thunder and lightning preceding the fast-approaching storm clouds were putting the nervous animals at risk. If excessively frightened, they might rear and buck in the tight confines of their stalls, causing damage to the structure and themselves.

Rory wasn't sure if it was a strike of lightning or an overturned lantern that sparked the flames. It really didn't matter. He only knew that once it started, the fire unleashed in the stables was alarmingly fierce. Fueled by the dry hay and gusting winds, the hot flames spread with great speed. There was no time to attend to the inferno. Rory's full attention was set on freeing the horses from their stalls before the walls of the old wooden structure collapsed around him.

Daniel heard the baying of the frightened horses. Their sounds of alarm reached through his passion-driven mind, alerting him to the danger. Pulling himself away from Kayla, he announced, "Something's wrong. We must go." He grabbed his long shirt and wrestled into it as he made his way into the courtyard. Kayla grabbed her cloak and followed close behind.

Out in the courtyard, they encountered rampant chaos. Winds whipped the wild flames were engulfing the stables. Frightened horses were scattered throughout the bailey. Through the smoke and flames, Daniel could see Rory heading back into the burning building, intent on releasing the horses from their confines. Seizing one of the horse blankets that had been dragged into the courtyard, Daniel dunked the heavy fabric into the nearest watering trough. He draped the soaked blanket across his head and shoulders and raced into the firestorm after his friend.

Rory was releasing the last stallion from its stall when the large animal panicked and bucked. It heaved its massive weight against Rory, knocking him firmly to the ground. The horse's hoofs descended with brute force, hitting him square in the chest, ripping flesh and shattering bones. A heart wrenching scream tore from his lungs. His body clenched into a ball as he lay gasping for air in the smoke-filled room. The horse bolted just as burning timber fell from the roof.

Dodging the path of the last stampeding animal, Daniel headed toward the screams of the fallen man, searching the far reaches of the stables to find Rory crumpled in a bloody heap surrounded by flames. Pulling him from beneath the burning wreckage, he hastily draped the sodden blanket over Rory and heaved him over his shoulder. The scent of blood and burning flesh shocked his senses. Drawing on an adrenaline-fueled burst of strength, he quickly retreated from the innards of the burning building.

When Daniel reached the safety of the open courtyard, he saw Duncan and his men in the throes of fighting the fire and rounding up the horses. Dodging the onslaught, he raced to the far side of the open yard, well away from the danger of the ensuing chaos. He gingerly laid Rory on the ground, still wrapped in the sodden blanket, and sent up urgent prayers of hope. He wished there was something he could do to minimize Rory's pain.

"Help him. We must help him," Kayla sobbed, reaching for Rory. She was nearly hysterical by the sight of her brother's burned and bleeding body.

Daniel had enough experience with medical emergencies to know that Rory's wounds and blood loss were too much for his body to endure. His heart and lungs were failing. Daniel held Kayla back, wishing with all his soul that it could be different. "There's no saving him," he said. "There's nothing we can do. It's best to let him go."

She dropped beside them, sobbing, reaching out her hands. "You must let me try. I have to try."

Daniel stared into the eyes of the man who had become his brother. "You understand, don't you, Rory?"

With a look of brutal determination, Rory nodded his acceptance. Yes, he understood. "It's time," he coughed. "Teressa's waiting."

Daniel's eyes blurred with tears. He squeezed them shut tight, trying to hold back the flow. The effort was useless. Tears rolled from his eyes, wetting his cheeks. "I'll see you in another life, bro," he offered with a sad, broken smile.

Kayla shook with fear and grief. "Is there no saving him? Is there nothing we can do?" Tears streamed down her face.

Daniel looked up. He saw her pain. "I'm sorry, Kayla. He's already gone."

She looked into the face of her brother and saw that Daniel was right. The light of Rory's soul was gone, leaving only a lifeless body.

Chapter 35

The sun was unable to break through the grey skies as the thick cover of clouds released a steady mist of showers. The MacNicols solemnly weathered the dampness as they laid Rory's body to rest in the clan's graveyard. The occupants of Scorrybreac were in a deep state of shock and mourning over the loss of their beloved son, brother, and friend.

The MacDonald chief and his assembled kin also attended the burial, showing heartfelt respects for Rory and his family. Soon after, they withdrew to their chambers, preparing to leave as soon as the summer storm passed. Any pleasure their visit might have offered faded and fizzled in the shadow of Rory's death.

After the burial was done and they had returned to the keep, Lady Lydia approached Daniel as he passed through the great hall on his way back to the barracks.

"Daniel, a moment of your time, if you please," she asked. The politeness of her address was unexpected, conveying previously unknown respect. The passing of Rory had left its mark. The loss of her favored son had broken through her hard-held prejudice.

"Yes, Lady Lydia," he answered. He gave her his full attention and mutual respect.

"I want to thank you for your efforts. Kayla told me how you pulled Rory from the fire. That you tried to save my son's life." She held herself proud and erect. She was the kind who shed her tears in private.

"I did it for Rory. I only wish I could have done more," he spoke without malice.

Nodding with understanding, she took no offense. "He's at peace now, I suppose." Her words came softly. He could see it wasn't easy for her to speak.

"He's with Teressa," Daniel declared.

"Are you sure?" There was hope in her voice. Hope that her son had found the happiness he deserved.

"Yeah, I'm sure. They were together before I left. Rory and Teressa are happily married and living in the future," Daniel confirmed, acknowledging his final acceptance of the soul mates' reunion.

Lady Lydia breathed deeply. "Thank you, Daniel. That's good to know."

They parted, each going their separate ways with newfound acceptance. Lady Lydia had finally accepted his presence in her time, and in her daughter's life. And while he couldn't agree with her actions, knowing how deeply her choices had hurt Rory, Daniel accepted that she'd been blinded by her love for her son. Right or wrong, selfish or not, she'd done what she thought was best.

Later in the evening, he sat alone under the eaves of the great stone archway leading into the keep, nursing a tankard of ale and keeping watch on the grey gloomy skies. Night had fallen, and still the storm showed no sign of ending its tearful showers anytime soon. It was as if the heavens and earth were morning the loss of a favored son, providing kindred company for Daniel's foul mood. He welcomed the summer storm as his quiet companion. He needed to feel its cold brush of wind against his skin and breathe its chilly damp air. He needed the storm to reaffirm his existence.

It was late, and most of the occupants of the keep had retired to their rooms. Unexpectedly, Daniel was pulled from his silent contemplation by the sounds of booted footsteps approaching from inside the keep. He was even more surprised to see it was Arlin.

Through his contacts in the kitchens, Daniel had learned all he needed to know about Arlin. He had heard all about Lady Lydia's aspiration to arrange a betrothal between Kayla and Arlin. He also knew Arlin wanted nothing to do with Kayla, preferring to bestow his affections upon the servant girl, Becky. Apparently, Arlin's preferences had stirred up bad blood between him and his parents. He wanted to marry Becky and work with her father as a blacksmith. He was the one who arranged for his mother take Becky as her personal maid.

"Drinking alone, are ye?" Arlin asked.

Daniel didn't look up to acknowledge the gate-crasher to his private pity party. He said nothing.

Arlin deliberately ignored Daniel's snub. "I understand you were close to Rory," he stated.

"As far as I'm concerned, we were brothers." Daniel's eyes remained fixed on the sympathetic summer storm.

"No wonder you show such a preference for Kayla." There was no mistaking the undertone of malice in Arlin's words.

"Just what do you mean by that?" Daniel cast a steely look toward Arlin. He wouldn't mind releasing his sorrow and pent-up anger in a good knockdown brawl, and he wouldn't mind at all if Arlin was the one to take the fall.

"The way you've been acting around her, pretending to be her suitor. I figure it must be for show, as a favor to Rory. The rumor is you'll be leaving soon, just like your sister, leaving Kayla high and dry." His words were accompanied by a sneering laugh.

"I should warn you, you're treading on very thin ice here." In all fairness, Daniel believed he should give the man a warning to back off. But if he didn't take it, he was perfectly willing to once again knock the snot out of the bastard.

Arlin foolishly disregarded the warning. "These aren't your people. You're just passing through on your way back to wherever it is you came from. Unless you have some grand plans of staying with the MacNicols, you don't belong here. Why should you care? It's not your problem."

Unfortunately, that was exactly his problem, not knowing how long he could stay, fearing that someday soon he would leave. As far as he knew, he could be sucked back in time without any warning, the same way he had arrived.

He wanted Kayla, of that he was certain, but he had no reason to believe he was the right man for her. She was a woman worthy of marriage, a marriage that would serve her and her family, and that didn't include a man with an unknown future.

"Kayla is my friend. My dear friend. If you know what's best, you'll leave her be." He struggled to remain civil toward the man. *Walk away,* he thought. *One of us needs to walk away.*

"Such nice words, 'my dear friend.' Ha, she's been a little too long on the shelf, if you ask me. I prefer them younger, like my Becky. Now there's a woman worth the taking."

Daniel clenched his fists, his anger brewing just below the surface.

Speaking with smug confidence, Arlin taunted him, "Or maybe you've already had your way with your 'dear friend.' Has she given in to wantonness in her old age?"

That was the final straw Daniel needed to push him over the edge. His tightly coiled anger and frustration burst forth with a satisfying release of brute force. His fist shot out across Arlin's chin, hitting its mark with bone-crunching power. Before Arlin could flinch, a second blow was delivered in rapid succession. It knocked Arlin several steps back, reeling toward the hard stone walls of the archway.

Daniel lurched at Arlin as he stumbled back, grabbing the unbalanced man. Together they rolled down the stairs of the keep, the hard stone steps biting into their backs. Rain-induced mud greeted them at the bottom of the stairs, making it difficult to secure a sure footing.

Slipping in the sodden mess, Arlin did his best to rise to his feet. Without gaining a proper balance, he lunged forward and slipped again, falling face-first into the mud.

Daniel had let the momentum of the fall take him away from their landing site. He drew on the energy of his rolling tumble to position himself into a crouch before he stood to recover his footing. Gaining a momentary advantage, he executed a swift high kick, bringing his foot to connect with the left side of Arlin's head just as Arlin was trying to stand. The man went down into the mud for a third time.

Daniel stood over him, ready to pounce again.

Duncan suddenly appeared at the door of the keep. "What the blaze is going on here? What the hell are you doing?" he demanded of Daniel.

Daniel didn't speak. His eyes darted from Duncan to Arlin and back again. Arlin lay sprawled in the mud groaning.

"Who caused this fight?" Duncan asked.

Daniel reached down to help Arlin to his feet with gruff assistance.

Bloodied and bruised, but still defiant, Arlin stared at Daniel, silently daring him to reveal the nature of their fight to Kayla's brother.

Daniel struggled to recover his senses and rein in his emotions. It was a mess. A dirty, ugly mess, and he was in no condition to discuss what had transpired with Duncan or anyone else. He wouldn't lower himself to repeat Arlin's hateful words.

"Trust me, Duncan," he stated flatly, "you don't want to know."

A look of understanding flashed between the two men. Regardless of the reason, the MacNicol chief understood. Daniel had been defending the honor of his clan. Giving a nod, Duncan turned to haul Arlin back into the keep. Daniel held his ground for several minutes longer, allowing the chill of the light summer shower to wash over him and cool his temper. Finally, he turned on his heel and slowly walked away.

Chapter 36

*D*aniel stepped into his room and kicked the wooden stool, sending it flying across the room. He thought about picking it up and smashing it to bits to help release his frustrations, but he didn't. Instead, he grabbed it and set it upright, returning it to its spot beside the table.

He stripped off his wet clothes and threw them in the corner. They were a sodden muddy mess. He'd have to see if he could get Bonnie to wash them in the morning. Naked, he stepped back out into the rain and ran a washcloth over his face and body, doing his best to clean up after the fight. It was a cold and sorry replacement for a shower, but it would have to do.

After drying off, he threw himself on the small bed of his dimly lit room and stared at the ceiling with his hands entwined behind his head. A single candle burned to keep him company in the dark. It was late and he was tired, but his mind was restless, busy assessing all that had happened since his arrival on Skye. He endeavored to come to grips with the plethora of emotions he was experiencing, trying to calmly and rationally sort through them one by one. It wasn't an easy task, but it needed to be done.

He didn't feel bad about losing his temper; it had felt too damn good to kick Arlin's butt. The man deserved a good thrashing for the way he spoke of Kayla. Usually, Daniel was in better control of his emotions; he knew he should've walked away. With grudging acceptance, he admitted his emotions had been too strong, too raw, and ready to boil over. He realized he had welcomed the opportunity to smack the crap out of the offending MacDonald.

Lying there alone in the nearly dark room of the thirteenth-century barracks, he felt the strength of his connection to the MacNicol clan. Rory had been like a brother. He felt much the same about Duncan and Michael. The old druid, Souyer, had become his friend and confidant. And there was Bonnie and Milly; they fawned over him like dear maiden aunts. The list went on and on. Even Lady Lydia had shown him respect. The people of Scorrybreac were becoming his people. He felt a connection to this time and place.

And God help him, he could finally admit it, at least to himself, he'd fallen in love. He was in love with Kayla, and nothing about it was easy.

With so much connecting him to Scorrybreac, he wondered why he still felt like an outsider, that he didn't belong.

Then it hit him, smack-dab in his face. Fear—it was agonizing to admit and impossible to deny. Fear was holding him back. Fear that he'd lost control of his life. Fear that he could be sucked back in time at any moment without any warning and lose it all. Fear prevented him from living fully in the moment—and now all he wanted was to stay.

It was a grand adventure, the thrill of a lifetime to experience ancient history. And yet he knew, as exciting as the adventure was, it was meaningless unless Kayla was a part of his life.

Unlike Teressa, he had no idea why he'd been brought back in time. Obviously, he wasn't brought there to cause Rory's death, and he certainly hadn't able to prevent it. If he'd been brought here to assure Rory that someday he would be reunited with Teressa, he had failed. He had never shared that information with his future brother-in-law. Besides, that alone seemed too weak of a reason to displace a man over seven hundred years in time.

He knew Teressa had been brought here to act as a relationship coach, a matchmaker for Duncan and Janet. She'd been given clear instructions on what was expected of her and when she would leave. His time-travel experience, on the other hand, seemed to be completely without reason.

As he continued to dwell on his dilemma, he realized there was one aspect of this experience he shared with his sister. They had both met someone with whom they felt a special connection, and like his sister, his first reaction had been to fight the obvious attraction.

But unlike Teressa, he contended, his efforts to fight the attraction weren't so much for his sake but for Kayla's. He'd believed he could protect her from a painful loss if he avoided getting too close to her. Then again, by trying to protect her from such pain, it seemed very likely he had actually created another, a different type of disappointment. He had refused to tell her he cared.

He felt the attraction between them, and he knew she felt it too. It was there in her eyes, in her smile, the way she looked at him, and the way she reacted to his kiss. He might have been trying to keep their relationship light and friendly, but in the end, who was he kidding? There was a connection, an attraction, and he was simply trying to avoid the obvious.

By denying their attraction, wasn't he simply exchanging one pain for another, inadvertently choosing the pain of undeclared feelings over the pain of a possible loss? And for now, that was all it was, only a possibility. But the feelings were so real.

He had come to accept that Teressa and Rory had found a way to be reunited across time. Rory had become Robert, and Teressa believed their souls were together. To her, that was all that mattered. She was with her soul mate.

Was it possible that some unknown solution existed for him and Kayla? Even if he didn't know right now what it was? Wasn't that the lesson his sister had learned, to let go of her fears and live, and yes, even love in the moment?

His head ached. He had lots of questions, but he still had no answers. His mind was dancing in circles, going round and round. He felt he was truly following his little sister's footsteps, too afraid of what might be to enjoy what was already right in front of him.

He leaned his head back and laughed. It was a cold hard chuckle, but he had to laugh. He laughed at himself as he thought. *Here I am, the biggest fool of them all.* He remembered Rory's mantra: "The pleasure of love was worth the pain." And Souyer had told him, "The greatest risk is to take no risk at all." Yes, this truly was a grand and glorious adventure, he mused. And one hell of a journey right through life's toughest lessons.

With renewed determination, Daniel realized Kayla needed to know how he felt. She needed to know he was from the future and be given an opportunity to choose. It was only fair they both be included in this adventure. He'd been trying to manipulate the relationship all by himself, to maintain his illusion of control, forgetting that she was involved. She had a right to her feelings. She had a right to be fully engaged in this experience. And she had a right to make her own choices.

Now he just had to figure out how he should go about telling her.

Chapter 37

Early the next morning, Kayla waited for Duncan in his study, sobbing. How many times had he found her like this? she wondered. Not often, if ever. It wasn't like her to pour her heart out to anyone, especially her eldest brother.

As soon as Duncan entered the room, he sat down beside her and gathered her into his arms, offering what little comfort he could. "You grieve so over Rory, little sister?"

"Oh Duncan, it's that and so much more." She could barely speak between sobs, her head burrowed into his shoulder. Kayla had been close to Rory, and it was only natural she would grieve so deeply, but that wasn't the only reason for her tears.

The events of the past few days had proved to be too much for her emotions. She needed a release from all the frustration and pain that was lodged in her soul. It was the reason she had sought the quiet comfort of Duncan's study, hoping he would soon arrive to provide his brotherly support.

"Tell me what pains you so," Duncan said.

"My life. It's a mess. I know I shouldn't think of myself at a time like this—but Rory's death, it could have been any one of us."

"Aye, Kayla. None of us are above such accidents." Duncan patted her on her back, trying to soothe her pain.

"It could have been Daniel. He was there, trying to save Rory." She rubbed a hand across her eyes, trying to dry her tears.

"Daniel! What does he have to do with this?"

Before she could speak, her brother offered an answer, "You care for him, don't you?" His voice softened with concern.

"Aye. And I hate that vile Arlin. I want nothing to do with him. If you and Mother push for a betrothal, I shall flee. I could never be married to such a vile man." She needed to let it all out. All the anger and pain her grieving heart had brought to the surface.

"You have no worries. No one is going to request a betrothal between you and Arlin," he tried to reassure her.

"And just like Arlin said, I'm all alone, and old, and nobody wants me." Her voice took on a woeful sound.

"Kayla, you can no think such a thing. Many women your age are able to find a suitable husband," he offered.

Her pained look told him that hadn't been the right thing to say.

"I mean, surely there are others who find you attractive."

"But that's just it. I want no others. I want Daniel." She looked up at her brother with weepy eyes, wiping a handkerchief across her nose.

"I know. I've suspected it for some time now," he confirmed.

"But I fear he no wants me." She struggled to regain her composure. Daniel had been avoiding her since her visit to his room, and now she feared the worst. She had thrown herself at the man, and he didn't really want her.

Duncan gave a weary sigh. "Are you sure about that? It looks to me as though Daniel has a very strong interest in you," he said.

A glimmer of hope tiptoed across her heart. "Do you think so? Has he said something to you?"

"Nay, but I have eyes. I've seen how he is when you're together. I believe he cares for you." Duncan paused, and she could see he was gathering his words, as if he had something important to tell her. "If he hasn't told you, it's because, well you see, there's a problem."

Her eyes opened wide, her imagination spinning out of control, filled with fearful thoughts.

"He's from the future," Duncan stated plainly.

"The future? Whatever can you mean?" Confusion and disbelief swelled in her belly. She fought back the nausea.

"Teressa and Daniel, they're both from the future, about seven hundred years. I've always known. Teressa was sent here by a fairy."

"Moezell?" Kayla interrupted.

"You know of her?" Duncan's brows shot up in a look a stark surprise.

"I've met her," Kayla admitted.

"You have?" Her brother's quizzical gaze told her they would be revisiting that subject.

"What has Moezell done?" she asked quickly.

Duncan gave her a scowl but continued to explain, "It was Moezell who brought Teressa here. She was brought here to secure the match between Janet and me. When her job was done, she was sent home. We think Moezell is also the one who brought Daniel here, but we don't know why."

"Did Rory know Teressa was from the future?"

"Not until she left. He saw her disappear on the beach when Moezell sent her back to her time. That's when she showed herself to Rory."

"But why? Why would she do that?"

"We don't know. We weren't told. All we know is that when her task had been completed, she was sent back to her own time. Rory was told he would see her again someday, but now, that no longer seems possible."

"And what of Daniel? When will he leave?" Kayla's tears welled up again. She fought to hold them back.

"I don't know. We think Moezell brought him here, but why or for how long, we have no answers. Daniel believes it was to bring news of Teressa, but that has long since been accomplished, and still he remains."

"Mayhap he was brought here to save Rory from the fire, but he failed. You should have seen him. I think he would have given his life to save Rory." She reached out to grasp Duncan's hands, adamant in her conviction.

"Rory thought of Daniel as a brother. I believe Daniel thinks the same of Rory. I know he grieves the loss."

"If that's true, that he was sent here to save Rory and he failed, he'll be sent back, like his sister. Oh Duncan, 'tis all my fault. What shall I do?" Her hand rose to cover her mouth, striving to hold back her anxiety.

"What do you mean? It's not your fault. None of this is your fault."

"I was there, in Daniel's room, at the time of the fire. If it hadn't been for me, he might have gotten to Rory sooner. He might have been able to save his life. If only I hadn't been there."

Duncan's glare turned dark. "As much as I'd like to question you about your presence in Daniel's room, this isn't the right time. We need to talk to Daniel. It's time we discussed this, together." He rose and stepped to the door. "Wait here," he instructed.

Kayla could hear Duncan out in the great hall. He ordered one of the servants to go fetch Daniel. When he returned to his study, he took his seat at his desk.

"While we wait, mayhap you can tell me what you know about Moezell. How did you meet her?"

Kayla took a deep breath. Her moment of truth had arrived. She had some confessions of her own to make.

"Moezell came to my bedchamber the night Daniel arrived. I was feeling resentment toward Daniel, being Teressa's brother. She told me I should no judge Teressa and Daniel so harshly, that I didn't know all the facts. She told me how much Rory loved Teressa and it was no Teressa's choice to leave. She confirmed everything you've told me, that Teressa had to return home. She just didn't tell me her home was in the future."

"Was that all?" he asked, looking somewhat unconvinced.

Kayla was unsure about what more she could say to Duncan. She couldn't tell him she was related to Moezell and the fairies. Her mother had asked her to keep that information secret.

"Nay," Kayla admitted after some thought. "She also told me that to find love, I must seek with an open heart. She told me my fear of pain is what keeps me from my greatest pleasure."

It was embarrassing enough to disclose to her brother how Moezell had counseled her on love. She wasn't about to admit she had wished for true love, although he could probably guess.

Then an idea hit her, filling her with renewed hope. If Moezell was the one who brought Daniel back in time, maybe he was here to grant her wish. Moezell had said that all she could do was provide the right opportunity; it was up to Kayla to do the rest. It was too grand to believe, but that must be it. What else could it be? Renewed excitement bubbled up inside her.

A knock on the door announced Daniel's arrival.

Daniel stepped through the door and surveyed the room. *This should be interesting,* he thought. He wondered why Duncan wanted to see Kayla and him together. He noticed her red swollen eyes and knew she'd been crying.

Dropping to the chair next to her, he asked, "Kayla, what's wrong? Are you all right?"

"We've been discussing Rory," Duncan began. "Now we've moved on to you."

"Me!" Silent alarms went off in Daniel's head. He quickly recalled his earlier visions of the MacNicol brothers exacting their revenge for his seduction of their little sister.

"I had to tell her," Duncan remarked.

"Tell her what?"

"That you're from the future."

"Is it true?" Kayla asked.

He paused, his eyes switching back and forth between Duncan and Kayla. So here it was, his moment of truth. Drawing a deep breath, he answered, "Yes, it's true." Relief washed over him. He realized he was grateful Duncan had told her. It was time she learned the truth.

"Why didn't you tell me?" Her voice was soft and low. She sounded hurt and betrayed, and rightfully so.

His chest constricted, seeing her so upset. "I wanted to protect you."

"Protect me! Protect me from what? The truth?"

Daniel shrugged. Suddenly, his answer didn't sound so good. In fact, it sounded rather lame. He knew secrets were a bad idea. They had a way of kicking you in the ass at the worst possible times.

"I was going to tell you," he said.

"When?" She glared at him through red swollen eyes.

"Today. Actually, I decided I should tell you today. And now you know." There was no saving this runaway pony. It had already left the stable.

"Were you sent here by Moezell?" Kayla asked.

"I guess so. I don't really know. I've never met the woman, or fairy, or whatever she is."

"You've never met her? She hasn't spoken to you?"

"No. Have you?" He looked from Kayla to Duncan for their response.

"Aye, she visited my chamber," Kayla confirmed.

"I have not, but she has shown herself to Teressa and Rory," Duncan offered.

"If she's responsible for bringing me here, why hasn't she shown herself to me? Damn, this is frustrating," Daniel groaned.

"I don't know." Kayla shrugged. "She just appeared in my chamber. I didn't summon her, at least not directly."

"Summon her? You mean ask her to appear?" Daniel questioned, feeling a flash of inspiration.

"Aye, it seems she only appears when she chooses, which isn't very often," Duncan said.

"Really. Well, we'll just see about that." Daniel grabbed Kayla's hand and led her out to the great hall.

Duncan followed close behind them.

"Wait, what are you doing?" Kayla asked as she followed him.

"You'll see." Daniel had enough of the fear and frustration from not knowing. It was time for a showdown with the elusive fairy.

Daniel led them out to the middle of the great hall, which was uncommonly vacant for the early morning hour. It was as if all of Scorrybreac had arranged to give them their privacy.

Standing in the middle of the great hall, Daniel began to shout, his voice echoing off the stone walls of the nearly empty space. "Moezell, get your fairy butt out here. It's time to do some talking. I've got questions, and by god, you're going to give me some answers. Do you hear me? Show yourself and do it now," he demanded.

For a moment, the room was silent, buzzing with the stillness. Then it grew as bright as the sun at midday, and a woman appeared, stepping through the veil of the unseen. She was beautiful to behold, dressed in a long liquid blue gown, with flowing white blond hair and ice blue eyes. It had to be Moezell.

"Greetings, Daniel." Moezell smiled. "I was wondering when you would get around to calling for me."

Duncan and Kayla gasped, while Daniel stared at her in wonder. He'd never seen a fairy before, and until now, he had never truly expected that he would. It took a few seconds for him to wrap his mind around the idea.

"You mean I could have summoned you at any time?" he asked.

"Nay, not until you were ready to face this moment. And now you are." Moezell's voice whispered like a calming breeze through the great hall.

"Teressa should have warned me what a mean-spirited meddling fairy you are." He spat at her. He had no fear of her power, believing the worst she could do was send him back home, which he fully expected her to do anytime her fickle fairy soul desired.

"Such anger," she mused in amazement. "'Tis to be expected when one feels they are out of control."

"Yeah, like how Teressa wasn't in control of being sent away from Rory. You didn't even let her say good-bye." Daniel felt his anger rise. He wasn't about to back down.

"That was not of my doing. Cousin Lydia was in control of that event. I was honor-bound by our agreement to fulfill her request. We are all bound by our agreements. You may not be aware of it, but your souls have agreed to these adventures, or you would not be here," Moezell graciously informed Daniel.

"When did I agree to all this? That's something I still don't understand." Daniel was beyond frustrated. He'd enough of her fairy games.

"Did you not ask to find a place where you belong? Did you not wish upon a star?" The fairy gazed deep into his eyes.

Daniel slowly nodded, suddenly recalling his whispered words as he traveled toward Scotland. "I remember."

"A wish expressed, a favor bestowed. To fulfill your wish, I chose to give you an option, provide you with the opportunity to find your destiny. Now you must choose," Moezell advised.

"You're telling me I can choose to stay or go, to return home?" Daniel's anger began to fade, replaced by new thoughts, new questions, and the possibilities held in the answers.

"Aye, that is correct. The choice is yours," Moezell confirmed.

"If I choose to go back home, will I be returned to the same time as when I left, like Teressa was?" He wondered how much control she had over his time travel.

Kayla pulled back, stepping away. "You want to leave, just like your sister. You want to leave and return home. You don't want to stay."

He reached out and grabbed her hand again, not letting her go. "No, Kayla, wait. You're wrong. I just need to know." He turned to glare at Moezell. "So tell me, will I return to the same time?"

Moezell answered his question with a smile, "Aye, be it an hour, a day, or a year from now, if you choose to go back to your time, you will be returned to the moment when you left."

"And if it was ten, twenty, thirty years from now, would that still hold true?" he questioned further.

"Aye," the fairy acknowledged with a slight nod. "However, you will still age and grow old with the passing of time, regardless of when or where that time occurs."

It was as he had hoped, but he realized it no longer mattered. He already knew exactly where he wanted to be. There was only one other question left to be answered before he made his choice.

"There's only one good reason for being anywhere, and that's to be with the ones I love." Turning to Kayla, he continued, "Kayla, if you could ever love me, could ever want me like I want you, well, then I'll know where I belong."

"Love you?" she asked. Anxious fear danced across her innocent features.

"Yes, do you think you could love me, as I love you?" Daniel asked, his voice unsteady with the weight of his emotions.

"Of course, I love you." Tears threatened to spill from her eyes.

For a brief powerful moment, Daniel silently connected with Duncan's watchful gaze. The eldest MacNicol brother gave his nod of approval. Corny as it might seem, Daniel knew it was important for him to do this right. Reaching for Kayla's hand, he dropped to one knee. "Kayla, will you marry me? Will you be my wife?"

She looked stunned. It took her a second to answer. "Are you serious? Are you sure this is what you want?"

"I don't think I could be more serious. What do you say? Will you have me?" A pensive look sheltered Daniel's emotions as he gazed into the depths of her bright green eyes. He wasn't known to be a betting man, and yet here he was, taking the biggest risk of his life, giving up all that he had known before for all that might be.

"Aye, aye, a thousand times aye." Tears of pure joy filled her eyes and spilled down her cheeks.

Daniel stood and gathered her in his arms, holding her body close as she melted into him. Home, she felt like home. Taking her face gently in his hands, he turned her face up so he could see the golden specks dancing in her sparkling green eyes.

"I have no more questions. I know exactly where I belong."

"You choose to stay?" Moezell asked.

Daniel turned to face the fairy. "I choose to stay," he confirmed, holding Kayla close in his arms.

"As you wish," Moezell said. She lingered a moment to connect with Kayla. "I expect we'll be seeing more of each other. We have much to discuss. You have much to learn."

Flashing a radiant smile upon the lovers, Moezell stepped back behind the veil and disappeared.

Daniel stared at the empty space, then blinked, still holding Kayla. He tightened his grip on her, holding her close, as if to never let her go. It was too much to believe. His grandest wish had come true.

Epilogue

$\mathcal{A}$ soft patch of tufted grass cushioned the back of Daniel as he awoke near the river. He wore a plain white linen shirt with faded old blue jeans and a well-worn brown leather jacket. The jeans were tighter than before, and the leather jacket had seen better days. These items had been tucked away in storage, waiting for this day. His footwear might look a bit out of place if you looked closely. His old riding boots had worn out long ago, and the soft but sturdy leather boots he wore were stitched by hand.

He opened his eyes to the face of an angel. Backlit by the sun, she was framed by a halo of glowing red hair. Her pale white skin took on an iridescent glow. Innocent green eyes peered back at him. He smiled, knowing she came from heaven.

"Are ye all right?" she asked.

"I think so," Daniel replied, still grinning.

"Then come along, Da." She reached out to help him sit up.

"Thanks, Bree." Daniel rolled to his side and welcomed the assistance of his strong, beautiful daughter as she helped him to his feet. "And thank you, Moezell," Daniel whispered. He turned his face to meet the fluttering breeze dancing through the air. "You've brought us both back."

He took a mental and visual scan of his person, confirming he was still whole and in one piece. Dignified strength was evident in his features, but years of a hard life and rugged living had taken their toll. He felt the stiffness in his bones as he rose to his feet and looked around. It was a dim memory, but everything was just as he remembered.

He spied Wilbur grazing a bit farther downstream. The sudden summer storm must have spooked the animal, but thankfully, he hadn't run back to the stables. Garrett had chosen a strong and reliable mount. Daniel was grateful the horse was still there, waiting, although he understood he'd only been gone for a moment.

Father and daughter slowly walked over to the horse, and with a fair degree of effort, Daniel vaulted into the saddle. *Old age is a bitch,* he thought, *no matter 'when' you are.* He then lent a hand to his daughter as she mounted up behind him. He spurred the horse into a gentle walking pace, taking the trail heading back to Portree. There was no hurry; he had all the time he needed. Not much, but enough.

He figured they would head directly to Robert's cottage instead of the Skyeland Stables. He'd let Robert return the horse for him. It would be better that way, fewer questions to answer.

Reaching into the inside pocket of his leather jacket, he pulled out a scroll of parchment. Unshed tears glistened in his eye as he unrolled it and gazed with undying love at the portraits sketched in charcoal. The artist had done a superb job of capturing the faces of his wife, son, and four daughters. His youngest daughter, Breanna, was the one sitting behind him. Missing from this family portrait were his five grandchildren, and there was another one on the way. He already missed them, but it was time. He knew his time was short and he had an old family duty to fulfill.

Looking up to the sky, he said a little prayer to his dearly departed wife. "We did good, Kayla. You and me, we did good."

Then he laughed, thinking what a surprise this would be for his sister and her husband. For Teressa and Robert, he had only been out riding for a few hours, but for him it had been over thirty years since he had last seen them. He had always known this day would come, a day when he would return to the future, his long-ago past, and say his final farewell. He knew he had some explaining to do and a lifetime of stories to tell.

Twelve days later, Daniel Ellers of the MacNicol clan peacefully passed away as he lay sleeping in his brother-in-law's cottage. His heart, which had been ailing him for some time, simply gave out. It was his time. In accordance with his final wishes, he was laid to rest near the ruins of the Scorrybreac castle. It was the place where he belonged.

About the Author

Tricia is a member of the Unity Community and a dedicated student of metaphysical spirituality. She has enjoyed a successful career as a Foreign Exchange Trader and International Banker and has lived in five states, on two islands, and on a farm. After successfully raising two amazing children, Tricia is living happily ever after with her soul-mate in Northern California.

12619318R00110

Made in the USA
Charleston, SC
16 May 2012